The Chapel

THE
CHAPEL

A Novel

MICHAEL DOWNING

COUNTERPOINT PRESS

Library of Congress Cataloging-in-Publication data is available

ISBN 978-1-61902-495-3

Cover design: Faceout Studios
Interior design: Domini Dragoone

Photos and illustrations courtesy of the author except: pg. 51 from *Giotto* by Francesca Flores d'Arcais; pg. 166 and 198 (top) © BananaFish/ DollarPhotoClub; pg. 167 and 195 courtesy of Matt Hobbs/Public Domain Archive; pg. 171, 172, and 265 courtesy of the Isabella Stewart Gardener Museum, Boston; pg. 193 and 198 (bottom) © Roman Sigaev/ DollarPhotoClub; pg. 194 and 199 (top) © Salvo77 Na/DollarPhotoClub.

Counterpoint Press
2560 Ninth Street, Suite 318
Berkeley, CA 94710
www.counterpointpress.com

Printed in the United States of America
Distributed by Publishers Group West

10 9 8 7 6 5 4 3 2 1

for Peter Bryant,

per tutto questo—assolutamente tutto

Memory, so complete and clear or so evasive,
has to be ended, has to be put aside,
as if one were leaving a chapel and bringing
the prayer to an end in one's head.

—HAROLD BRODKEY

PART I: PADUA

I

The first time I got lost in Paris, I was not alone. Mitchell was holding my hand, a habit he'd suddenly acquired while we were boarding the airplane in Boston to begin our belated honeymoon. We'd never flown together, so I initially chalked this up to nerves. But he latched on for the entire taxi ride from the airport to our hotel, and during the next few days he often reached across a café table and squeezed my hand or laced his fingers into mine as we left a museum, pulling me nearer to him, as if he wanted to reassure me, as if our three-year marriage had been a trial period and this trip signaled his decision to stay and brave the future with me at his side. Despite the city's amorous reputation, most of the hand-holding I noticed among Parisians that week involved teenage girls or children under the age of six, but that was true of short pants and white socks, too. Mitchell had packed only one pair of full-length trousers. He did bring a suit, his wedding attire, which came out for a fancy dinner and never saw Paris again.

After that trip, neither did we. But we got lost together that breezy blue day in the Marais.

We had set out from the Louvre to find a famously cheap bistro recommended by one of Mitchell's colleagues at Boston College. However, the promise of a hot pile of *pommes frites* receded block by block as we passed window displays of increasingly pricey petits fours, perfume, and pearls. Finally, Mitchell said, "I don't think any of these places would serve French fries."

I said, "These places wouldn't serve us."

"You look like a native," he said. "I look a little too beatnik."

More Boy Scout than Left Bank, I thought. Mitchell was a handsome, barrel-chested man with a close-cropped mat of wavy dark hair slightly receding at the top of his big head. When he put on a sport coat and tie, he looked pensive and strong, but he was only a few inches taller than I was, so he was not quite as big as the sum of his parts. In short pants, he looked top-heavy.

But if Mitchell's legs were exposed on that warm June day, so were my pretensions. I was wearing one of three Marimekko shifts I'd purchased for this trip. It was still the '70s. For the newly appointed interim assistant reference librarian at the Cambridge Public Library, I looked rather chic. In the better neighborhoods of Paris, I looked like a bolt of upholstery.

"I'm not sure I'm up to asking for directions," I said, knowing he hoped I would take the initiative.

"I love your accent," he said. "Indulge me."

I could get us safely through a menu, and to boost my confidence about speaking in French, Mitchell had taken to pointing quizzically as he lay down on *le lit* in our hotel room, or raising his *stylo bille* before he signed *un Travelers cheque* at a restaurant or jotted something down in his *cahier*—words I would speak and he would repeat as many times as it took for me to approve his pronunciation. He surely knew more French vocabulary than I did, so this pretense should have been annoying or demeaning. But Mitchell had just finished a rough semester, and I wanted him to know that I was game for anything, that I'd be on his side whether or not he got tenure, that wherever we went, we were in it together. So I decided to believe what Mitchell had repeatedly told me, that he was a competent reader but could not speak or follow a conversation in French. And after a few days, those language lessons turned into something more rewarding, something like flirting in public.

I also guessed that Mitchell couldn't tolerate some shopkeeper calling him out on his pronunciation. He didn't want to be chastened again. I didn't blame him. At his year-end tenure review that spring, he had been rated "underperforming" in the scholarship category. This was a man who regularly lectured in Italian, was fluent in Spanish, and taught illiterate undergraduates to read Latin. He had written his dissertation on *De vulgari eloquentia*, a treatise on the virtues of plain-spoken Italian, which Dante, ironically, wrote in Latin. Mitchell had always been happy to expound on this irony and all things Dante until one night a few months before we left for Paris, when we had dinner at our apartment with a college classmate of his.

Tom Moulton had come to Cambridge for a medieval-history con-ference. He was on the tenure track at Princeton and had just published his first book, "just under the wire," he said a couple of times, until I finally asked what that wire was, and he said, "Thirty." His emaciated, viciously polite wife, Kitty, spent most of the evening squealing words and phrases—Galley kitchen! Ham roll-ups! Venetian blinds! Blush wine! You two! No car? Fondue! When she finally exhausted her sup-ply of astonished nouns, Kitty excused herself for a minute, and Tom seized the opportunity to grill Mitchell about his long-overdue book.

"I'm calling it *Who Stole Dante?*"

Tom glanced at me and said, "Catchy title."

Mitchell had a knack for titles, perhaps because he'd written more titles than pages in the last three years.

"It's probably going to need a subtitle," Mitchell added, "much as I hate writers who spell out the whole thesis on the cover."

"When can I get my hands on a few chapters?" Tom hadn't shifted his gaze away from me yet. He knew there was no book. "Or is Liz your only trusted reader?"

Mitchell said, "Liz is a dynamite reader. And don't forget, she's a researcher of sorts, in her own way."

Tom pulled a folded-up piece of stationery from his blazer pocket. "Before I forget," he said as he bent back the creases, exposing an embossed Harvard logo. He handed the sheet to Mitchell. "They want someone with a Ph.D., and it'll definitely help that you have teaching experience."

Mitchell said, "This is the job listing?"

Tom said, "I know someone on the search committee."

Mitchell was still reading when he said, "It's not a faculty position."

"It's in FAS," Tom said argumentatively. He shot me an accusatory glance, as if I ought to back him up.

I felt panicky. "FAS?"

Mitchell said, "Faculty of Arts and Sciences." He wouldn't look at me. "It's not a teaching job."

"It is a job in academe." Tom looked my way and winced—conspiratorially? Apologetically? "Most administrators at Harvard and Princeton have Ph.D.s," he added petulantly and then retreated deep into the sofa. "Anyway, they want to fill the position quickly."

"Oh, Tom," I said, slathering my voice with feigned disappointment. I snatched the stationery from Mitchell's fingers and pretended to read the text. "I was truly excited for a minute there. I honestly thought you were about to tell us that you'd been offered a job at Harvard—a ticket out of New Jersey for you and Kitty."

Tom tilted his head and gave me a wan little grin as if to apologize for any embarrassment he might have caused. He said, "Let me know soon if you think of someone who might be interested."

I topped off his wineglass.

He asked about Mitchell's students at Boston University.

"Boston College," Mitchell said amiably.

"Right," Tom said, "the Jesuits," as if B.C. were a seminary and not a legitimate university.

Mitchell explained that the Italian department was small and not getting more popular with undergraduates, so he was still saddled with two intro Latin classes every semester on top of his literature classes, which left little time for research and writing.

Tom said, "Italian scholar wanders off course into a thicket of undergraduate ablatives. Didn't you notice the sign?"

Mitchell looked confused.

Tom raised both his hands over his head and carved out an arc as he said, "Abandon hope, all ye who enter."

Mitchell smiled at me. "That's from Dante."

I nodded. "Gates of Hell."

"Cozy powder room!" Kitty was back, and I left to slice the Cherry Cheesecake! And plug in the venerable Electric Percolator! I was twenty-five years old, and as I stood in that too-small kitchen and tried to scrape the sugary red goo off the store-bought dessert, I absolutely believed that Mitchell would have been tenured had he married a skinny woman who made coffee in a French press.

All of this was in the bags we had packed and taken to Paris. And then we got lost.

We were so lost that we couldn't find a French fry in Paris.

Dozens of taxis were whizzing by us both ways through the Marais, but when I suggested we could splurge and catch a ride back to our hotel, Mitchell pointed at the window of a clock shop behind me. Seven filigreed gold pocket watches with faded ivory faces were suspended on invisible wire from an iron dowel. A few feet behind this priceless mobile, an elderly man in a three-piece suit and a thin slick of silver hair was wielding a feather-duster like a billy club, slapping the wooden handle against his open palm, as if he thought we were casing the joint.

"*Les cloches*," I said.

Mitchell smiled. "That's the word for *clock*?"

"The plural," I said.

He said, "*La clutch?*"

"Not quite," I said.

He said, "*Clush.*"

I said, "Try *cloash.*" The more didactic I became, the more delighted he looked.

"*La cloach?*"

"More like the *O* in *closet. La cloche.* And I am not asking that shopkeeper for directions. He looks like he's about two minutes away from calling the *gendarme* to get rid of us." But by then the pomaded proprietor had pushed the door halfway open, his disapproving gaze aimed at Mitchell's bare knees, and I surprised all of us by uttering a few halting sentences with present-tense verbs and several repetitions of the name of our hotel, and there poured forth from the shopkeeper a mercilessly detailed walking route, replete with landmarks where we were meant to veer off to the *gauche* or the *droite*, and when I thanked him, the shopkeeper winced and said to no one, *Une autre canadienne*, and closed the door.

I was elated.

Mitchell said, "Did you get all that?"

"Only a few words," I said. "But who cares? He thinks I'm Canadian. Not that he meant it as a compliment."

"It's a left-handed insult," Mitchell said, taking my hand and confidently leading me through the crowded streets, turning us *droite*, *gauche*, *droite*, *gauche*, this way and that, right back to our hotel, like clockwork. He had understood every word the clock-shop owner had spoken.

That night, Mitchell put on his wedding suit, and we were whisked off in a taxi to the Monte Carlo, an absurdly elegant little restaurant with a maître d' done up in tails and mustache wax. Mitchell ordered for us both, *les escargots* and *Chateaubriand pour deux*—"surf 'n' turf à Larousse," he called it, surprising me with his pitch-perfect pronunciation. And then he told me he'd been offered a job at Harvard. "No more conjugations and declensions," he said. "An assistant dean in the Faculty of Arts and Sciences," he added quickly.

"Harvard," I said too loudly, because I knew it would make him happy. And even in Paris, heads turned. I laid my hands on his and leaned in, lowering my voice. "Harvard? Since when?"

"The money will be a big boost," he said.

I said, "Not teaching just to start with, or not teaching ever again?"

"We can buy a house," he said. He slid his hands out from under mine and flapped open his napkin with a flourish. "No teaching. I'm strictly Administration from here on in."

The restaurant seemed suddenly too small, too dark and smoky, too loud with incomprehensible conversations, too much like the rest of my life. But soon the sommelier was popping open a bottle of champagne, compliments of a tuxedoed gentleman at a neighboring table who confided he was Class of '29, and Mitchell stood and proposed a toast to his blushing bride, and though the honeymoon was over by then, the chef sent out a complimentary dessert course of cheese and fruit on a circular slab of green marble under a large bell-shaped crystal dome, and the waiter bowed to me and said, "Shall I remove the *cloche, madame?*"

"*La cloche,*" I said.

Mitchell said, "*La cloche.* The bell."

"Ah," I said. "I gave you the wrong word at the clock shop. Why didn't you correct me?"

Mitchell shrugged, letting me know it was his pleasure to indulge my ignorance.

I said, "Please remove *la cloche, monsieur.*"

The waiter backed away.

Mitchell said, "*Horloge.* I think that might be the word for clock."

"*Horloge,*" I said.

"As in horology, or horologic," Mitchell said. "From the Greek, I think."

"I'm sure you're right," I said. "So." The cheese smelled like a sewer. "Harvard!"

THIRTY-TWO YEARS LATER, I GOT LOST IN PARIS AGAIN, BUT this time I was alone with no one but myself to blame. My flight from Boston had landed twenty minutes early that Saturday morning in June, saddling me with even more time before my connecting flight took off at three-thirty. I was running on ninety minutes of sleep, two issues of *Vanity Fair*, two vodka tonics, and one defrosted Valium from Mitchell's icebox pharmacy of expired prescriptions, so I was better prepared to kill myself than to kill four hours in Charles de Gaulle Airport.

The flight attendants had assured me that my checked bags would make the transfer without my assistance, but I headed for the nearest information booth in the busy terminal to confirm this and squander some time. I chose the longest and most unpromising of three lines, directly behind five tiny women wearing colorful silk head scarves and tennis shoes, who were cooing in a language sure to stump the middle-aged stewardess manqué at the counter. Before I got my "*Bonjour!*" from Martine, the blue-uniformed woman who, up close, looked even older than I did, I unzipped my bulging red canvas wheelie bag (borrowed from my daughter, Rachel, at her insistence) and extracted the leather-bound *Journal of Discovery* (going-away gift from Rachel and, allegedly, her brother, Sam) to jot down information for surviving the layover. Perhaps Martine would be willing to map out the route to my departure gate, and recommend a lunch spot where English was spoken, and maybe I could persuade her to check an Italian weather forecast and let me know if I should expect rain when I got to Venice, as I was wearing espadrilles instead of my ugly new water-resistant walking shoes because I'd got seized with a fit of nostalgia right before leaving the house in Cambridge and pulled off the stretchy jeans (late-night catalog purchase strictly intended for travel days) and put on a venerable black-and-white Marimekko block-print belt dress, which still fit if I treated the belt as an ornament, casually knotted at the back.

I said, *"Bonjour."*

"Bonjour. Où allez-vous, madame?"

"Yes," I said, as if Martine's question were philosophical. I was trying to remember why I had left my quiet house, my sofa beneath my bay windows, my pile of books, my remote control, my too-big TV mounted on my off-white living room wall at a slightly annoying angle to my pale blue chair rail and crown molding.

Martine smiled and optimistically said, "English?"

"Yes," I said deliberatively, sticking a finger into the gutter of the journal before I closed it, as if that blank page might yet be filled in with some charming anecdote from the first day of my monthlong Italian adventure, the deluxe surprise Mitchell had painstakingly planned with the conspiratorial assistance of the children to celebrate our thirty-fifth wedding anniversary even though—Surprise!—I would have preferred a week of watching movies in bed with takeout Chinese for dinner. Even after—Surprise!—several hundred little malignant tumors, metasta-sized from a vicious cancer on his liver, had been discovered during Mitchell's annual checkup on the Monday after Thanksgiving, and the likelihood of his being alive in June was in grave doubt, his itinerary-making and optional side-trip selecting went on, each choice dictated by an annotation or a footnote he found as he paged through his Dante box, which he referred to till the last as his book.

He left me everything, just as he promised. "Everything," he liked to say during his last month on the sofa as I leaned in to feed him rice pudding, "everything will be yours," as if it weren't yet. I was left with that and two adult children who could not tolerate my sitting at home by myself—admittedly, rather too often in a capacious pink flannel nightgown and the green cardigan Mitchell was wearing on the afternoon he died.

Martine said, "Where are you going, *madame?*"

"Nowhere," I said, unpleasantly, for no good reason, or maybe because I had not been brave enough, or confident enough, or honest enough to say so to my children when they prevailed upon me to trade the bittersweet squalor of my sofa for their father's idea of romance.

"Okay," Martine said. "*Bon voyage, madame.* But remember you are not alone."

"Oh." I felt a swell of camaraderie. "What a sweet thing to say."

But Martine had just wanted me to move along. She was pointing at the long line behind me and waving forward a young German couple and their backpacks. "*Bonjours! Où allez-vous?*"

I wheeled my way to an empty row of red plastic chairs and sat down. According to the sign behind the Air France booth, I had arrived at Gate 2D, and according to my ticket, my next flight departed from Gate 2D. I really was going nowhere. But without coffee and a sandwich, I knew I would soon pass out, so I got up and rolling. Fueled only by instinct, I rolled right past the first café, and then another, and then a newsstand and a crêperie on the edge of a vast, international food court that looked like the Seventh Circle of Hell, a throbbing pit of currency conversion and halting translation and hungry, hopeful travelers staring with disappointment at the cooling blobs of stuff on their Styrofoam plates as they waited for seats to open up. I veered off into a glass breezeway and onto an electric rubber sidewalk. The passage was echoey with the laughter and shouting of schoolkids in blue blazers and caps running the other way, but I could see to the end, just beyond the point where the conveyor belt bent back underground, to a bright, empty bank of gates and rows of empty blue plastic chairs. That was just where I wanted to be—nowhere. And I felt precisely what you are supposed to feel in France, a frisson, a splendid little chill of illicit delight when I realized what I was about to do.

I aimed for the first open row with an unobstructed view of the runways. In a fit of inspiration, I tented my magazines on the nearby chairs, as if their occupants would return at any moment. I was not going to Venice. I was going to sleep. And then I was going home.

A few rows away, a black man with a cockney accent was hovering over two plastic infant carriers, whispering reassuringly. When he noticed me, he waved.

I held up my hand and raised two fingers, smiling sympathetically.

He took a few wary steps my way and looked back at the babies. "Be asleep. Please be asleep," he said, and then he turned a smile to me. "Twins."

I said, "Aren't we lucky?"

He looked confused.

I spun my hand in little circles a few times in the air, indicating the unlikely silence and unpopulated room. "So peaceful."

"Oh, yeah, no Jews," he said.

This was odd enough to make me rethink the benefits of my isolated perch.

He took a few more steps my way, hands in the pockets of his hero jacket, flapping the plackets, making himself bigger.

I froze, but my head didn't. It kept twitching back and forth—*no, no, no, stay away, stay away.*

He stared at me, narrowing his gaze, and his lips tightened into a tiny smile. Finally, he closed his eyes, snorted dismissively, and then dipped his shoulder and headed back to his babies.

At the other end of the room, three men in turbans and business suits emerged from another breezeway, each of them texting with one hand and dragging a carry-on case with the other. They looked like a modern-dress version of the Three Wise Men. They settled into seats facing me and the man with the babies, their backs to the traffic on the tarmac. Above them, I saw that each of the unmanned booths belonged to El Al airline. And this was the Sabbath. No flights for the Jews. Maybe that's all the young father was trying to tell me. I wondered if I should clear up the awkwardness between us. I could have approached him. I could have apologized for my performance. I could have tried to explain that my panic had nothing to do with the color of his skin, as he had huffily assumed. It was the jacket that made him look like a thug. Would it have killed him to put on a button-down shirt and a blazer when he was traveling? His snorting at me didn't help, either. Of course, he might say it wasn't a snort but a yawn, or just nothing. Maybe he wasn't even insulted. Maybe he had just walked away because I'd clammed up and he figured we'd run out of things to say to each other. His head was tilted back in his seat—probably sound asleep. And I was exhausted. And I was sure neither of us wanted to wake the babies.

Sometimes, it seemed that I was married to every man in the world.

I closed my eyes.

I was roused a few times by noisy passersby and a couple of interminable public-safety alerts, but it was a screaming baby that finally woke me up. I felt fine until I stood, and then I felt like I did most mornings after a night on the too-soft sofa. But my soreness was tempered by triumph. I had successfully overslept and missed my flight. I also had thirteen new messages—a bonanza for a hermit like me. My semi-private quarters in the Jewish ghetto had filled up, but the twins and their father were gone, and so were the turbaned texters. This gave me a sense of status as the veteran, the queen of the displaced. I scrolled through my missed calls and texts—six from Rachel; two from Sam; one from Sam's girlfriend, Susie; one from EurWay Travel; and one from the company that sold stretchy jeans to women who shouldn't wear jeans.

Sam was the softest target, but out of loyalty I dialed Rachel. She had done more than anyone to get me this far. It was seven o'clock in Paris, one in the afternoon in Boston. I imagined Rachel would be strolling the aisles of Whole Foods, shopping for something yummy. Her ex-husband took the two boys most weekends, and Rachel had been dating lately—that's what she called cooking dinner, sleeping with a man, making him breakfast, and then getting him out of the way with time enough to complete the *Sunday Times* crossword before David dropped the boys back at home.

She didn't answer her phone. This was a surprise. I dialed again. Since Mitchell died, Rachel took my calls whether she was writing a brief or taking a bath with a new beau.

I didn't leave a message. Evidently, she'd got the message already.

Sam answered on the first ring. "You're alive."

"Hello, dear boy. I fell asleep in the airport, so I'm a little stiff, but otherwise unscathed."

"You missed your flight to Venice." No questions. No recriminations. No proposed remediation. I was so grateful Rachel had not picked up.

"I guess it wasn't meant to be," I said. A long silence followed, and I heard young girls squealing in the background. "Are you at school today?"

"Volleyball tournament. I've been whipping up their spirits because we're going to get crushed. Are you really okay?"

"This was your father's dream, not mine. It never really made sense, did it?" Jumbo jets were gliding up and out of sight every few seconds. "Me on a bus for a month? With other people?"

Sam went silent. Maybe he was really thinking about my question, maybe he was downloading a new app, or maybe he was tying his shoe. Whenever I called my children, they treated me like one more member of the audience tuned in to the latest episode of their reality shows. Finally, he said, "What can I do?"

I said, "Nobody has to do anything. Just don't expect a postcard from the Vatican. I'm flying home tomorrow."

Sam said, "So what I could do is drive to Boston tomorrow and pick you up at Logan. We'll be knocked out of the tournament by three, and Susie has to run the box office for the matinee at the theater tomorrow, so I'm on my own. Should I try to find you a hotel near the airport where you can sleep tonight?"

He'd do anything short of calling his sister. I said, "Have you spoken to Rachel?"

"No. I've had thirty or so texts since noon, but I told her I was being hauled off the sidelines to referee and couldn't talk till later. I wanted to know what you wanted first."

When I wanted the huge flat-screen TV, which I had never wanted in the house, taken out of Mitchell's office and installed on the living room wall so he didn't have to use a walker to watch a ball game, Sam took the train from New York and did the job, despite Mitchell's objections about the ruination of the living room, and his complaints about my underestimating his stamina, and Rachel's insistence that her father's pride was more important than his physical comfort. The TV did hang at an odd angle, true. Unbeknownst to Mitchell and Rachel, there was a hole about the size of a volleyball in the plaster where Sam had badly misjudged the location of the stud on his first attempt—also true. And Sam had driven away that day in his father's two-year-old BMW, and that loan, like so many others, had aged into a gift.

Rachel got less and gave more. Once Mitchell took to the sofa, she rearranged her mornings and drove the boys to school herself so she could come by the house with the *Wall Street Journal,* which Mitchell had always read at the office. It pleased him not to have to belly up for home delivery. It pleased him to speculate wildly about Rachel's salary as legal counsel for a pharmaceutical start-up frequently featured in the pages of the *Journal.* And after he died, I think it pained Rachel to see me sprawled out on that sofa for three months running, wrapped up in a sadness that was, at least, in part hers.

"Listen, Mom, I have to go soon." Sam had moved closer to the action, presumably to authenticate the sense of urgency with sound effects. "But I have to warn you—Rachel got in touch with Susie when she found out you didn't get to Venice with your plane. I think Rachel wanted Susie to call her friend." During the pause, the background noise got louder.

"Tell Susie not to bother her friend." Neither Sam nor I said *again,* but surely the word had bounced into our respective courts. This was not my first missed flight. Mitchell's itinerary for the Italian adventure had anticipated a Thursday departure from Boston. But when Thursday afternoon arrived, and the taxi Rachel had arranged beeped from the curb, I gave the cabbie twenty dollars to get lost. When I called Rachel to tell her the trip was off, she offered to find me a therapist who specialized in agoraphobia, and by midnight she had a confirmation of my reservation on Air France for Friday evening from Susie's friend at the online travel site, who had ticketed all of my international flights, and Rachel had also persuaded EurWay Travel to send a driver to meet me at Marco Polo Airport in Venice on Saturday afternoon. And now I'd missed my connecting flight. "Listen, Sam. Nobody has to do anything." I'd been saying so for months.

"Okay, okay. But just so you know—you are booked on a midday flight to Venice tomorrow," Sam said. "Susie was going to text you the details." The little volleyball players were chanting, *Our turn, Our turn, Our turn.* "You don't have to go, Mom."

My cell phone binged with a new email from Rachel. "You have to go, Sam. And god knows I have to go somewhere they're serving coffee. I hope your girls win. Give Susie my love. And a million apologies."

"Love you, Mom, wherever you are." Sam clicked off.

I rolled all the way back to that first crêperie, pointed to two dinner crepes on the illustrated menu, and accidentally ordered *deux cafés au lait* when I begged the waiter for some coffee—*du café*. I was halfway through the second cup before I felt up to reading Rachel's message.

Dear, dear, dear mother of mine—
Six things.
1. *Your reservation number at the Novotel hotel for tonight is*
   9WX877YUSA. The hotel is a three-minute walk from
   Terminal 3. You are in Terminal 2.
2. *Your flight to Venice leaves tomorrow (Sunday) at 12:35 PM from*
   Terminal 2. Susie's text has your boarding pass and gate info.
3. *The same driver (Pietro) will be at Marco Polo (again) tomorrow*
   with your name on a sign. Don't stand him up again. And don't tip
   him—he's made a fortune off you already.
4. *The driver will take you to the train station, where the smaller*
   group going to Padua will pick you up in the tour bus. (The driver
   is prepared to escort you to the bus. I've licensed him to be firm—
   up to and including handcuffs.)
5. *You haven't missed much. Daddy had never thought of your initial*
   stay as anything but recuperation from jet lag, which is why you
   have three full days in Venice at the end of the month.
6. *Don't call me until you are in Padua so we don't say what we'll*
   only wish we hadn't said.

Everything went according to Rachel's revised agenda until my Venetian driver pulled into the train station almost half an hour before the tour bus was due. "We are too early," he said, "and giving thanks to me for this favor." Pietro stepped swiftly around his car, opened the back door, and offered me his hand.

"I better just wait right here," I said.

Pietro took this as a rebuke, dropping his gaze to the pavement. His disappointment was exaggerated by his three-piece suit. He was old enough and bald enough to be an appropriate suitor. "This bus you must take is nowhere. Always, is always *molto tardi*. I promise you. *Tardissimo*."

"I really don't speak a word of Italian."

"Me neither," he said, pulling me out of the car.

"My bag," I said, as if having that in my grip would assure me of safe passage.

Pietro obligingly dragged my canvas wheelie out of the trunk and led me around the side of the huge, squat train station. "Everybody in Venezia is not speaking just like you, right? See?" He pointed to a herd of elderly tourists ahead of us. Each of them was wearing a yellow baseball cap. "*Tutti in ferie!*" Pietro turned to me for confirmation.

I understood nothing he'd said, but I was not happy about those yellow hats. "Does my tour come with a uniform?"

"You see now? *Si, si*, there she is for you."

We were perched at a railing, about ten feet above a busy dock at the edge of a dark, deep canal with a profound current churning up waves along the stone wall. "Is this the Grand Canal?"

Pietro proudly said, "*Canalasso*."

"So—not the Grand Canal?"

"We say here *Canalasso*."

Here at the train station? Here in Italy? Here in Venice? Our conversation had ping-ponged like that from the moment we met. We were both trying to be good sports, but we were whacking these balls at two different tables.

Staring deep into the center of the canal, Pietro said, *"E' bella, no?"*

We had seen the canals from the car, and I had brought with me many memorable descriptions from novels, and images from the movies, but everything else was eclipsed by this first true glimpse of the watery world. From where I was standing, the dark sea surging through the city seemed ancient, and unnerving, and fantastical, like a dragon's tail on a medieval map.

Very softly, Pietro said, *"Canalasso."*

I said, *"Canalasso,"* which made me cry, as if Mitchell were streaming by below me, just beyond my reach.

Pietro kindly let a lot of water pass beneath us before he moved. Calmly, he led me out of the sun to the shelter of an open café table outfitted with a red-and-blue Cinzano umbrella. He insisted on buying me my first coffee in Italy, and I insisted on paying. Actually, he said, *"Café?"* and after he paid, and wagged his hand dismissively while I dug out my wallet, I put a fifty-euro note under his espresso cup, and then he took off without a word for just long enough to make me wonder if that was the end of him. When he returned, he presented me with three accordion-pleated postcard collections. The top card on each stack was a view of the Grand Canal from just about the spot where we'd stood in silence together, but when Pietro spread the cards out across our table, what followed from Venice was unpredictable— the Tower of Pisa, a mosaic church ceiling in Ravenna, a sheep on a Tuscan hillside, the Colosseum.

"Oh, they're all different. From everywhere," I said. "So now I have to choose one set?"

Pietro said, "Okay."

"I can't choose," I said. "I really can't. Which one is the best?"

Pietro smiled at me, at the umbrella, at the canal.

I tried again. "Really. You choose, Pietro. Please."

"Tutto," he said. "Choose everything."

II

❋

The bus ride from Venice to Padua was a little less than an hour long. The trip was slightly longer if you counted the fifteen-minute wait at the Venice train station for the widow from Cambridge, who was already famous for going AWOL at airports. At least eight of my twelve fellow passengers on the EurWay minibus counted the wait time against me, and so did the driver, an American college kid. As he crammed my red wheelie into the overhead luggage rack, he advised me of my obligation to be present at designated pickup locations fifteen minutes before departures.

I thanked him and apologized for not knowing the routine.

Somebody—one of the five men—shouted, "Read the contract."

"Sit here, if you like." This offer came from a woman seated directly behind the driver. She pulled a skein of ivory yarn from the unoccupied seat beside her and skewered it with her two-foot-long bronze knitting needles. She had short dark hair parted on the side—she couldn't have been fifty—and she was wearing pink capri pants with a pink bolero jacket over a white turtleneck, which made me think she lived alone and didn't have any close friends. Surely, someone who loved her would have suggested a simple cotton cardigan. I didn't want to appear ungrateful, so I reached up and rummaged for my cell phone while I assessed my options.

No one else moved.

The seats across the aisle from the knitter were occupied by a trench coat. The next two rows on both sides were apparently reserved for retired married couples, the four wives tucked neatly into window seats, their husbands with newspapers and maps sprawled out, legs crossed, their big shoes blocking the aisle. Behind the couples, next to the only open seats, was a tall, silver-haired gentleman with his eyes closed. Even at a glance, he was much too composed to be sleeping, so maybe he was meditating, but more likely he was praying I wouldn't sit in the open row beside him. In the aisle seats at the very back, two women with identical silver perms and shiny navy blue jogging suits—sisters or suburban lesbians—were happily passing a digital camera back and forth, reviewing the record of their two days in Venice.

Huge raindrops splattered against the windows, and the sun retreated across the concrete parking lot like an outgoing tide. This turn in the weather didn't improve anybody's mood, so I smiled apologetically at the knitter and said, "Are you sure you don't mind?"

She waved me down. Once I was settled and the bus had pulled out of the parking lot, she pointed her thumb at the trench coat on the empty seats and whispered, "He's the one who yelled at you. Welcome to junior high school." She took up her knitting.

I had a text from Rachel, which read: √

The day had gone dark, and the Italian weather was being compared unfavorably to summer days in Raleigh, North Carolina, by the couple behind us, and they were also annoyed at the tour guide's failure to clear up their confusion about Venice, the Veneto, and Vicenza, which was creating some anxiety about Tuesday.

I saw the month ahead as a wall calendar, each day an empty window I wanted to jump out.

"My name is Shelby Cohen," said the knitter, never looking up from her lap, "and if you prefer peace and quiet, just say so."

"I was admiring your needles," I said. On the top of the one nearest me was a shiny, piercingly blue stone disk in a silver setting.

She said, "Do you knit?"

"Oh, god, no," I said, and into the awkward silence that followed, I tossed another conversation stopper. "I really don't do anything."

"I don't either, not in the summer," she said casually. "I'm an accountant, and so is Allen, my husband, so we each take a month off in the summer, after the late-filing madness dies down. He's a climber, and me—well, I'm a shopper. I found these needles last summer in a little hand-forging operation in a tiny town on Galway Bay, would you believe."

"Is that a gemstone?"

"Lapis lazuli," she said.

I'd only ever seen that in museums. "So they are really precious."

"No, fifteen euros or something for the pair, but I think they were meant to be displayed and not used." She showed me the top of the other needle. The silver setting was empty. She examined a patch of ivory wool ribbing she'd finished. "One cuff," she said. "I am so sorry your husband died. I hope there's some comfort for you in being here."

The *Boston Globe* obituary for Mitchell had been sent out as an addendum to the little biographical notes compiled by the tour company, which were meant to give us a head start on getting acquainted with our fellow travelers. I had never gotten around to reviewing the roster, but I wasn't looking forward to being the sad sack of the group, the distraught widow. "I'm frankly not sure what I expected, but I am not very well prepared for this," I said.

"This—you mean the trip?" Shelby was working up a sleeve to go with that cuff.

"The trip, Italian vocabulary, sticking to a schedule, holding down my end of a casual conversation on a bus. Being alone."

She leaned forward in her seat and pointed to the middle of her back with her needles. "Is something all ruffled up back there?"

Something was amiss. I tugged tentatively at the wrinkly pink ruching between her shoulder blades, which dropped down, as did the puffed-up fabric on her shoulders, which I'd mistaken for epaulets. It was a cashmere cardigan.

"Thanks," Shelby said flatly. "That's one of the downsides of traveling alone. You never know the condition of your hind quarters. But there are benefits, too." She leaned back. "After the group meeting at the hotel, we're on our own for dinner, and the doctor offered to take me along to a place he wants to try in the Piazza del Erbe."

The meeting, the doctor, the piazza—I should have grabbed my itinerary and welcome packet instead of my phone and memorized a few useful facts. I wasn't even sure Shelby was inviting me along for her outing. "I don't want to be a third wheel," I said, the anthem of all third wheels.

"Oh, don't worry, you might be a fifth wheel," she said, and she didn't explain because my cell phone rang.

It only rang twice and then stopped, but one of the men behind us said, "No, she didn't turn her ringer off because she's above the rules. Harvard, you know."

Shelby turned around quickly, as if she might say something in my defense, but I put my hand on hers.

Shelby smiled. "I guess you're used to that—occupational hazard."

"More like guilt by association," I said. "I was a reference librarian until my children were born. Now, I teach reading to public-school kids. Or I did before Mitchell was diagnosed." Well, about five years before the diagnosis, the public schools cut reading specialists out of the budget and I agreed to roam around the city as a fill-in librarian and substitute teacher's aide. I spent many days portioning Gummi Bears into little paper cups under the scrutiny of women younger than my daughter. Mitchell urged me to quit and do something more rewarding, but I told him it was a point of pride. "With italics for emphasis on *a point*," he'd said. This past September, I retired because I was finally fully vested, with a pension that might cover the rent for a third-floor walk-up studio apartment on the Somerville side of the Cambridge town line—if I went easy on the utilities.

The woman directly behind us said, "No, it wasn't because he was rejected." She amped up the volume, or else she leaned forward so I could hear her clearly. "And I heard there were at least two other boys in his class who got into Harvard but went to Duke."

Shelby shrugged.

I said, "I think Harvard is infuriating because all the self-important monkey business somehow preserves something people still look up to. It's like the Vatican. I almost feel like skipping Rome because I know I'll have to be grateful to the scoundrels after I see the Sistine Chapel."

Shelby said, "Are you a Catholic?"

Not much of one, not since my sophomore year in college, when my mother died suddenly of a cerebral aneurysm. She'd been plagued by migraines for months, and instead of bothering her doctor with complaints about a silly headache, she had decided to give up coffee for Lent on the advice of a parish priest whose sister was a missionary nurse in Guinea-Bissau—"formerly known as Portuguese-Guinea," my mother reminded me each time we spoke that spring. My mother was all for the natives, who'd overthrown the repressive colonial government, but she was also sending ten dollars a week to the Portuguese convent and hospital to make sure the poor Africans didn't throw out the quinine with the bathwater.

My mother was not a fanatic. I'm sure she didn't expect to be miraculously cured of her headaches. She had taken to religion as a young widow, and her piety and her devotion to her parish did not go unrewarded. She offered up the inexplicable and unbearable circumstances of her little, often lonely life and they acquired significance in the ancient and worldwide project of the propagation of the faith.

Unlike my older brother, Richard, I had not really gotten to know my father before an industrial transformer he was installing exploded and killed him and three other young men, so I was vulnerable to the appeal of a heavenly father and stories of brave young saints whose gruesome deaths won them celebrity status in heaven. And when I got my first look at the graphic reality of pregnancy in a grade-school Hygiene and Holiness class, I got very interested in a career as a virgin martyr or a nun. Richard never succumbed and eventually got himself tossed out of two Catholic colleges in one year and dropped out of my life for a long time. I was in high school by then, and my friends' older brothers were teaching them to drive, and their fathers were buying them flowers for just being in the chorus of a play, and I irrationally aimed most of my resentment at the Church and the big fuss everybody made about the Crucifixion, which seemed less tragic than my lot in light of the Resurrection three days later.

But I was practiced and pious enough as a young Catholic girl to be an asset when Mitchell was navigating the implicit moral and social codes at Boston College. I also came in handy as a theological resource when he was still working on his Dante book in earnest those evenings. Whether I was reading a recipe or pondering the persistent blanks in a *Times* crossword puzzle, I was delighted when Mitchell interrupted me with a question about the hierarchy of angels or a miracle. I was amazed to discover that stuff had value, and Mitchell and I were both astonished by my recall.

On any given evening, in the midst of preparing dinner, I could recite the Seven Sacraments or the Seven Deadly Sins or the Seven Cardinal Virtues. I was no scholar. I was more like Wikipedia with a cocktail shaker. But I had other skills, as well, and Mitchell's readiness to exploit them registered as a compliment, elevating my degree in library science from technical training to an academic accomplishment and raising my hopes about my own prospects in the world. During my last year at the Cambridge library, I happily devoted more time to cross-referencing arcane 14th-century sources than to reshelving periodicals, but then we went to Paris, and he came home to a new job, and I came home pregnant.

We didn't lose Dante when Mitchell veered off into the secular world of academic administration, but an unlikely passion we'd shared was downsized to a hobby. And nothing in my girlhood qualified me as a guide to Harvard Yard. I stayed at home until Rachel and Sam were in school. And now, I was no longer a wife, no longer a librarian or a teacher, and not really a mother anymore. Not a lot to go on conversationally. So, as no one in the Church hierarchy had bothered to excommunicate me for my many sins, I said, "I am a Catholic. Why do you ask?"

"I thought Berman might be Jewish," Shelby said. "One of my aunts—her maiden name was Effie Berman."

"Mitchell's father was a Jew," I said.

Shelby said, "He's passed on, too?"

"Years ago," I said. "And Mitchell's mother, too." Mitchell had insisted we move her from a nursing home in Philadelphia to a facility near us. He couldn't tolerate the idea of her spending her last days alone, and though she had long since forgotten who he was, he visited her religiously, every Sunday morning, till she died three years later. I visited her three days a week after school, and spent the better part of my time in her room collecting compliments from her roommate and the nurse's aide for Mitchell, whose devotion to his mother deeply impressed everyone.

Shelby said, "And your parents?"

I felt like Typhoid Mary. "I do have a brother," I said.

I couldn't tell if Shelby was afraid to ask another question or if her curiosity about me was waning. She had taken up her knitting again. I closed my eyes and tried to come up with something interesting to say. It seemed a safe bet that Shelby and Allen Cohen were Jewish, but I'd been wrong about the bolero. I didn't know where she lived or if she had children, but I didn't want to insult her by proving I hadn't read her personal profile.

"Do you want to see something beautiful?" Shelby passed me her phone. "Allen just sent me this. He's climbing the Three Saints this month in Southern California."

Above a foreground of palm trees, a vast snowcapped run of ridges and peaks rose right out of the desert, topped off by an impossibly blue sky. I said, "Put your needle there—the blue one—put it right there, on the sky."

Shelby tilted the stone toward the screen and smiled. "Lapis lazuli," she said.

I nodded. It was bluer than the familiar blue sky—it was the empyrean, the brightness Dante had imagined beyond the bounds of heaven and earth, beyond past and future, beyond the beyond.

Shelby aimed her finger at the top of the little screen. "That's San Jacinto, the tallest of the peaks. Ten thousand feet high. That's where he's headed right now. I can show you a picture of Allen on the mountain."

Her shoulder pressed into my arm and our hands touched again as she searched for the right button on her phone. I didn't move. I held my breath. I wanted to extend this contact, this oddly intimate moment, extend my readiness to believe in that blue above and beyond the Three Saints, that immaterial place where Allen and Mitchell might someday meet.

"THE HOTEL ARENA IS PERFECT. IT'S IN A LONG, MODERN, arcaded concrete building with balconies, but inside it looks like the sort of place Thomas Mann might have stayed—a tiny wood-paneled reception desk, where a mustache in a tuxedo orchestrates dozens of dark-haired valets in green vests, and the elevator is smaller than your walk-in refrigerator. It's all so charming." I was determined to make Rachel believe I was happy to be here.

"Is the bathroom tiny?"

"Compact," I said. The sink was a cereal bowl. "Handsome old green-marble floor and white-tile walls. And I have a perfectly Italianate view of red-clay rooftops." This was true if you lay in bed so that you couldn't see the tin ductwork directly below the one window. "I'll send you some pictures."

"That's okay," she said, "I've already seen the pictures on the Web. Daddy didn't want to upgrade to a balcony room because he'd read something about traffic noise at the front of the building."

"I prefer it here at the back. It's so peaceful." So was the front of the hotel, which faced Largo Europa, a two-lane street with a leafy pedestrian park separating it from the next block, but maybe it was trafficky on weekdays. Admittedly, I hadn't spent much time outside after we got off the bus, as it quickly became apparent that I was the only one in the group who'd paid the supplement to bring a second suitcase, and I didn't want to hear about it from the married couples. "My luggage arrived, safe and sound," I said.

The boys were fine, work was busy, Rachel was proud of me but I shouldn't feel I had to call every day, just have, you know—and then a long pause. It was about noon in Boston. I guessed she was doing the Sunday crossword and had hit a bad patch. "You know, have fun, and—" Another pause. "Eat pasta! Or just, you know—"

"Sweetie, I have to wash my face and leave for dinner soon."

"Of course. Okay, so, let's see," she said. I heard pages flipping. "Tomorrow is the Arena Chapel and St. Anthony's Basilica. And then you go to Vicenza on Tuesday, but that's only a day trip from where you are, so that will be easy. And then—is it Wednesday you go to Florence or Thursday morning?"

"Wednesday afternoon," I said, "and then Moscow on Thursday and Tokyo on Friday."

"Sorry. I'm acting like your mother," Rachel said. "Or your father. I mean, Daddy. I'm sorry. I'll let you go."

I said, "Kiss those two beautiful boys for me."

Rachel said, "But you really are happy to be in Padua?"

I said, "I wouldn't be happy anywhere else."

OUR FREELANCE TOUR GUIDE IN PADUA WAS SARA, A THIRTY-year-old local woman in a white trench coat and thick black plastic horn-rimmed eyeglasses, and she had wound her long dark hair into a face-lifting bun. She spoke almost impeccable English, explained almost nothing, and narrated everything she did, occasionally nodding at questions and ignoring them. "I will now pass to each of you a personal copy of the itinerary for tomorrow, which is Monday," she said as she slowly made her way to the twelve Padua side-trippers scattered throughout the hotel's windowless Executive Business Event Conference Center, a blank room with one hundred red restaurant-supply dining chairs, a long table, and a pull-down movie screen. From my perch near a desktop computer at the back of the room, I noted that the doctor with the silver hair was missing. "While I am now passing out the prepared itinerary, I will remind you that we must meet in the lobby at nine-fifteen tomorrow morning after you have had time to enjoy a complimentary breakfast buffet of your choosing."

One of the wives asked for dinner recommendations.

"Yes," Sara said, "and you will notice there is no change from the itineraries you were issued in Venice except for the addition of details, including a local post office, which you can see is marked right here on the top left of the itinerary I am now holding up to show you in case you have some postal cards for that purpose."

Two of the husbands momentarily commandeered the event to complain about the private balconies, which weren't private but one long, undivided balcony, so anyone could walk the length of any floor and look into everybody else's room, as if you were staying in a motel.

"The balconies are reserved for paying guests at the front of the hotel," Sara said, "and there will be no flash cameras allowed inside the Scrovegni Chapel, which I point out now to your behalf on the back of each itinerary, where you can see the marked *Arena Chapel*."

One of the women asked, "Which name do the locals use for the chapel?"

"Of course," Sara said, "the famous frescoes painted by Giotto more than seven hundred years ago had no equal in the world, as you will see. Interesting for all of you is Dante, the greatest poet for all time. He tells everyone in *Divina Commedia*, the greatest poem for all the world, that Giotto was the greatest of all painters in the world, better even than his own master, Cimabue." Sara picked up an index card from the table behind her. "In painting, Cimabue thought to hold the field / Now Giotto is acclaimed by all / So that he has obscured the former's fame."

Mitchell would not have approved. Sara was reading from the Mandelbaum translation, which Mitchell considered authoritative but tame. He preferred the wilder, woollier early translations that delivered a more rousing narrative voice and served up plenty of errors and infelicities for him to annotate as he read. The reason I had been booked on this side-trip to Padua was for Mitchell to point out how heavily Giotto had leaned on Dante's ideas. Giotto was one of many answers to his title question, *Who Stole Dante?*

"Lucky," Sara said, "you will also see in the Bargello how Giotto painted a portrait of Dante."

A woman who'd found time to curl her hair into a perfect platinum flip asked, "But isn't the Bargello museum in Florence?"

"Both of these great artists were, how you say, *Fiorentino.*"

The same woman said, "We actually say Florentine."

"*Si, si, si, Firenze,*" Sara said.

"No, no, no, *Florence* is what we say. Like you say *Padova,* we say *Padua.*"

Shelby swiveled in her seat near the front of the room. "Potato, *Padova.* Let's call the whole thing off."

"Agreed." The blonde conceded the point with a shake of her flip. "But we still don't know whether we should refer to it as the Arena Chapel or the Scrovegni Chapel."

"I will show you next this church of the Eremitani," Sara said, her voice a little shakier now. "Next, not walking too far," she stumbled on, sliding her finger down the map, "we will enjoy this ride on the tram for visiting the very holy basilica with the very holy tongue of St. Anthony looking even today almost like new, saving time to stop in many other famously beautiful chapels along the way."

This went on for fifteen minutes. The frustration in the room was palpable, but it was held in check by the anxiety evident in Sara's earnest performance. Shelby shot me a couple of exasperated looks from the front of the room, and I nodded, but I wasn't eager for the event to end. I was dreading my dinner with strangers, and then sitting alone Monday morning with some panicky assortment of sweet rolls and exotic-fruit nectar from that breakfast buffet, so I was hoping Sara would talk until Tuesday.

I felt someone's hands on my shoulders.

"Have I managed to miss absolutely every tedious detail?" As I turned, the silver-haired doctor slid into the chair beside me. He had changed into a blue linen blazer and a starched white shirt, unbuttoned at the collar. He was at least six feet tall, and his taut, pale skin was deeply etched around the eyes and mouth with tiny, dark age lines. When he leaned toward me, his severe, angular profile widened into a delighted grin. He whispered, "At this moment, we are the only people in Italy not having a drink." I got a whiff of gin and lemon and instinctively looked at my watch. It was almost seven. He nodded.

"Is there some questions at the back of this room?" Sara was peering at me.

Very loudly, the doctor said, "I suppose it might just be me, but—" He paused so everyone had time to turn around. He leaned back, rocking a bit in his chair, staring at Sara. "I'm a little bit on pins and needles back here. I just know, at any moment now, you are going to toss away those eyeglasses, shake your hair loose, and turn into Gina Lollobrigida. You are so very beautiful."

One of the husbands yelped, "Exactly!" He started a round of applause that caught on as everyone laughed and nodded in agreement. Relief swept through the room like an unexpected wave, and as it receded, one of the wives said, "It really is true, Sara. You're just lovely."

Sara leaned back against the table and waved her hand. "We can go enjoy the evening now." Soon, she was surrounded by the couples, and the doctor wagged his head, which was suggestive enough to make me follow him to the hotel bar, a counter with six steel stools tucked into a dark alcove between the kitchen and the restaurant.

"Gin okay?"

I nodded.

He nodded at the bartender, who pulled down two tall glasses from a shelf, scooped a tablespoon of frozen lemonade into each, added an incautious amount of gin, topped it off with tonic water and a slice of lemon, and shoved them our way. The doctor clinked his glass against mine and said, "To so-and-so, who invented this perfect marriage of sour and bitter."

It was a very good cocktail. "Who is so-and-so?"

"Long story," he said.

I said, "What's the drink called? It's delicious."

"We have time for two," he said. "St. Shelby volunteered to escort the two elderly sisters with the wigs to the restaurant, and that won't be a quick trip. The drink is called a Perfect Marriage. Is it Elizabeth or Betsy or Liz or Mrs.?"

"Oh," I said. "Me?" Either he talked too fast or I was drinking too fast.

He said, "I'll go with E. until further notice." He waved at the bartender.

I panicked. "You're not serious about a second?"

He urged the bartender to mix up another round. "Let's just agree that you're sad and I'm sad, and we're both old enough to have our reasons."

I said, "How old *are* you?"

"Jesus, I thought we were friends," he said.

I said, "I don't have friends anymore, so I'm out of practice." To make myself stop talking, I polished off my drink, which did not work. "I'm fifty-six," I said, as if that qualified as a boast. It was a lie. "Fifty-seven, I mean. What year is it? I'm at least fifty-six." To stem my rising anxiety, I just kept telling myself, *He's a doctor, he's a doctor, he's a doctor.*

"I would have guessed younger for you. Honestly. I'm fifty-four."

I was into the second drink. "What's your name?"

He said, "T."

I said, "As in T-shirt?"

He said, "Before we go any further, I should warn you. The great restaurant in the Piazza del Erbe doesn't have a table for us. We'll be dining on pizza in the Piazza dei Fruitti. If that doesn't put you off, let's take one more sip and head out."

And we did.

We threaded our way through a couple of arcades and several short, tilty cobblestone streets that justified my espadrilles if not a third day in the block-print dress. The streets were filled with ambling families and pairs of men with their heads bent toward each other, often staring intently into a plate-glass window of a small shop selling ties or cheese or shoes or cell phones, and then we were in a vast courtyard, and T. turned us toward a collection of ten square tables under a yellow canopy and waved. "They look very happy to see us, which can't be a good sign."

That was the first sentence either of us had spoken outside of the hotel, as if we really were old friends already.

The elderly sisters were both wearing neat dark suits, and Shelby seemed to have herself wrapped in a maroon sari, though it might have been a twisted-up shawl and slacks. I felt a little rush of something as we approached the others—disappointment, or the gin—as if the best part of the evening was ending. But T. held up his hand, and a waiter shoved another table toward the one Shelby had chosen, and T. rearranged everyone, seating the sisters together, and Shelby and I at his sides opposite them, as if we were three journalists assembled to interview two celebrities, a fair summary of how the evening went.

Shelby and T. settled on the house wine and five varieties of pizza for sharing, most memorably a crispy cracker of a crust with ricotta salata and anchovy oil, and a sweet tomato, provolone, and baby artichoke pie. I sobered up on sparkling water and the heavy air of an almost-summer night. I mightn't have said anything at all, but T. occasionally prompted me to ask a question by bumping his knee against mine.

The sisters had been born in Malo, just a few miles northwest of Padua, but Anna, the slightly taller and slightly younger of the two, had married an American when she was twenty. She lived with her son and his family in Tallahassee now that her husband was dead, and this was her first time coming home to Italy. The trip was a gift from her six children. Here, the older sister, Francesca, held up both her hands, extending three fingers on each, looking wowed. She spoke almost no English, but whenever Anna or T. translated bits of the conversation for her benefit, she would retranslate the essence into a little panto-mime. Anna told us that, as a girl, she had never even traveled as far as Florence or Pisa, and Francesca leaned sideways in her chair, as if on cue. Both sisters broke out in laughter. Francesca had once been to the States, when Anna's husband was still working for Ford in Detroit, and after a brief pause, Francesca took hold of an imaginary steering wheel. "Uffa, you and your big Ford cars." She pointed to the piazza. Every citizen of Padua was walking by. "Better, no?"

Shelby took the lead, asking the sisters about the kind of food their mother cooked and recipes she'd passed on, until the bill came. It was only then I learned that Francesca still lived in Malo, with her husband, and this was her last night with her sister until Anna circled back up north with the tour at the end of the month. Apparently, this was not news to Shelby or T., but I was surprised enough to thought-lessly ask, "Wouldn't it be lovely if you were able to see the whole country together?"

Francesca understood that much English. She held up her hands, rubbed her fingers together, and shrugged.

I was humiliated. "Of course, it is expensive. Forgive me."

Anna shook her head, not happy.

This was bad enough, so to torture myself further, I conjured a little ramshackle stone hut with a thatched roof, a chicken in the living room, Francesca bent over a black cauldron of soup. Feeling in need of an ally, I turned to T., whose gallant nature had apparently been diluted by the wine. He just raised his eyebrows at me.

"*Denaro, denaro, denaro.*" Anna spit out the words. "*Troppo denaro* when it's something for her. Her Mario is a rich man with his boats and two-thousand-year-old brandies and suddenly he comes down with this fever about how she has to save for the future? He is the reason I never visit my home. I promise you, no money will be enough money if this one dies. Mario will have to hire ten nurses, and two cooks, and a secretary and a gardener to replace her. Him, he's been to China and Dubai. Right, Francesca? Francesca? She's never even seen Rome."

Francesca ignored her sister. She held her wineglass toward T. for a refill. He did the honors. She pointed at Anna's empty glass, and though Anna told T. she'd had all she wanted, Francesca took the bottle and filled her sister's glass. She said, "Anna, Anna, Anna. *Abbiamo questa sera.*"

Anna's face softened. "She says we have this night." She leaned into her sister's shoulder and said, "*Ecco, ecco, ecco.*"

T. tilted toward me, pressing his arm against mine, as if goodwill was circuiting the table, bringing us all into contact with each other.

We traded partners for the walk home. Francesca grabbed my hand, and Anna looped her arm around Shelby's, and T. patiently followed, alone. As we neared the hotel, he said he felt like Father Goose. One of the green-vested valets held open the door. T. waved us all inside and didn't even pause to pretend that he would follow along.

Shelby stopped in the middle of the lobby and said, "We've lost our guide. Where did he go?"

Anna said, "Oh, handsome men." She led us to the elevator and waited until the door slid closed to say, "At night, they are forever young."

III

�֎

I woke early, and warm, and absolutely convinced that Mitchell would turn up at any moment with two coffees and an English-language newspaper. Delusions like this were often the high point of my day, and I had learned to lie still whenever I sensed the possibility of him, which was real but evanescent, like a single note struck on a piano. Had I been at home, I would have eventually rolled off the sofa and followed the well-worn path to the kitchen or the mailbox, but in Italy every next thing involved strangers, and street maps, and translations, and confusion, and two huge suitcases to pack and unpack and repack. I didn't want to think about what came next every hour on the hour for the next thirty days.

I had done my duty. *Veni, vedi, pizza.* Now, I wanted to go home.

For a few grim minutes, I forced myself to lie there in bed, eyes closed, trying to imagine how I would explain my return to Rachel. But even that excruciating inevitability seemed inconsequential next to the delightful image of me standing in the lobby beside a young man in a tuxedo with my suitcases, waiting for a taxi to take me to the airport in Venice.

I was going home. The only obstacle in my way was breakfast.

I opened the window, and the hum and buzz of traffic poured into my room, followed by a stream of cool, damp air that soon chased me right into the shower. All went well until I had to choose a blouse or pull-over for the long day of travel ahead. After rejecting the obvious options, I caught sight of myself in the full-length mirror on the back of the closet door. My damp hair was dark, and the expensive new layers and soft fringe of my semi-permanent caramel-brown dye job were clinging to my neck and forehead like a black tattoo. I was slimmer than I'd been in years, thanks to a diet of coffee, Cheerios, and a weekly plastic vat of yogurt-covered raisins (I was in mourning). Still, the overall impression was not improved by the godawful walking shoes, which made it clear I was not really five foot five as I liked to believe, and the stretchy jeans weren't doing my thighs any favors. But what did me in was the superfluous sheath of skin that drooped like a sausage casing from just beneath my bra and pooled up at the pleated-elastic waistband. If I'd seen me in those jeans in the changing room before yoga, I'd have nixed the raisins.

Thus the invention of the shirtdress. I unrolled the three I'd packed and hung them in the closet. Beneath them, I lined up the espadrilles, the open-toed pumps, and the leather wedge sandals. This improved my spirits. I didn't immediately choose the navy blue, beige, or lilac. I unhitched Rachel's clever red canvas bag from its wheels, tossed in my wallet, cell phone, and reading glasses. I dried my hair, occasionally glancing at the dresses in the closet, as if conferring with three girlfriends. After I strapped on the Swiss Army watch Mitchell wore every day of his working life, which fit me like a bangle, I stuck my hand out the window. It was still cool, so I opted for the navy blue and the espadrilles.

It was 7:04. Breakfast was now officially not being served at the buffet. But as I walked past the desk in the lobby and turned to the restaurant, three of the touring wives and one husband were blocking the entrance. One of the women turned hopefully to me and then said, "Oh, hello there. I don't suppose you know where the staff is?"

"I'm meeting a friend," I said, and headed for the front door.

Outside, two green-vested men were smoking, leaning back against the sill of one of the windows of the restaurant. As I approached, they both looked at their watches and said something apologetic.

"I'm looking for a café," I said.

One of them knocked on the window and said, "Free coffee. We come now."

The other one pointed to his left. "*Il Metro. Per la strada, da questo lato.*"

I said, "*Perfecto*," not sure if that was Italian or Spanish or an invention. Halfway down the block, I was relieved to see the steel sign for Café Metro, backlit with blue light, as was the bar inside. It was perched at the corner of the arcaded alley we'd walked through last night on the way to the piazza. Its exterior walls were huge sheets of plate glass, and one pane on the front was pivoted open to a street-side café, where two singles were braving the traffic. I headed inside and veered toward the darkest seats on the arcade wall and hoped the young aproned woman with long henna curls leaning on the crowded bar could be roused into table service. Most of the business seemed to be espresso shots at the bar. After a few minutes of graciously expectant smiling and waving, I pulled my journal out of my bag, as if I'd just had a noteworthy thought, and I immediately realized I hadn't brought a pen.

"Don't ask." T. was standing beside my table with a tray. He was still wearing his blue linen blazer. He set down something dark with white foam in a clear glass, and then a second. "Latte macchiato," he said. He pushed my journal to the far corner of the table and then added two tiny cups of espresso. "Shots and chasers," he explained. Between the beverages, he slid a white saucer with three little biscotti on a white doily. He raised the steel tray in his right hand, and the redhead swung by and picked it up.

I was so happy to see him, I said, "You were wonderful last night. Thank you."

"Don't look now," he said, "but every man at the bar is staring at you."

"Last chance," I said. Two moon-faced men in dark suits were turned our way, both gazing at T. I sipped from the glass. It was the perfect morning coffee. "I'm going home today."

"Oh, did you forget something?" He knocked back his espresso.

"Yes." Even in the peculiarly evasive code language we'd adopted, it was a relief to announce my intentions. It made my departure real. I shoved my espresso his way. He hadn't shaved. "I forgot who I am," I said. I immediately felt my face redden with shame. It was meant to be a joke, but it sounded a lot like a confession, perhaps because it was true. In the silence that followed, my confession ripened into a plea for help. "I have to be at home," I said defiantly, which only seemed to highlight the psychiatric aspect of my decision.

T. smiled—maybe sympathetically, maybe diagnostically—and then he said, "I almost forgot what I wanted to tell you." He cleared some space at the edge of our table and opened my journal. He flipped through several blank pages. "Oh, very shrewd," he said. "Invisible ink." He turned back to the first page and pulled a silver pen from his jacket. He looked up at me.

"Permission granted," I said. I really expected him to jot down his home address, or maybe the name of a shrink he knew in Boston.

He drew this:

"Roman arch," he said.

"Greek to me," I said.

"Basis for the greatest empire in the history of the world. Also, the basis of the barrel vault, if you imagine one of them as each end of an enclosed space, like that brick arcade." He closed the book, pocketed his pen. "What time does your flight leave from Venice?"

"Let's find out." I pulled my phone out of my bag.

He covered the phone and my hand with his. "It leaves tomorrow," he said. "I won't be going with the others to Vicenza. I'm renting a car—a convertible—and we'll take the scenic route to Venice. You have to see some of the countryside, and I'm dying to see the airport one more time. At dinner tonight, I'll steal a cotton napkin. You'll want a hair scarf to tie under your chin."

I said, "You have me confused with Gina Lollobrigida."

He checked his watch. "So, if you will tell Sara not to expect me today, I'll meet you this afternoon at the Arena Chapel at three-fifteen or so."

I drew back my hand. "If I do stay, I'll have seen the chapel by then." This day was shaping up like a Roman arch, and I had the feeling I was on the downside already.

"Perfect. You will know how to get there. There are benches just outside the visitor entrance." He picked up a little biscuit but thought the better of it. "I have two tickets for a lecture at four."

I consulted my itinerary. "I'll be at the basilica."

He pointed at my phone. "Where's the camera on that thing?"

I turned it on and handed it to him. "Press here." I resisted the urge to fix my hair.

He stuck out his tongue and snapped two pictures of his open mouth. "Now, you can tell everyone you went to the basilica and saw St. Anthony's eight-hundred-year-old tongue." He drank the second espresso and stood up. "Three-fifteen. Look for a man dressed up like a Catholic priest." He left via the arcade, heading away from the hotel.

I picked up my phone. No new messages. It was two in the morning on the East Coast. Rachel and Sam were asleep. For the first time in months, I was ahead of them. For a moment, I felt like their mother again, comforted by the idea that I would have advance knowledge of any global catastrophe and could warn them, urge them to take cover.

Before I left the café, I had a conversation with a helpful young man at Air France. For twenty dollars, he sold me a twenty-four-hour hold on a reservation for a Tuesday afternoon flight from Venice to Boston. If I left at three on Tuesday afternoon, I would be in Paris by five, and in Boston by eight-thirty on Tuesday night, which seemed a little breathtaking, as was the pricing—$10,000 for first class, $4,500 for business class, and $2,500 for coach. Added together, all three options equaled the cost of the deluxe holiday I was tossing away. I opted for coach, despite his warning about the hefty charge for a second suitcase and other bulky items. I assured him I'd only be checking one bag.

Back in my hotel room, I emptied the second suitcase, the banged-up match to mine, Mitchell's better-traveled bag. He'd made it to Rome on Harvard's tab several times, and once to Milan, but he'd never been to Florence, having waited to see it with me. He'd never get there now, a permanent exile, like Dante, who never entered the walls of his beloved hometown after he got himself tossed out when he was thirty-six.

This biographical fact and everything else that remained of the Dante book was in the suitcase whose contents I had spilled onto the bed, all of Mitchell's copious notes and the few furiously marked-up pages of his own fragile prose he had preserved. I'd even brought along a sampling of his photocopied pages of *The Divine Comedy* translated by the great British mystery writer Dorothy Sayers in her spare time, annotated and crammed with Mitchell's marginalia. He'd left me thousands of similar pages, and I'd been stuffing the duplicates and triplicates into the newspaper recycling bin week by week.

Many of the pages I had saved were crazy quilts, photocopied bits of esoteric literary exegesis Mitchell had taped to blank pages and then drowned in scribbled counterarguments and probably very witty or sardonic exclamatory bits of Italian that were lost on me. I'd sorted them into folders, one per artist—Botticelli, Blake, Rodin, and Dalí—as well as writers ranging from Chaucer and Milton to T.S. Eliot, Freud, and Jung. Some of the pages I'd saved were puzzling curiosities, including his notes for Chapter One, the chapter devoted to Giotto. There were a few photocopied pages of notes and anecdotes about Giotto from early Italian sources, but most of what constituted this chapter was basically a single page, a fragmentary chronology of Giotto's career. Over the years, Mitchell had evidently made dozens and dozens of copies, each one covered with a new batch of annoyed annotations and exhortations to himself, as well as asterisks and underscores and arrows, skid marks on a stretch of road he never mastered, a curve that apparently threw him off course every time he approached the task of writing his book.

I HAD TRIED TO PERSUADE WIDENER LIBRARY TO TAKE THE whole business off my hands, and in deference to Mitchell's lifetime of service to the university, a graduate student was dispatched to my house and spent the better part of two hours in Mitchell's study. He was a smoker, and he took several long breaks in the backyard before pronouncing the whole lot "a testament to the best tradition of citizen scholarship," but not archival quality. He did give me the names of two rare-book dealers who might be interested in a couple of the oddball editions he'd noticed on Mitchell's Dante bookcase.

blue-skinned devil!
see Last Judgment!

n | BONDONE

WHO STOLE DANTE?

DEZ 1996
(~~10 JUNE 1993~~)

Giotto di Bodone(notes to address ~~very basic~~ fundamental questions, i.e., Who? What? Where When? Why?)

WHY DID POPE BONIFACE LOVE GIOTTO? (CIMABUE STILL ALIVE)

DANTE b. 1265 > 1267? 1268? Giotto di Bodone born near Florence.

1275? 1280? Giotto's studies with master painter Cimabue

1285 Cmiabue takes Giotto to Rome(leaves him there to study?)

1290-01? Giotto joins Cimabue in Assisi, where Cimabue is beginning frescoes for Basilica of St. Francis (project goes on for decades) NO PROOF OF GIOTTO PAINTING ANY ENTIRE SCENE IN ASSISI — DOZENS OF PAINTERS IN CIMABUE'S WORKSHOP — G. GETS CREDIT RETROSPECTIVELY? (TO STIMULATE TOURIST TRADE!)

1297 Giotto back in Rome to make frescoes for Lateran for ~~Pdep~~ Pope Boniface VIII

EIGHTH CIRCLE - SIMONIAC

1300 Giotto back in Florence

Dante sent to Rome on behalf of commune of Florence to meet with POPE BONICFACE VIII, who sets in motion plot against him

(Giotto goes to Rimini)

1302 Dante permanently exiled from Florence. — COINCIDENCE?! SAME YEAR GIOTTO GOES TO PADUA?

Cimabue dies.

1302-09 & 1312?

SEVENTH CIRCLE - USURER

Giotto back and forth to Padua to make frescoes for Basilica of St. Anthony (eroded? painted over?), SCROVEGNI CHAPEL, and Palace of Reason (lost in fire, mid-15th C.)

MUST EST. CLEAR DATE FOR COMPLETION OF CHAPEL 1306? 1309? 1317?

1306 Dante completes plan for *The Comedy* and begins to write "The Inferno"

TURNING POINT - GETS COMMISSIONS FOR BARDI AND OTHER BANKERS' CHAPELS IN FLORENCE

GONE - ALL OF IT

1307-37 Giotto in Assisi again, also Padua, Florence, Rome, Naples?, maybe Milan — scant evidence

Most famous painter in the world. Named master architect of Florence.

(All he designed was bell tower for the duomo.)

AND YET NO EVIDENCE HE EVEN ACKNOWLEDGES DEBT TO DANTE — DEAL W/ THE VATICAN?

1321 Dante dies in exile.

1337 G. dies in Florence.

DANTE FORCED TO LEAVE BOLOGNA - DOMINICAN FRIEND OF ~~SCRO~~ SCROVEGNI WAS AT BOLOGNA UNIV. FOR YEARS!

SCROVEGNI WENT TO ROME TO BUY INDULGENCES FROM POPE BONIFACE!!

For a few weeks afterward, I managed to believe I would have the wit and the wherewithal to hire a raft or a little skiff in Florence, pack it with all this paper, light it on fire, and send it down the Arno under the Ponte Vecchio like a funeral bier, the sort of honorific send-off Dante didn't get. Now, I couldn't even imagine getting myself on a train to Florence. Unless I could enlist T. to invent a more fitting conclusion to this sad story, it was obvious I was going to leave the suitcase under the bed.

Before I repacked the whole mess, I put on my reading glasses, found the Sayers folder, and pulled out Mitchell's preferred version of the lines Sara had read aloud, Dante's assessment of Giotto's fame.

> *Oh, empty glory of our human deeds!*
> *How brief it's green upon the topmost bough,*
> *unless perhaps some grosser age succeeds.*
> *In painting, Cimabue thought as how*
> *he held the field; but Giotto rules today*
> *so that obscure the other's fame is now.*

The margins were crammed with Mitchell's exclamatory huzzahs to the genius of Sayers and Dante: *topmost (golden) bough! the painter's and the painted FIELD! rules (like a monarch? or a pope!).* In a fit of inspiration, I got my nail scissors and clipped out the six lines to preserve them as a tribute to Mitchell, Dante, and this brief moment when we were all together in Padua. I laid them onto the second page of my journal, wishing I had some glue or a roll of tape. I finally settled for a slick of lip balm, which held the patch of poetry in the middle of the blank page. I stepped back to admire my work.

I closed the cover, opened it, turned the page—and it had stuck. But Dante's praise of Giotto had not. From my distance, *Giotto rules today* sounded a bit equivocal. I sat down and read the lines again.

It was the Renaissance that succeeded Giotto, not "some grosser age," which sort of confirmed the opening lament: "Oh, empty glory of our human deeds!" This was not exactly an endorsement of Giotto's enduring greatness. True, Dante conceded, Giotto held the field for a while, but so had Cimabue—human deeds, empty glory. Dante, on the other hand, had strolled into Paradise at the end of his poem—a supernatural, unearthly accomplishment.

Had Dante dissed Giotto?

The whole passage was weirdly reminiscent of the patronizing tributes Mitchell had so often received from the more eminent deans and senior-faculty grandees, pats on the back that kept him in his place. Mitchell had read the Giotto passage from *The Inferno* a hundred times, a hundred ways. Surely, he hadn't misread Dante's meaning. I read it again to the end. "Obscure the other's fame is now."

Mitchell had been half-right. Dante had bestowed upon Giotto a form of immortality. He'd damned him with faint praise.

SARA WAS STANDING ALONE IN THE LOBBY WITH A CLIP-board, her long hair gathered with a yellow rubber band high at the back of her head so it cascaded down several inches away from her neck, like a real pony's tail. She was wearing skintight blue jeans and a tiny jean jacket with a pair of lime-green high heels that probably cost more than Mitchell's BMW. I was relieved to be the first in line, above reproach. Sara was texting so I kept my distance, leaning on the front desk.

From a swinging door behind the desk, a new character in a tux-edo emerged with two silver ice buckets. He was just about my height, with buzz-cut silver hair and a square, German jaw. He said, "*Prego.*"

I looked around. "*Prego?*"

He said, "*Prego.*"

I got the sense he wanted me to want something, so I said, "Glue?"

"Blue?"

"Glue." I licked my finger and pretended to get it stuck on the desk. "*Ah, francobollo.*"

This seemed unlikely. "No, glue." I rubbed my finger on the desk and flattened my hand against the spot, and then leaned back, pulling on the wrist.

"*Si, si, si. Adesiva, adesiva.*"

I said, "*Adesiva!*" We were both delighted.

"*Adesiva, ha! No, no, no. Diciamo colla.*"

Cola? I blamed the ice buckets. "No—no cola, *grazie.*"

"*Prego, prego.*" He bowed, ducked under the desk, and headed for the elevator.

I waved at Sara, and as I approached, she politely lowered her phone. I took the opportunity to report on T.'s decision to skip the day's activities.

She said, "*Il medico?*" She sounded exasperated.

I nodded.

"Everyone tells me nothing," she said. "*Arrivederci!*" She crossed his name off her list.

I had intended to tell her about my altered afternoon plans, but I chickened out when Sara pointed at the four impatient couples staring at us from the sidewalk. She barked, "*Andiamo!*"

As we stepped outside, one of the men said, "Which way?"

Sara pointed to a crosswalk at the end of the block and the post office just beyond.

I said, "Aren't we waiting for Shelby?"

Over her shoulder, one of the wives yelled, "She went ahead with that elderly gal. We were all waiting on you again."

I brought up the rear next to Sara, who towered over me, texting furiously. Corso Garibaldi was a major thoroughfare, with several lanes of two-way traffic, trams running on embedded tracks, and a broad sidewalk bordered by an unbroken run of waist-high iron-pipe railing that prevented pedestrian crossings for anyone who wasn't ready to limbo. Within half a block, Sara pointed out the Church of the Eremitani on the far side of the street, a biggish, dark building oddly angled inside a curved brick wall. The church appeared as part of the Arena Chapel complex on the map she'd given us. "We will go there," she said.

I couldn't see how.

The shops we were passing were just opening up, and I asked Sara if the odd lot of cameras and ponchos and religious statuary was the edge of a shopping district.

"For tourists who must buy something, sure," she said. "The station for trains, it is one kilometer up there. You will see Wednesday when you leave for Firenze."

I wouldn't, but I nodded agreeably, as we were about to catch up with the couples. They were waiting at a traffic light where the railing opened up for a tram stop and crosswalk. The men were edging out into the street, their wives clotted on the curb behind them, smiling indulgently at their impatient boys.

Sara never even paused to look at the light. She yelled, *"Pronto!"* and took off across the street like a model down a runway, her green shoes flicking, her tiny hips still, and her ponytail swishing around her swaying shoulders. She was showing off, and she wasn't getting any criticism from the husbands behind her. She never turned around. She raised her long arm and pointed to the right, leading us halfway back to the hotel along a six-foot-high brick wall until she veered off through an open iron gate into a courtyard of paved pathways lined with waist-high brambles bursting with pink roses and the occasional park bench. She opened the door to the visitor center and leaned back to keep it ajar, handing a brochure and a ticket to each of us as we entered and saying, again and again, "Fifteen minutes to enjoy the wait."

The room was a big, spare white rectangle, with a long white counter for unticketed visitors to the left, and an open-shelf and table-top display of scarves and ceramic coasters and postcards to the right. I followed the couples past the gift shop to the coat check, where a sign warned us not to try to carry bags, cameras, food, drink, or pets into the chapel and to switch off our cell phones. I grabbed my glasses and left everything else in the red bag. I was headed back outside to the roses when I spotted Shelby and Anna, seated on a bench on the far side of the room.

Anna waved. She was wearing another handsome knit suit.

Shelby stood up. She was wearing a crinkly white button-up jumpsuit with a pair of camouflage binoculars, big as bazookas, slung around her neck. You had to admire her nerve. When I was still about ten feet away, she hollered, "That shirtdress is killer! You go, girl!"

I said, "You always look ready for anything." I had left Mitchell's compact black-rubber binoculars at the hotel.

Shelby hugged me and held on long enough to say, "Our friend is a little blue. We took Francesca to the train station this morning."

"Okay," I said. When she let go, I bent to kiss Anna, as if she were my aunt, and then sat down between them.

Sara was standing right in the middle of the room, leaning into her big leather purse, her jacket and white shirt pulled up, exposing a few inches of her tiny waist.

Anna said, "God forgive me, I'm grateful my husband isn't here to see that."

The four live husbands had staked out spaces at the front of the line by the door to the chapel. Their wives were wending their way past the other ticketed visitors, holding their opera glasses overhead as if they were swimming upstream.

Shelby stood up and said, "Shall we dance?"

I stood up.

Anna said, "Where are we going now?"

"We're halfway there," Shelby said. "We have to be dehumidified. Apparently, we go from here to a special air-conditioned room and watch a video about Giotto for fifteen minutes, and then we have our fifteen minutes in the chapel."

Anna said, "Only fifteen minutes?"

I said, "Andy Warhol meets Giotto."

Anna said, "When I came here as a girl, none of this museum business existed."

Shelby said, "Did you come to Mass here?"

"Oh, no. I don't think it was ever used like that. It was just a place my mother loved. *La mia piccola cappella*." She stood up, but her mood was sinking. "She wouldn't recognize it now."

As we joined the line, Shelby said, "We're so lucky to be alive and here today. It's only a few years ago that they finally finished the restoration. Imagine—the frescoes could have just peeled and flaked and faded away."

Anna said, "In Florida, there's black mold on everything."

The line snaked out through the door, along a paved path, which dipped as it neared the unadorned side of the little dusty brick chapel on our left. A vast woodland park spread out to the right with walking trails twisting around massive black boulders and disappearing into the glimmering greenery. The line stalled outside a dark glass vestibule, a kind of modern greenhouse attached to the chapel. From some angles, you could see the people inside, seated on folding chairs, watching a TV monitor while they were dried out.

Someone well ahead of us said, "Three minutes."

Anna said, "Now what are we waiting for?"

Shelby said, "There's another group of twenty-five ahead of us."

Anna didn't seem to approve of the glass vestibule or the wait.

I asked if she wanted to sit on one of the nearby benches.

She said, "I just hope it still feels like her little chapel."

We heard a woman yell, and the whole crowd turned to see Sara streaming down the path like one of the Furies trying to catch up with her crazy sisters, holding some sort of baton in her right hand. She came to a teetering halt next to Shelby. Instinctively, the whole crowd closed in. Sara bent over to catch her breath, and when she straightened up, she yelled, "*Attenzione! Attenzione!*"

"That goes without saying," I whispered to Shelby, a little too loudly. I got several approving nods from the women on the periphery.

Sara slid a rubber band from her baton and peeled off a single sheet and handed it to Anna. "My EurWay guests only and not the others did not yet receive these helpful maps I am now passing to them," Sara said breathlessly. She was already starting to move away from us. "These are perfect preparation for the chapel."

Shelby grabbed several sheets as Sara passed and handed two to me.

Anna looked at the diagram and said, "This can't be right. Did they make it bigger inside?"

Shelby said, "It's not a floor plan. It's flattened out. It's a guide to the frescoes on all four walls and the ceiling."

The door to the vestibule opened, and the three of us slid into one of the open rows near the back. I watched the tour group ahead of us filing into the chapel through a glass breezeway at the other end of the room. Another group was filing out of the chapel down a ramp behind them. They were there, we were here, and there was already another group congregating outside, and twenty-five more tourists picking up their tickets behind them. All the coming and going made my time in the chapel seem both precious and pointless. Several people in our group were unhappy with their seats and kept popping up and

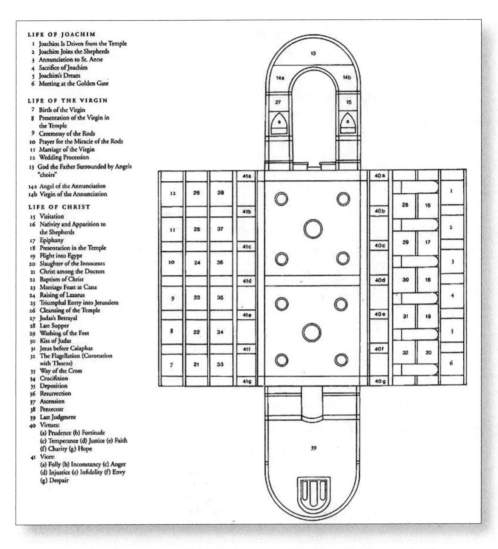

LIFE OF JOACHIM
1 Joachim Is Driven from the Temple
2 Joachim Joins the Shepherds
3 Annunciation to St. Anne
4 Sacrifice of Joachim
5 Joachim's Dream
6 Meeting at the Golden Gate

LIFE OF THE VIRGIN
7 Birth of the Virgin
8 Presentation of the Virgin in the Temple
9 Ceremony of the Rods
10 Prayer for the Miracle of the Rods
11 Marriage of the Virgin
12 Wedding Procession
13 God the Father Surrounded by Angels "choirs"

14a Angel of the Annunciation
14b Virgin of the Annunciation

LIFE OF CHRIST
15 Visitation
16 Nativity and Apparition to the Shepherds
17 Epiphany
18 Presentation in the Temple
19 Flight into Egypt
20 Slaughter of the Innocents
21 Christ among the Doctors
22 Baptism of Christ
23 Marriage Feast at Cana
24 Raising of Lazarus
25 Triumphal Entry into Jerusalem
26 Cleansing of the Temple
27 Judas's Betrayal
28 Last Supper
29 Washing of the Feet
30 Kiss of Judas
31 Jesus before Caiaphas
32 The Flagellation (Coronation with Thorns)
33 Way of the Cross
34 Crucifixion
35 Deposition
36 Resurrection
37 Ascension
38 Pentecost
39 Last Judgment
40 Virtues:
(a) Prudence (b) Fortitude (c) Temperance (d) Justice (e) Faith (f) Charity (g) Hope
41 Vices:
(a) Folly (b) Inconstancy (c) Anger (d) Injustice (e) Infidelity (f) Envy (g) Despair

scanning the room, as if they belonged in first class. Shelby was busily tearing and folding her diagram. Anna looked lost.

As the lights dimmed, Shelby passed Anna the fragile paper box she'd made by crudely tearing Sara's handout along the perimeter of the diagram and folding up the four numbered panels. She had turned the map into a diorama.

Anna looked inside the box. "That's it. That's her chapel."

The video crackled and popped on the TV screen at the front of the room, and a vaguely medieval melody drifted back toward us.

Apologetically, Shelby whispered, "But the ceiling is on the floor."

Anna whispered. "We'll stand on our heads."

BLUE.

Had Mitchell been standing beside me, where he belonged, he would have whispered, "First impression?"

My first and enduring impression of the chapel was blue.

The ceiling was a deep azure evening sky flecked with golden stars. The residents of the heavens were provided with golden portholes on either end, and from the smaller of these windows on the world bearded saints and patriarchs looked down approvingly. The bigger, central lookout above the altar end was occupied by Jesus in his middle age, and near the original entrance, above the Last Judgment, the Virgin Mary held her infant son for all to see.

But wherever I looked, no matter which sainted gaze held mine, I felt the pulsing of that beautiful blue, not watery but viscous, as if all of us, the living and the dead, were swimming in that intergalactic amniotic fluid.

Blue was my first impression every time I turned and looked to the top of another wall, the blueness of sky above and beyond the figures in each frame of the painted story circling around above us.

This blueness was not constant. It faded from top to bottom, the sky in each succeeding row of pictures a little paler, each sequential layer of the story a little less saturated with the immensity and depth of eternity.

Eventually, I had to give my neck a rest. Staring straight ahead, I ran my gaze along the row of pale greenish-gray panels at eye level, the Seven Vices on one side, the Seven Virtues on the other, rendered not in lifelike hues but colorless, pallid, like stolid marble statues of themselves.

Second impression?

Had one of the strangers wandering around me asked, I would have said my second impression of the chapel was the crazy smile on the white snout end of the big gray equine head of a donkey. He was giving Mary and Jesus a ride, but that didn't really account for the smirk.

My third impression was that T. had drawn the chapel perfectly. It was just one big barrel vault. There was a sanctuary with an altar embedded at one end, a window at the top of the other end, and six big windows cut into one side. And that was it for structural detail. The rest—not just the human figures and the landscapes, but what I had first seen as supporting columns and arches, elaborate pilasters and medallions carved in relief, and even the beveled and chamfered frame around every separate frescoed scene—was an illusion. The gloriously illuminated and architecturally complicated chapel was not really there. There was nothing but paint painstakingly applied to the smooth plaster walls of a brick-and-mortar barrel vault.

The pleasure of this masterful illusion was complicated by my turning and turning and not seeing Mitchell. If I stood still, I could almost conjure his voice, but it was mixed up with the baritone narration that had accompanied the introductory video we'd watched. I closed my eyes to concentrate, but everything was jumbled up, a stew of half-remembered facts and speculation from which I plucked a pet confusion of mine about Dante and this chapel, which Mitchell always called Scrovegni's chapel. He'd meant this as censure, not praise.

As far as I knew, Dante had never seen this chapel. And yet in Dante's visionary poem, Scrovegni had been singled out and labeled as an unredeemable scoundrel. I never understood, despite Mitchell's many little lectures, why Dante had picked on Scrovegni, made his name infamous by identifying him alone among the crowd of otherwise anonymous moneylenders suffering in the Seventh Circle of his Inferno.

According to the video, both Reginaldo Scrovegni and his son Enrico figured in the history of the chapel. Reginaldo had been infamous, one of the most ruthless and successful moneylenders of the 13th century. But Dante never met him, and there were plenty of rich usurers in Florence, whom Dante would have known personally and despised. Reginaldo was dead by 1300, when his son Enrico paid to have this chapel built and then decorated and offered up to the Virgin Mary.

The dedication of the chapel—Enrico's flamboyant act of contrition for the sins of his father—was memorialized by Giotto in the Last Judgment, the huge fresco Number 39 on Sara's map. In the bottom left quadrant, Giotto painted Enrico and a priest hoisting the chapel building up to the Virgin Mary. This exchange was taking place while Jesus, high above them, was separating the haloed and pious figures from the eternally damned, several of whom were serving as snacks for a giant horned ogre with a potbelly.

According to Giotto's painting, Enrico and his chapel were firmly fixed on the side of the saved. Yet Dante's poem had relegated the Scrovegnis to the deepest-down depths of hell.

Giotto and Dante were contemporaries, and I knew they were both alive in 1300, but when I tried to recall who did what when— well, I couldn't remember my children's birthdays, never mind the speculative and often wildly revised estimates for the completion of a pre-Renaissance painting or a poem. Mitchell had shown me reproductions of Giotto's Last Judgment many times, tracing his finger through the layered lines of saints and sinners to demonstrate the painter's debt to Dante's spiraling circles of hell. Mitchell believed that Giotto had been compelled to paint Enrico and his chapel into the scene because Scrovegni and everyone else in Italy had read *The Inferno* and Scrovegni wanted a happier ending for himself and his family name. This all made sense and, as was so often true of my conversations with Mitchell, did not really address my question. Why did Dante pick on Scrovegni, of all people?

One startling detail from the video, which Mitchell had never mentioned and maybe never knew, wasn't swallowed up in this historical stew—a teardrop. I was looking for a tear. It was the reason I had migrated to the corner of the windowed wall near the Last Judgment and looked up to the second row of panels from the top. It was somewhere in Number 20 on Sara's map, the Slaughter of the Innocents.

In that frame, a central patch of deep blue sky was bordered by two white towers. From a windowed parapet on the left, the red-robed King Herod pointed a finger, directing the attention of the hooded and helmeted soldiers beneath him. On the right were the white buttresses and arched windows of a church, half-hidden by a crowd of grieving mothers. One woman was cradling her baby, only its head visible above the back of a bigger soldier with a metal rod poised to break the woman's embrace, and next to her a blue-robed woman was losing her grip as a bearded soldier tugged at her baby's ankle with his left hand, a sword in his right hand aimed at the child's bent spine. At this man's feet, and piled shin-high against his comrades, were the bodies and severed heads of dozens of pierced and broken children, bent limbs, a bruised buttocks, and feet splayed at impossible angles. The babies were bulging out of the bottom of the frame, blurring the border between then and now, as if their broken bodies might fall down into your arms.

"You need these. Trust me." Shelby had sidled up to me and slid her hand around my waist. She passed me her binoculars and slipped away.

Every hair on every child's prone or thrown-back head had been imagined and painted with a separate, singular, delicate stroke of a bristle or two of Giotto's brush. I felt a rush of tears, and the magnifying lenses were wet before I could pull them from my eyes. I was sobbing, and I was impatient with myself because I knew our time was almost up, but the vicious vulgarity of the murders and the tender hand of the painter who had labored over every hair on every baby's head were combining and recombining in some sort of chemical reaction I couldn't control.

A uniformed man called *"Tempo di andare!"* from somewhere just behind me, and after the hushed groans of disappointment from the other guests died down, he called out again, "Time!" and I rubbed my sleeve across my eyes and looked through the lenses to the farthest-away woman at the front of the clot of mourning mothers. She was wearing green, and her empty hands were crossed in front of her hollow face, and there, from the sad slit of her eye, at the outside corner and tracing its way down her pink cheek until it gathered into a tiny dark drop as it fell from her jaw, I saw it. I saw where Giotto had painted, for the first time in the history of the world, a human tear. Behind her, a second tear fell straight from the inside of the almond eye of a red-veiled mother, streaking past her unbelieving, open mouth. And a faint tear stained the upturned, pleading face of the woman behind her, too, the mother in blue whose wide-eyed, terrified baby was being wrenched from her embrace.

SHELBY, ANNA, AND I SAT FOR A LONG WHILE ON A SUNNY bench, the gusty breeze buffered by the abundance of roses on either side of us. We had wordlessly agreed to sit out the tour of the 3-D presentation in the visitor center and the collection of Paduan paintings in the museum next door. Moreover, none of us wanted to visit the Church of the Eremitani, and Anna and I didn't want to take the tram to the basilica, either, but only Shelby was bold enough to break all of this news to Sara. While she did the heavy lifting, I braved the ticket counter in hopes of securing us a return visit to the chapel, but all of the spaces for the remaining tours had been sold.

On my way back to the bench, I saw Shelby waving me over to the gift shop. She had already picked up a commemorative T-shirt and two silk scarves, and I could only hope they didn't stock togas in her size. I didn't say a word, but I must have been making *that* face, which had staved off any number of fashion disasters for Rachel, because Shelby claimed the shirt was for a niece and then decided she would wait on the scarves.

I told her we were locked out of the chapel for the rest of the day.

"Well, we're on our own for a while. Sara was not happy," Shelby said, "but mission accomplished. I do think I may have spoiled any chance I had for getting in on the trip to Vicenza tomorrow."

"Is Sara the guide for Vicenza, too?"

"Oh, if Lewis was here—you haven't met him yet, but he's a doll. He's traveling with the bigger bunch in Venice. He's one of the co-owners of EurWay, so he can make executive decisions. He'd let me ride in the luggage rack if there wasn't a seat."

"You have to take my place," I said. "I'm not going to Vicenza." I didn't continue. I wanted to tell her I was leaving, tell her she'd been one of the bright spots on this ill-begotten adventure, but I knew she would feel it was her job to talk me into staying.

"Are you on the list? A seat on the bus is not the problem," Shelby said. "It's the meals and the pass for the Palladio building that will matter to Sara."

"I am signed up and prepaid, and I am absolutely not going to Vicenza tomorrow." This was a pleasure and a relief, like giving away opera tickets. "You have to take my place."

It was clear Shelby wanted to ask why I wasn't going on the side-trip, but instead she said, "Then I won't take a run till later this evening.

You go on to the basilica, and I'll take Anna to lunch and back to the hotel for a nap, if she wants."

"Take your run now, and then you can meet up with Sara and the others at St. Anthony's. Ushering Anna back to the hotel is just about what I can manage by way of social life this afternoon."

Shelby said, "Okay."

Her readiness to countenance my antisocial tendencies did sting. "Okay, then."

She said, "Let's plan—tentatively—to have dinner, the three of us."

"I'd like that," I said. I hoped T. was up for another night in the role of the dashing younger man.

Anna and I ate an early lunch of frittatas at a window table in the hotel's surprisingly bustling restaurant. We agreed they were good, but not good enough to make me rethink the plan to return to the Piazza dei Fruitti for another round of those superb pizzas. Midway through our meal, we saw Shelby jog by in pink spandex biking shorts and a matching tank top.

"It's lucky she found herself a husband, isn't it?" Anna said. "She's awfully kind."

She asked a few questions about Mitchell, and I learned that her husband had been an autoworker, not an executive as I had imagined. From her stories of her early days in Detroit and what she'd said the night before, I patched together a life that made Anna almost eighty years old. This made me feel a little glum about abandoning Shelby for the rest of the month, leaving her to attend to the vagaries of Anna's tolerance for the rigors of the tour.

As casually as I could manage, I asked Anna if she had a telephone number or email contact for Lewis. I felt I should tell someone I was going home so I didn't get reported as a missing person, apt as that designation seemed.

Anna reached under the table for her purse and pulled out her itinerary, which she handed to me. On the first page, in the margin beside her Venice hotel information, in careful little capital letters, she had written TWO DAYS WITH FRANNY!

My eyes welled up.

Anna said, "Are you missing your husband?"

"I'm fine," I said. I hadn't been thinking of Mitchell. I had been thinking of people who belonged together.

Anna said, "It comes on like that, the loss of him."

"Like a migraine," I said, too cavalierly, though it was true. Marriage had been a mixed blessing for both Mitchell and me, but missing him was debilitating. Almost my entire adult life had been lived in response to him, or in reaction against him, and now the thought of him just occasioned a kind of paralysis. "I'm not even sure if I miss Mitchell, or if I miss being a wife."

Apologetically, and maybe a little reprovingly, Anna said, "That's none of my business."

"But it is," I said. I flipped ahead to the Contacts page and copied Lewis's number into my phone. "I have to tell you something," I said.

Anna looked alarmed. "Maybe you've said enough for now."

"No, I want to give you something," I said quickly, "but I'm not certain I will be allowed." This sounded vaguely like the beginning of a smuggling operation. "I have to go home, to Cambridge, soon."

She looked aghast. "Is it one of your children?"

Again, announcing my intention had calmed me down. "No, it is not any kind of emergency. I need to be at home." None of this registered as reassuring to Anna, so I said, "It's all set. I've already scheduled my flight. But I need your permission—I need to know if this is really what you want."

"I don't want you to go away," Anna said. "What gave you that idea?"

Thank god, the waiter came by and recited the dessert specials, which restored a sense of normalcy. I ordered an espresso. Anna opted for the lemon tart.

I didn't wait for the waiter to return. I said, "I want to ask Lewis if my reservations and tickets and meals—if they can somehow be transferred to Francesca, if she can take my place." I couldn't decide if this plan was inspired or insane.

Anna looked past me, her gaze darting around the room, as if maybe I had been talking to someone else. "My sister?"

This tipped the balance toward the insane. "I don't have a sister," I said. "I barely have a brother."

Anna drew her napkin from her lap to the table. "Well, I'm sorry about that," she said.

I felt queasy, as if I'd arranged this lunch so I could sweet-talk her into selling me a sibling.

Anna folded the napkin along the ironed-in creases. I couldn't tell if she was mulling over my offer or waiting for an apology. Finally, she said, "My sister? Franny?"

I said, "Only if you want her to join you."

"You barely know her."

This was starting to feel like a warm-up for the conversation I'd be having with Rachel when I tried to explain why I didn't get even a partial refund. "It's something I can do," I said. I instantly regretted the phrase. I could see it had registered with Anna as a boast.

She folded her hands, and then she tilted her head. "Why would you do such a thing?"

I said, "To salvage what will otherwise be wasted?"

Anna's face tightened. She didn't say anything.

Two women at the table beside us burst out in laughter. I watched several tiny cars zip down Largo Europa. I could have used that espresso.

Anna finally said, "I don't know why I ordered that pie." She placed her purse on the napkin, as if she were building a barrier between us.

I said, "It was just an idea."

Anna unsnapped the brass clasp of her purse. "Should I call Francesca?" She had suddenly lit up, and she had her phone in her hand. "I mean, are you serious?" She sounded giddy.

I wasn't prepared for this change of heart, or her eagerness to seal the deal. "I'm not certain it can be done, but I do want to try," I said.

Anna was way ahead of me. "I can call her right now."

I should have put on the brakes, but I said, "Okay." I was unnervingly aware that I had cooked up this plan on the basis of nothing but Shelby's favorable review of Lewis's disposition. It occurred to me that this could easily end badly—with me secretly paying Lewis another ten or fifteen thousand dollars for Francesca's fare, and a FOR SALE sign in front of my house in Cambridge.

Anna didn't reach Francesca, but she left her a long, exuberant message in Italian. I couldn't translate word for word, but the spirit of it was, *Call me immediately, and pack a bag.*

The waiter returned, and I dropped a couple of ice cubes from my water glass into the little white cup and took a big sip of courage. Anna asked if she could take her dessert up to her room. The waiter bowed and backed away with the tart.

Anna looked exhausted—dreamy, but half-asleep. She said, "I don't know what to say."

I said, "I'm going to call Lewis. I'll call you as soon as I have his answer."

"The awkward thing is that Francesca could pay you," Anna said. "I can't."

"The lucky thing is that the money doesn't matter," I said, feeling that my voice might shoot up into the soprano register at any moment. "It's already spent."

"Surely, you could get a refund," Anna said. "If you said it was an emergency, they'd have to give you something back. You've barely been here two days."

I shook my head, as if lying for profit was simply out of the question. But I was thinking, *Two days? Two days?* I was going to have to concoct a heartbreaker of a story to get Sam on my side before any of this leaked to Rachel.

We sat in silence for a few minutes. I was anticipating a wave of relief or delight, or at least a little jolt from the caffeine. Nothing.

Finally, the waiter returned and handed Anna a small white pastry box tied with blue string. Under the perfect bow, he had tucked a fork wrapped in a red napkin. From our table by the window, through the lobby, to the elevator, and up to the fourth floor, where Anna hugged me and then waved good-bye, I envied her that beautiful little box and all of the tiny, unpredictable, tender touches of Italy to come.

MY OWN SURPRISE PACKAGE WAS WAITING FOR ME OUTSIDE the door to my room. I found a small white paper bag, its top neatly folded over, and a sheet torn from a notepad with the hotel's crest stapled to the front. In a fancy hand, someone had written *Sig.ra Berman, 414—Ricardo.* I had never met anyone named Ricardo, but it was my last name and my room, so I assumed it was something distributed to members of the tour group.

I peeked inside the bag. My door prize was a disappointment—a little jar of honey. I had just about an hour before I was due back at the chapel to meet T., and I knew Anna would be eager to have confirmation of my proposal, so I briefly rehearsed my plea and dialed Lewis Thayer at EurWay Travel. The first message I left was a series of halting preambles assuring him that I did not want a refund or a ride to the airport, so I called a second time and exhausted his voicemail's time limit with a biographical portrait of Anna and a disquisition on the difficulties for a widow traveling alone, and when I replayed that message in my mind, I worried that Lewis might think I was actually angling for a refund. My third message was, I thought, a triumph of clarity, though I did end up feeling like one of those women who try to return a pair of absurdly expensive shoes after wearing them to one black-tie event.

And I still had forty-five minutes to kill.

I pulled my door prize out of the white bag. It was not honey. The little glass pot was outfitted with a complicated printed label that meant nothing to me until I read these words: *La colla più affidabili!* Not cola, but *colla*! I opened the jar, and the familiar scent confirmed my delight. It was a jar of amber glue with a bristled brush attached to the inner lid of the tin screw top.

I opened my journal on the desk beside the window and found the six lines of poetry curling away from the second page. I pulled them up, rubbed what was left of the lip balm into the page, and painted a square of glue around the stain. I pressed the Dante down and smoothed the patch of poetry several times. This small victory was so gratifying that I scanned the room for something else to glue into the journal. From a pocket of my dress, I rescued one of Sara's maps of the chapel and evened out the worst of the wrinkles and folds. I placed it on the next blank page of the journal. It fit, but just. After a quick trim with my nail scissors, the map could be more elegantly centered on the journal page. In the drawer of the desk, I found a pen and made a few dots to mark the perimeter of the cut-out map, and then I painted a thick frame of glue, and, within the frame, I added three very delicate vertical brushstrokes to hold the center portion flat, but before I laid the map down, my cell phone rang.

I didn't recognize the number on the screen. If it was Lewis politely turning down my request, I knew I wasn't prepared. I decided it was best to let him leave a message. Within the hour, I could enlist T., and together we could surely come up with some way to pressure Lewis into accepting Francesca as a substitute for me.

I waited a few minutes to give the new message a chance to register, and then my phone rang again—Rachel. This sent me into dead panic. Had Lewis called her to report my unstable behavior? I dropped the ringing phone on the bed, as if that would serve as an alibi when Rachel later asked why I hadn't answered.

I returned to the journal, but the glue had already hardened, spoiling a whole page. I turned to the next page and made another glue frame and hastily pasted in the map. Then I checked my messages.

Lewis was noncommittal, but he had a British accent, so he sounded amused, which gave me hope. He was tied up until five and promised to ring again. Rachel had called to say she was on her way to an all-day deposition and guessed I would be asleep by the time she was free, so she promised to call again on Tuesday. She'd also picked up my newspapers and arranged to have delivery of the *Times* and the *Globe* suspended until the end of the month. She didn't mention that she'd done this once before, after my first false start. Rachel wasn't argumentative, but she was persistent. It occurred to me that I could get through the week in Cambridge without her knowing I had come home if I was willing to live without the daily papers—the only reason I ever turned on the lights.

And just like that, I teared up again. I could feel myself sliding down from panic toward my sofa and the familiar furrow of my depression. To check my descent, I put the red bag on the chair beside the door. I still had fifteen minutes to kill. I turned around twice, looking for something else that could be glued into the journal. That ruined page was haunting me. I sat down with the scissors and pressed hard on the spine, but the leather binding was too sturdy to open up for a clean cut. I turned to the spoiled page. The thick lines of the square frame of dried glue were immediately apparent, but the three little vertical lines I'd painted inside were invisible. I traced my finger slowly across the page. I could feel them, each one. I tilted the page toward the light, and there they were—pale, smooth stains, like tears, so insignificant no one might ever notice. I pulled the pen out of the drawer and labeled this page: #20. Slaughter of the Innocents.

IV

✵

O n my way to the chapel, I stopped at the desk to thank Ricardo for the glue, and an unfamiliar green-vested man asked me for my room number.

I said, "414. Why?"

He said, "Signora Berman, yes?"

I nodded, and he handed me my passport, which I'd forgotten to collect after checking in. I was another step closer to Cambridge. I said, "Ricardo?"

He said, "At night only."

"I see," I said.

He said, "And the mornings, yes?"

"Okay," I said. "Later, he will be here?"

"Sometimes, *si, si, si,*" he said, smilingly.

Every conversation I had with an Italian was like walking on the beach and watching the tide erase our trail.

I followed Sara's roundabout route to the chapel, certain that any attempt at a shortcut was likely to land me in Bologna. I paused at the post office. Before he died, Mitchell had printed sixty labels for me, thirty addressed to Rachel and her boys and thirty addressed to Sam and Susie—"To save time," he'd said. He wrote postcards to me and the children whenever he traveled farther than the grocery store, and I think he really believed I didn't send postcards because I hadn't paid attention to his routine, which made it easy. He even suggested a few pat phrases I might adopt and repeat. "Don't try to be original, or it will turn into a chore for you," he'd said. It was after three, so I convinced myself I should not stop, that I could buy stamps in the airport tomorrow, possibly from someone who spoke English. With a few strategically placed air mail stickers, I could even get away with sending the postcards later in the week from Cambridge.

In the courtyard of the chapel, there were at least thirty Catholic priests, some in full-length black cassocks or brown hooded robes, others in black suits with white Roman collars, and a few of the men in jeans might have been Jesuits. Inside the visitor center, there was a large contingent of nuns in full headdress. In an American museum, they would have looked otherworldly, like visitors from another era, but here they looked like Management.

"You have to take a vow of silence." It was T. in the same blue blazer, a new white shirt. He had apparently been perched on the roof and swooped down when he spotted me. "And I need your passport. Follow me." He led me inside to the ticket counter and introduced me to a priest in a black suit, who shook my hand. His name was Ed.

Father Ed said, "You must be E.?

I nodded.

T. and the priest headed to the counter, and I stayed where I was. T. handed the priest my passport, then leaned on the counter, and handed his passport to the priest as well. The priest pulled an envelope out of his jacket pocket and handed it and the passports to a stern, squat, blue-uniformed woman. While she examined the contents of the envelope, T. smiled blithely, as if he often traveled with a priest as his personal valet.

I heard T. say, "No, no, no," and then the priest nodded toward T. and said, *"Egli è il medico."* He turned, pointing to me, and said, *"Lei è la vedova del professore. Dottore Berman, Decano dell'università di Harvard."*

The uniformed woman disappeared with the letter and the passports. T. stayed at the counter, and the priest sidled up to me and said, "All set," and led me across the room to a corner of the gift shop. He was not a lot taller than I was, but he had a reassuring, muscular presence under all that black, or maybe I was inferring too much based on his dark hair and eyes, and his impressive five o'clock shadow. "I hope the lecture won't bore you," he said.

"My husband worked at Harvard," I said. "I've been inoculated. Will it be in English?"

"English and Italian."

"So it will be twice as long as necessary," I said, as if I had been drinking.

"Yes, we'll see how that goes over." He had a strong, square, impassive face, which was probably an asset when people confessed their sins to him. "Most of the priests here are traveling from the States." He glanced at his watch.

I knew I was breaking my vow of silence, but getting a fact out of T. could be tricky, so I plunged ahead while I had the priest alone. "How do you and T. know each other?"

"Oh. Caroline," he said, and he paused long enough that I realized he expected me to recognize the name. "His ex-wife?"

I nodded. This was news to me. I knew T. lived in Houston and was a partner in a general surgical practice, which was all he'd provided by way of facts for the EurWay passenger biographies.

The priest said, "Caroline is my older sister." He put his hand flat against my back. "But I knew him first. Now, I really am late, so the rest will have to wait until this evening." He waved as he disappeared out the door.

The clerical crowd was breaking up outside, so I took to one of the benches. When T. finally emerged, he flashed me the victory sign. As he joined me on the bench, he handed me my passport with a large white envelope. On the flap was an embossed gold seal that featured the words *Commune di Padova*. He said, "What time is your flight tomorrow?"

I said, "Three o'clock or so. I have to buy the ticket before dinner. Is this an official city document?"

"Yes. And since you've paid for Tuesday night in the hotel, I agree that a Wednesday departure makes more sense."

"Tomorrow is Tuesday," I said.

"And we have unlimited access to the Arena Chapel. It's like being a Scrovegni for a day." He opened my envelope and held up a letter typed under the same gold seal. "Ed arranged it for us."

"Is he the bishop of Padua?"

"A medievalist at Georgetown. He's on sabbatical here till December, writing a book about the First Jubilee."

"It sounds festive, anyway."

"I didn't know what he meant by that either, so you'll have to ask him. He won't take it so hard coming from you. We're having a drink with him after his lecture."

"Ed is giving the lecture? Even better." I was pretending not to be lamenting my comments to Ed about the boring lecture by pretending to read my letter. "Who did you tell them I am?"

T. said, "The widow of the late Professor Doctor Dean Berman, Dante scholar."

I said, "Mitchell was never dean of the college, or dean of the Faculty of Arts and Sciences. And he wasn't faculty. Or a scholar, not in any practical sense. He ended up as a vice president—"

I stopped because T. had pressed the back of his hand to my forehead. "Post–Harvard stress disorder. It will pass, like sunstroke. Was your husband not a dean? Did he not have a passion for Dante?"

"Once, long ago."

"Over here, he gets to keep all of his titles. It's like ringtoss. Can we say one word about Shelby's jogging outfit?"

I said, "Impetuous."

"Thank you. Unlike Shelby, I disapprove of your bequest to Anna."

It was like junior high. Everybody knew everything. I said, "Actually, Francesca is the beneficiary."

"Whence my objection," said T. "I'm certain she speaks more English than she lets on."

"That will make it easier on Anna," I said. He might be able to talk me out of a Tuesday flight, but the sisters were my business.

T. said, "Folly."

I said, "Call me impetuous."

"But you're here now." T. grabbed hold of my hand. "Are you really that unhappy?"

Everybody touched each other here, even Americans. "Sometimes," I said. Every day brought a new measure, so it was hard to get a fix on it. She's so unhappy that she didn't shower today. She's so unhappy that she forgot to return three phone calls from her brother in Atlanta. She's so unhappy that she got down on her knees and scrubbed the walls of her self-cleaning oven. Most unnerving of all, sometimes she was happier than she let on.

T. was looking disapprovingly at my Swiss Army watch. "A memento mori," he said. He looked right into my eyes. "You are here."

I nodded.

"It's Italy," he said urgently. "There are all kinds of wonderful drugs to improve our moods, and we can get them right over the counter."

"Are we missing Ed's lecture?"

T. stood up. "Park bench to church pew," he said.

"Pilgrim's progress," I said. I stood up and fell into step beside him. For some reason, he led us away from the chapel and out the gate. If the signs we passed were any indication, Ed was lecturing in the Church of the Eremitani. I was thinking ahead to Thursday and Friday, thinking it should probably be unthinkable, but thinking I would miss T. for a couple of days as much as I missed Mitchell, and maybe more.

THE FIRST JUBILEE WAS DECLARED IN 1300 BY POPE Boniface VIII—aka, His Holiness P.T. Barnum—to drum up business for the dilapidated shrines and cemeteries and churches in Rome. It was a financial bonanza. On any given day, there were about a quarter of a million heat-stroked pilgrims trampling ancient ruins as they fought their way into old St. Peter's to buy pizza and plenary indulgences, hoping like hell to end up with "full and copious pardon of all their sins." There were also all-night block parties in Sienna, and no end of Paduan pageantry parading through streets crowded with pilgrims who couldn't make the trip to Rome, not to mention knights errant galloping around, lances up, looking for a fight or a free drink or a reasonably priced damsel in Venice and Florence and many of the other independent communes throughout Italy—which was just a notion and not a nation for another five hundred years, and only then if you were willing to define a nation as a conglomeration of cities that changes prime ministers more often than the citizens change their underwear.

That's how Ed spoke. I didn't object to the breakneck pace, but his offhand, derisive tone was bewildering. He might have been saving his more academic material for the Italians. I couldn't see how his lecture was going over with the American priests, but from the way wimples were whipping around, I could tell he wasn't scoring a lot of points with the nuns.

I nudged T. to get his verdict.

He shrugged and whispered, "This is my first visit to a Christian comedy club."

The setting wasn't doing Ed any favors. Even by the dour standards of the Dark Ages, the place was a downer, a hulking bulwark of a building. The ceiling of the church was built like the hull of a ship, all shellacked dark-wood beams and rafters, and the walls were dull marble, alternating rows of green and maroon horizontal stripes, which were no more flattering to the Romanesque architecture than they were to a middle-aged woman's midriff. The only relief was the light behind Ed, where the altar was set inside a bright domed space, its ceiling and walls decorated in the suburban Catholic paint-by-numbers style—a pale blue sky with cartoonish, cottony clouds and a pastel Jesus surrounded by some sacred stuff I couldn't really see. T. and I had been late so were stuck in the farthest-back benches.

Before he crossed the language barrier, Ed hammered home the significance of the Jubilee Year, reminding all of the English speakers that Dante had been in Rome in 1300, sent as an emissary by his friends in Florence to beg Pope Boniface to butt out of their secular business. Years later, in *The Divine Comedy*—"that conniving fever-dream of worldwide condemnation and self-promotion in verse form"—Dante dated the launch of his famous trip through the Gates of Hell as Good Friday, 1300. And it was 1300 when Enrico Scrovegni sold off a town he owned in the Veneto and plopped down a pile of gold to purchase the decrepit site and tumble-down ruins of the old Roman Arena in Padua, with plans to build himself a new home and a little chapel.

T. whispered, "It *was* a banner year."

One of the American priests raised his hand and shouted, "You're saying Scrovegni owned Venice?"

"No, you're saying *Venice*, and I'm saying *Veneto*," Ed said, alienating one of the few people in the pews still paying close attention. "The Veneto is the region that extends north of here, and Enrico owned a lot of it. The town he cashed in to buy the Arena is called Malo."

T. elbowed me, but I would not look his way. I did not need to be reminded that Malo was Francesca's hometown. And I didn't like the feeling that, like Enrico, I was meddling in Malo in an attempt to buy myself absolution.

Ed said, "Okay, exercise time." Nobody moved. He seemed almost heroically unfazed by the crowd's animosity. "You're going to have to stand up eventually. So if I can coax you out of those rock-hard wooden pews, I'll ask you all to follow me to the chapel on my left. If you didn't bone up on your Italian, just look at the pictures and wait for the English portion of our program to resume."

As he stood, T. said, "I will say not one word about Malo, but you must know my tongue is bleeding."

"They have a spare at the basilica, courtesy of St. Anthony," I said. "Do you think Ed explained what *Eremitani* means in the English part we missed at the beginning?"

"Hermit," T. said, and he handed me a photocopy he'd plucked from a rack in the vestibule on our way in. "But these hermits couldn't shut up about Scrovegni." He was leading me to the back of the church, and when I glanced guiltily toward Ed, I saw a couple of priests following us. "They even wrote to the pope in 1305, complaining about how fancy the Arena Chapel was looking, so the powers-that-be forced Scrovegni to scrap his plans for a big bell tower."

"1305?" I was thinking of Mitchell's many chronologies. He had always assumed that Giotto did not finish frescoing the chapel until after Dante had begun to write *The Inferno*. "Did those hermits happen to mention the state of the interior? Had Giotto finished painting in 1305?"

T. shrugged off my question. "I think the proposed bell tower was their big gripe. The Eremitani had been here since 1260-something and didn't like competition."

"You should be giving this lecture."

T. stopped at the back of the church and turned around. "I'll tell

Ed there was a medical emergency." The two priests zipped right past us, their heads bowed. Ed had moved to the edge of one of the two chapels that bulged out of the nave on either side, forming a modest transept, anticipating the familiar crucifix shape of later churches. T. said, "These monks hired Mantegna to fresco that little chapel at some point in the 15th century."

"Mantegna who painted the Foreshortened Christ?" That famous view of the shrouded, ashen body of Jesus seen from the end of the marble slab on which he is laid out is unforgettable.

T. nodded.

I didn't add that I only knew the painting because it hangs in a museum in Milan, and I had a postcard of it in a bin at home, courtesy of Mitchell.

"Mantegna is also credited with the first painting that applied the mathematically worked-out theory of perspective," T. said. "That masterpiece is in a church in Florence, by the way—in case you ever have the chance to get there."

"Perhaps Francesca will send me a postcard," I said, which sounded more like a rebuke than I'd intended. T. looked as surprised by my tone as I was, but I didn't offer an apology, and I couldn't explain it. I just knew everything in my past was in tumult. The ground of my life had been shaken, and I didn't want to outrun the spreading fault lines and fissures. Whatever was happening, I wanted to let it catch up with me, overtake me. I had spent thirty-five years persuading myself to keep going, stoking my faith in the power of the next day, the next phase, the next promotion, the next graduation, the next book club, or concert series, or grandchild to vindicate my perseverance, to make something whole and smooth and strong of my married life. I no longer believed in the annealing power of the future. I couldn't see why I should go to Florence and Assisi and Rome and Venice just to get to Cambridge. "I want to see this Mantegna," I said. "As you would say, we're here now."

"Mantegna, unfortunately, is not," T. said, turning to the door. "Apparently there are some fragments of the fresco that they pieced together into a re-creation, but this whole structure is ersatz. The original was blown to bits during World War II air strikes."

"By whom?"

"I'm guessing someone with a plane. We'll ask Ed." He held open the door but stuck out his foot to stop me before I went outside. "Considering his performance, probably best not to ask Ed about bombing."

THE DAYLIGHT WAS STARTLING, AND THE PALE BLUE OF afternoon was overrun with puffy clouds—as implausible and silly as the painted sky above the altar inside. T. and I agreed that we needed a drink before we had a drink with Ed. Around the block, across the street from the low profile of the Eremitani cloister, we spotted two white metal chairs and a tippy white table about the size of a dinner plate. T. went inside and soon returned with two tumblers filled with something precisely the color of orange Kool-Aid.

He said, "He claims it's just called a spritz. I've seen them all over town."

I said, "Is it fizzy?"

T. raised one of the glasses to his nose. "Fizzyissimo," he said and sat down. "It's something called Aperol, which looks suspiciously like Campari with a dye job, and some prosecco, and sparkling water."

After a few sips, I said, "This makes me very happy."

T. said, "At this guy's prices, we can afford to get ecstatic."

Our little street wasn't much of a thoroughfare. A few cars cruised by, and three dark-haired girls in white short-sleeved blouses and pleated blue-plaid skirts came close and then disappeared into a doorway. That was enough for us for a long time, and then my phone rang. I saw that it was Lewis, and I turned it off.

"Not urgent," I said.

T. gulped down his drink. "I have to make a call, too. Ten minutes or so?"

I watched him wander away toward the church. The sun had slipped right into his path, so I had to use my hands as visors. His blue back got darker and smaller with each step, not disappearing but becoming something compact and dense, something I could hold in my hand, the essence of T.

A young waiter came out of the café and smiled sympathetically. He had a mop of curls, and he was wearing a butcher's apron over a T-shirt and blue jeans. I shook my head to let him know I'd had enough. He left me alone.

I pulled out my phone, but I didn't dial immediately. I didn't know what I wanted Lewis to say, and I'd had just enough to drink to believe my desire would influence his response. While I dithered, the waiter returned. He nodded in the direction T. had taken, and from behind his back he produced a white saucer with an almond biscotti glazed with a thin strip of chocolate on the bottom. Then he handed me a small wax-paper bag.

"To take away," he said.

I realized he was feeling sorry for me. "I'm okay," I said. "He's coming back. Really."

The waiter smiled knowingly. "My gift, okay?" He turned back toward the café.

"Orange and chocolate," I said. "*Perfecto.*"

He hesitated, then slowly said, "*Per-fet-to.*"

I said, "*Per-fet-to?*"

"*Si, perfetto. Preciso.*"

What the heck? I said, "*Perfetto. Perfetto.*"

He laughed. "*Essato!*" He left it there and went back to work.

I made the call. Lewis was delighted to speak to me, delighted that

I had enjoyed my abbreviated stay in Italy, and delighted to be able to accommodate my request. Anna, too, was delighted, just delighted.

Something I said must have struck a less delirious note because Lewis flattened out his voice and asked if I could bear to go over a few practical details. As Anna and Francesca would not be traveling back from Rome to Venice via Ravenna, he was preparing a refund for me for that leg of the trip. I assured him that was not necessary. He insisted it was already being processed. "I don't suppose you have any of your paperwork right there in front of you?"

I assured him I didn't.

"Why would you?"

The silence that followed was long enough that I thought we might leave it at that. I hadn't scrutinized a bill or a bank statement since Mitchell had gotten sick. This was not a matter of incompetence. In fact, it had been a point of pride. I had always been the bookkeeper and tax accountant in the house, and when Cambridge Trust offered to digitize our accounts and organize the whole operation online, I signed up immediately. When paying attention to Mitchell's care and comfort became a full-time occupation, and when missing him was all I could do in the course of a day, it was a relief to know the credit cards and the cable bill were being paid. Right to the end, Mitchell had grave doubts about the stability of the paperless world, and as long as he lived he accumulated enough ballast for both of us.

Lewis said, "Perhaps it would be better if I had this conversation with your daughter."

"Oh, no." I was prepared to write Lewis a check, not to call Rachel. She had managed all of the arrangements with EurWay for the last three months, including my many false starts, so I guessed that Lewis might have some sense of her impatience with my indecisiveness. "I'm afraid my daughter has resigned her post as trip advisor," I said, aiming for a confidential tone of voice. "You'll have to deal with me."

"A pleasure, I assure you," Lewis said. "This is a minor matter of accounting. The refund will be issued as a credit on your charge card."

"That makes it very easy for me. Thank you."

"The amount refunded for hotels in Ravenna and Venice will not match the amount on the original statement from us."

"Taxes and processing fees," I said, trying to make it clear I was on top of this.

"Quite," Lewis said, "but the differential largely reflects your choice to downgrade from A-Prime to Category B accommodations. We will refund at the lower rate, of course."

I said, "Quite." Apparently, sometime after Mitchell died, Rachel had decided to address my concern about the extravagant expense of a monthlong Italian adventure. I had raised the financial aspect only once, a few weeks after the diagnosis. Maybe I was being miserly, but I was imagining years ahead with Mitchell in and out of hospitals, second opinions and experimental drug therapies not covered by insurance, and when I'd added up the first EurWay itemized estimates, and the unforeseen add-ons and why-not dinners at overpriced restaurants with Michelin stars that might mean something to someone who mattered in Mitchell's office, I suggested to him that we could choose less luxurious hotels. I had said all of this to Mitchell, but I had never complained about the costs to Rachel. To me, at the time, Mitchell had said, "We're worth it."

"And one more detail, if you can manage it," Lewis said.

I said, "Of course."

"Very well. Unless you would prefer we handle this as two distinct transactions, we will roll in the credits owed you for the other hotels, as well, which were in-process this week."

"The Category B savings all over Italy," I said.

Lewis said, "Quite."

"Rolling it all into one refund makes good sense," I said. "You're being very gracious about all of this. Thank you."

"Delighted," Lewis said. "Delighted."

I hung up before he said it again. While I waited for T. to return, one of the three plaid-skirted girls reappeared from a doorway. She stood still, facing the street, as if she wasn't sure she wanted to leave. A third-story window opened above her, and the other two girls stuck their heads out. One of the girls upstairs yelled, "*Fottiti!*" The loner on the street didn't move. The two girls in the window yelled a few more times and then disappeared. A couple of seconds later, a little red canvas knapsack with long, loopy straps flew out the window. It looked like a parachute failing to open as it fell and thudded in the gutter. She still didn't move. Finally, I heard the window above her slam down. She picked up her bag, stuck her hand inside, and pulled out her phone, which she shook and held up in front of her face, as if it were a snow globe. She slung both straps of her red bag over one shoulder, and as she crossed the street, and maybe all the way home, she said, "*Porco dio, porco dio, porco dio.*"

T. AND ED WAVED FROM THE FAR CORNER, NEAR THE church, and as I headed up the street to join them, T. took hold of Ed's shoulders and bent toward him. Ed dropped his gaze, as if T. was saying something Ed didn't want to hear or didn't believe. When I got near enough to eavesdrop, T. backed off. For a moment, nobody seemed to know what to do.

Ed turned to me and said, "At my request, we are going to pretend that lecture never happened."

T. said, "What lecture?"

It was clear this was not what they had just been discussing. "Oh, Ed," I said, "are you that displeased with how it went?"

T. said, "How what went?" To Ed, he said, "Which piazza?"

Ed said, "Piazza dei Signori. It's the one behind Fruitti."

T. led us out to Corso Garibaldi, and after he zigzagged across a couple of intersections, he cleared a path through a wide pedestrian mall clotted with window-shopping and gelato-eating tourists and a separate, fast-moving, steady stream of dark-suited pedestrian commuters that eased around the tourists like a river around rocks. Ed stayed by my side, his hand hovering protectively behind me.

Within a few blocks, the public space opened up, and the building facades acquired granite columns and marble porticos roped off from the confusion for after-work drinkers and early diners. "This is really beautiful here," I said.

"This is the edge of Piazza del Erbe," Ed said, pressing his hand to my back to turn me into the dark, arcaded sidewalk of a narrow street bordered by smaller shops and dozens of tiny restaurants, each with about four tables, ten waiters, and forty happy customers. I'd lost sight of T. "There are some really good places to eat in these blocks," Ed said, "and the top-tier bars and cafés."

"Let's get out of here, then," I said.

"I owe you a drink at a decent bar," he said apologetically. "But I'm addicted to these crackers with little crispy bits of kale that they make at this one place near San Clemente, a sweet little church." He suddenly stopped walking as a blast of short beeps from a horn echoed around us.

A woman with long hair flew by on a pale-blue scooter, and as she passed, we saw a helmeted little kid on the back holding to his mother's waist for dear life. I couldn't take my eyes off them.

Ed leaned in and said, "What are you thinking?"

"When you're unhappy, everything seems exemplary."

Ed said, "And when you're happy?"

"How would I know?"

Ed put his hand behind my back, and we veered off to the right again. "I apologize for the hike," he said. "I'm indulging myself—another symptom of unhappiness."

I said, "What does *porco dio* mean in English?"

"Literally? God is a pig," he said, smiling. "Did someone say that during my lecture?"

"I heard it on the street," I said, "not from a nun."

"It's not really foul. It's an all-purpose curse," Ed said. "Or more of a cosmic complaint, like *goddammit.*" He stopped again. "That's actually a perfect example of what I was trying to get across today; that was the tone I was aiming at. I mean, it was not for nothing that Dante wrote about heaven and hell in the vulgate, in the vulgar Italian of silk merchants and moneylenders and carpenters, not Church Latin. That same impulse turns up everywhere in 1300 in the art— something coarse, or bawdy, or just the sense of bodies pushing through the veils of mystery and mystification."

"Like Chaucer," I said, aiming for something old and familiar.

"Right," Ed said. "Like Boccaccio. Not sex jokes and toilet humor—I mean, there was plenty of that, but there was something else, something aggressively human. And happy to be human, not ashamed of themselves. Oh, E., you know all of this."

I didn't. And until that moment, I didn't realize that Ed was genuinely ashamed, embarrassed by his performance. Whom had he hoped to impress?

Ed said, "It's the difference you see when you look at those golden Byzantine icons of the Virgin, or the saints in early Gothic paintings, and they're elongated and impossibly thin and angular, and then you see what Giotto did in the Arena Chapel—people with thighs and heavy hands and big heads."

"People like us," I said.

He sheepishly shook his big head.

I was staring at T., who was standing at the sunny end of the arcade, looking absurdly tall and lean and serene, like an elegant Byzantine portrait of St. Somebody of Constantinople. From his point of view, Ed and I must have looked like a couple of barn animals in Giotto's manger scene. "I wanted to use words to do what Giotto did with colors and light and shadows," Ed said. "That's exactly what I wish I'd said today. I didn't get it right, did I? But that's what I was aiming at, not another sermonette with footnotes by a Jesuit with an ivory tower up his ass."

"Nobody mistook that lecture for a sermon," I said.

Ed said, "What did T. say about it?"

"We both have a million questions for you," I said.

"I see," Ed said.

Had I understood earlier that T.'s reaction was all Ed really cared about, I would have happily lied about it. But we had caught up with T., and Ed took the lead, and T. fell into step beside me. He told me Shelby and Anna were hoping to meet us for dinner in about an hour, and then we turned into Piazza dei Signori, a big enclosed square, hemmed in on one side by the colonnaded balcony of the old Carrara family home, a block-long white granite palace centered on a bell and clock tower. By comparison, the little brick-front church where Ed was headed looked inconsequential, like one more of the many little row houses that lined the rest of the piazza. Ed waved to us from an unoccupied table he'd found in the middle of a fenced-off corral, one of dozens of ad hoc patios lining the perimeter of the piazza. The crowds spilled out so far from the storefronts that it was impossible to tell which café you were patronizing when you got to your seat. It was six-thirty, and as far as I could see, everyone in Padua was required by law to stop on the way home for an Aperol spritz. The orange cocktails glowed in the late-day sun like votive candles. T. casually said we should come by some morning for the famous open markets, as if we'd both rented villas for the summer season.

We sipped our spritzes, and Ed ate most of the kale crackers, politely leaving the ashtray of olives for me and T. to enjoy. For the better part of an hour, we didn't speak. We just exchanged smiles, turning to acknowledge an especially well-groomed passerby or a waiter with a hot plate of something we wished we'd ordered. But every time I turned my head, I sensed that I was seeing through a frame into the wider world beyond.

"Do you see someone you know?" I felt Ed's warm hand land lightly on my forearm.

I said, "Déjà vu," which was almost true. Ed's curious smile, the half-illuminated faces and shadowy bodies spread out around the widening spill of white tables behind him, the dim crimson facade of San Clemente at the edge of the piazza—I was seeing everything as if I were still standing in Giotto's chapel, staring into the open sky above the figures in the foreground of one of the frescoes, seeing us in their future. The past, the landscape of the life I had lived, was altered, unfamiliar, as I saw it now. But this inverted perspective seemed fragile or tenuous—a fleeting sensation that dissipated even as I attempted to describe it to myself.

T. said, "Exactly how big is the Arena Chapel?" He was snapping the edges off a kale cracker.

Ed said, "About sixty by thirty. Why?"

I said, "Feet?"

He nodded. "And just about sixty feet high."

I said, "How can it be so small?"

T. waved his paper napkin so it opened to a thin square and laid it on the table. "I don't see why those Eremitani were so upset about it," he said.

Ed said, "Well, if Scrovegni had been allowed to build the side chapels he'd planned, and the bell tower at the altar end, he would have been real competition for the monks. A bell was a way of calling all pilgrims, calling for alms, and attracting other paying customers. Plus, Scrovegni had Giotto, the most famous painter in Italy, running around on scaffolding, making everybody else's painted heavens and hells look like yesterday's news."

In one corner of his napkin, T. placed a little rectangular shard of his cracker. "Let's say this is the Scrovegni Chapel." A bit below that, he formed two larger rectangles into a cross. "And this is the Church of the Eremitani."

Ed said, "Maybe a little closer."

T. said, "I'm not working to scale. Where was the old Roman Arena?"

Ed said something to a passing waiter, who handed him a red felt-tip pen. He drew a big *U* at an angle on the napkin. The right arm ended at the chapel, and the Church of the Eremitani was outside that line.

T. said, "Were the monks mad because they were outside the arena?"

"No. They'd chosen their site. They were mad because Scrovegni had outdone them—and by an order of magnitude. I think they realized they were going to be living in the shadow of Enrico Scrovegni, a moneylender, and the son of a moneylender, for all time."

T. put his finger on the cracker chapel. "This couldn't have cast much of a shadow."

Ed said, "You know how it feels when you're in a crowded theater and the guy in front of you is tall, much taller than you? There's nothing you can do about it, but it's annoying. And then he doesn't take off his hat. You ask him, and he doesn't just refuse to take it off, he sticks a big feather in his cap." Ed looked around but didn't see what he wanted. "The chapel was Scrovegni's fancy hat, and the bell tower was the feather he wanted to stick in it." He looked around again but gave up. "If either of you can catch somebody's attention, order a biscotti."

I bent down to my red bag. I felt like Merlin when I pulled out the gift from my curly-haired waiter and handed it to Ed.

T. said, "I'm a little peckish, too. Do you have a panini press in there?"

Ed pulled the biscotti from the wax-paper bag and placed it at the open top of the U-shaped Arena he had drawn on the napkin. "*Perfetto,*" he said. "Before he built the chapel, Enrico built himself the biggest, fanciest house in Padua. It was torn down by Napoleon's troops," Ed said, tilting the biscuit to make it fit properly, "but this biscotti is the palace Enrico built for his wife and kids, an arching mass of marble and gold-leaf wrought iron and who knows what all. From the front, it was a long crescent of imperial columns—massive and opulent and galling to everyone in the neighborhood."

"So Giotto was an afterthought." T. shoved the Arena Chapel closer to the palace on the napkin. "I see. Like Charlemagne, Enrico added a little palatine chapel to heighten the majesty of his domestic arrangements."

Ed nodded.

T. pulled out his phone and took a picture of the arrangement, and then he divided the palace into three equal lengths, which we ate.

I said, "Have either of you been to the Gardner?" All the talk of palaces had made me mindful of Mitchell's favorite museum in Boston, which had been built to resemble a Venetian palace. Hidden among the crowded confabulation of Italian paintings and drawings, Asian artifacts, and precious who-knows-what stacked up in corners of every room were several rare early editions of Dante with lavish illustrations and illuminations.

Ed said, "You mean the Isabella Stewart Gardner Museum?"

T. said, "Not to put too fine a point on it."

I said, "There's a painting by Giotto there." It was a tiny tempera painting on a board washed in gold, so easily overlooked amidst the grandeur and glamour of the Renaissance masterworks that Isabella had propped it up on an easel draped in red velvet. While Mitchell attended lectures on Michelangelo's appropriation of Dante's poetry, I stared at that painting of the baby Jesus suspended between the arms of his mother and a bearded priest alongside a few long-robed attendants at a temple simply rendered as a kind of four-poster gazebo. I was as confounded by my affection for it as I was delighted by its miraculous presence, seven hundred years after its creation, right where I needed something beautiful to call my own.

T. said, "Is it a fresco?"

Ed said, "No. The Gardner Giotto is a wooden panel painting. One of only a handful in existence. It's a version of one of the frescoes in the chapel."

I said, "My little Giotto is here in Padua?"

"The original," Ed said. "It's commonly called the Feast of the Circumcision."

Mitchell had called it charmingly naive—his admiration spiked with condescension. I swallowed a lot of those Harvard cocktails. I said, "I think the Gardner painting is actually *The Presentation of the Infant Jesus in the Temple*."

Ed said, "They presented him for circumcision."

T. said, "Why?"

Ed said, "Jewish custom."

"Thank you, the doctor of theology," T. said, "but I wasn't talking about foreskin. I was speaking to E." He ate the last olive. "Why did you ask if we'd been to the Gardner?"

"I don't know," I said. "It's just somewhere I'm always happy to be." I wanted to anchor this day in the deep past so it wouldn't float away when I did, so I might find it tucked in under that velvet-covered easel if I ever managed to rouse myself from my sofa and visit the Gardner alone.

"I was there once, when I was rather young," T. said. He didn't explain why he'd been in Boston or pinpoint his age at the time. I didn't ask.

These elusive facts didn't register as secrets or mysteries. Any mention of his life before we met made him seem remote, as if his past was a sealed-off space, not contiguous with the present. I wasn't even sure I'd recognize him there. Of course, I didn't know who I thought I was—drink in hand, chumming around with a couple of unmarried men, handing out free trips. And T. never asked me to square any of that with the last thirty-five years. Sometimes, I felt we had woken up in adjacent tombs, relieved to discover a companionable neighbor who didn't expect to be invited inside for tea and sympathy.

"What I remember is that beautiful courtyard in the middle of the museum with the mile-high glass ceiling," T. said, "all of the windows looking out as if onto the Grand Canal—but actually looking in on the other exterior walls."

"Inverted," I said.

"That's exactly right." T. smiled, remembering what it was like inside the courtyard. "It inverts your expectations. Every window opens onto a view of an interior life. I remember that courtyard glowing with light. And it was surrounded by darkness at eye level—those low-ceilinged, narrow cobblestone arcades."

I said, "Roman arches."

T. said, "Where would we be without them?" He stood up, looked at his watch, instructed Ed to walk me over to the Piazza dei Fruitti in about fifteen minutes, and then left to meet Shelby and Anna and accompany them to our dinner reservation.

After a few silent minutes, I thanked Ed for the all-day pass for the Arena Chapel. I was eager to see the antecedent for the little Giotto panel I so loved. Evidently, I was not leaving until Wednesday.

"Don't throw that pass away," Ed said, staring at the clock tower. "It's good till December. They got your dates mixed up with my dates. Maybe we can plan a reunion." He sounded deeply sad, or maybe T.'s departure had pulled the plug on his hope of something more for the evening. I urged him to join us for dinner, but he said he was due back at the basilica for a dinner with some visiting priests, who'd also attended his lecture. "I'm debating whether I have time for one more drink," he said. "A bracer."

"Was it important, the lecture? I mean, to you."

"I just have to get through dinner. After that—well, I'm mostly surrounded by Franciscans at St. Anthony's, and they take vows to be kind to dumb animals. It should be fine." He stood up, and we angled our way into the adjoining piazza, where I surprised myself by spotting the restaurant from the night before. Ed stopped well shy of the yellow awning. He rested his hand lightly on my elbow. "Evenings like this," he said, but when I turned to him, he let go of his hold on my arm. "Goodnight, E.," he said.

"Goodnight, Ed," I said, and I watched him wend his way through the incoming hordes, head bowed, shoulders hunched, his hands clasped behind his back, looking like the much older man he might one day be.

I didn't see any of my familiars as I approached the restaurant, but a man in a black suit and a white shirt unbuttoned at the collar waved and yelled, "*Ancora?*" He was bald—the gleaming top, back, and sides of his head shaved to within a freckle of his life—and he had a pair of black plastic eyeglasses balanced above his forehead, which made him seem officious, someone who might demand to see my passport. I said I'd prefer to wait, and he said, "*Sì, sì, sì. Ancora* tonight, *signora*, you join us." He was older than I was, or he looked older than I felt at the moment. Before I could explain that I was meeting friends, he led me past several open seats to a table for four. By the time I spotted T. in the distance, a waiter had delivered four tall, narrow juice glasses and a bottle of Chianti—*classico*, he assured me, smiling at someone over his shoulder while he filled my glass to the rim. As Shelby ushered Anna through the rope gate to the table, I bent my head to the glass and sipped out an inch or two of the wine to prevent any settling-in spills.

T. slid his way quickly to my side and said, "Ed called. He's under the impression that I promised to dine with him at the Inquisition. Shelby said the tour bus leaves for Vicenza tomorrow morning at eight, so if you are still talking to me, I'll meet you for breakfast at eight-thirty." He handed me a photocopy of something folded in half. "I printed this at the hotel. Promise me you will rescind your offer to Anna and come to Florence. She's got six children. I'm certain she's good at dealing with disappointment." He shook hands with the bald man, and he was waving good-bye as Shelby eased Anna into a chair. I unfolded the page he'd handed me and then slipped it into my bag so it wouldn't get stained.

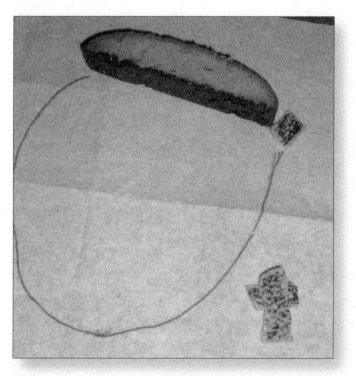

Shelby and Anna agreed that they weren't very hungry, so we only ordered two pizzas. We were all dressed as we were when we'd met at the chapel in the morning, and the only news any of us had was Shelby's report on St. Anthony's Basilica, which might have accounted for the cheerlessness of our attempts at conversation. Or maybe T.'s decision to dump us had dampened everybody's expectations for the evening.

Anna asked me several stilted questions about hobbies and magazine subscriptions, and I finally figured out that she was hoping to buy me an appropriate thank-you gift. To relieve her of that burden, and to save myself the problem of what to do with a needlepoint kit, I asked if she would take one picture of each city she and Francesca visited. I'd remembered the fun they seemed to be having with a camera at the back of the bus when we left Venice. Anna said, "Francesca is the photographer in the family, but I suppose I can ask her to do that," turning my request into a gift tax.

Shelby said, "It seems loud here tonight." She had been occasionally massaging her temples, and I could feel a migraine coming on, too.

I said, "The air is lovely, though."

"It is very crowded," Anna said, ignoring me. "Maybe we should have had dinner at the hotel."

The pizzas arrived. One was a simple classic—basil, tomato, and cheese—and the other featured a big mound of baby arugula at the center, lightly dressed in something spicy, which disappointed Shelby, who had expected roasted red peppers.

Shelby said she wasn't hungry, and she pulled out her knitting.

Anna poked her fork under the arugula in a couple of places, as if she suspected the greens were covering up a burned patch or a hole. She seemed to be offended by the presentation.

I pulled off a slice, rolled up the sides, and took a giant bite. It was my new favorite pizza of all time. "There's something sweet in here," I said, still chewing. "Maybe raisins?"

Anna said she preferred her salad in a bowl on the side. "I suppose I'm old-fashioned," she added.

Even Shelby looked surprised by the sharpness of Anna's tone.

I realized then that Anna was offended by me, or by Francesca's willingness to accept the gift from me, or else she felt my readiness to give away my place had devalued the trip her children had given her.

I was the only one eating, and though I was not eager to find out how long it would take for this conversation to shift into an open confrontation, I was not leaving before I polished off the arugula pizza. I asked about St. Anthony's tongue. Shelby said it was displayed in something that looked a lot like a sterling silver medieval knight's helmet with the face guard open. "And the tongue is black," she said.

"I voted for Obama in November," Anna said. "Did you?"

Shelby gracefully looped this dangling thread into the evening. "I think it's safe to assume we three were all on the side of the saints in that election."

I nodded and ate another piece of pizza. My history with our president was a little more complicated. Mitchell had been an early Obama enthusiast, and during the primary season he was initially amused and then offended that I nullified every check he wrote with a check of my own to Hillary Clinton's campaign. It hadn't been easy living in Cambridge, surrounded by liberals congratulating themselves for finding a candidate whose very existence made it noble and righteous and imperative not to vote for a woman.

When the check came, I insisted on paying. Shelby offered to split it, but I persisted, and she thanked me. To my surprise, Anna didn't object. She seemed pleased, as if the offer was an acknowledgment of something she'd been waiting for me to admit. "Even if it's not a lot of money, it means a lot to me," Anna said. "You've been very kind." I think she really believed I was a dowager with a debit card perpetually refilled from Harvard's $30 billion endowment.

Instead of the waiter, it was the bald man who brought me my credit-card slip to sign. While I was digging for my eyeglasses, he tipped the plastic pair off his head and offered them to me. They worked.

While I signed the receipt, Anna said, "Do you know him?"

The bald man said, "*Si, si, si*, we are old friends."

I looked up at him. I expected him to look pleased with himself, but his smile was tentative and hopeful, and it undid me, or undid a button somewhere inside me, somewhere near enough my heart to make me feel grateful—and a little nervous. I slid the glasses to end of my nose. I said, "*Grazie.*"

He said, "*Prego.*"

I said, "Really."

He said, "I know." He narrowed his gaze and his smile faded, and then, very softly, he said, "*Permesso,*" and, with both of his hands, he lifted his glasses from my face. He bowed and went to tend to the indoor customers.

Anna said, "Thank you again for dinner," and slid her chair back from the table.

Shelby leaned toward me and said, "The bald man—you two were having a moment."

"Oh, Shelby," I said, and then I surprised us both by kissing her on both cheeks. "I am going to miss you."

She stood up, nodded toward Anna, and whispered, "Are you regretting your decision?"

"No," I said and stood up. The sun had disappeared, and in the endless twilight of that early June evening, the crowded piazza was streaked with crenellated shadows shot through with pale, flickering flames. It was thrumming with life. I turned back to say something to Shelby, but she had moved away to guide Anna through the maze of tables.

I wanted to shout to Shelby. I wanted to call T. and Ed. I wanted to rush into the little restaurant and beg the bald man to join us. I wanted us all to run to the west, catch the sun where it was, and hold it up. I didn't want anything to happen next.

V

✶

I woke too early on Tuesday. The morning sky was slate gray, and I vaguely remembered a pounding rainstorm in the middle of the night. Something had washed away my good mood. From the window in my room, I saw evidence of the downpour puddled around the duct-work on the black roof below. I briefly lay down on the bed again. I looked around the room. For the umpteenth time, I noted that the red desk chair and the red chair by the door were not an exact pair. I got up and stared at myself in the bathroom mirror, a mistake, and then sat at the desk. There was a black metal safe under the desk, attached to a fiberboard shelf with two bolts I could've loosened with a pair of nail clippers. I returned to the window, put my hand on the white vinyl lever, and thought the better of it. Whenever I twisted that lever, I couldn't tell if the window was going to swing out on its gate latch or flip up from the sill like a tropical shutter.

All of this, and the surprising puffiness of the pillows (good), the mysterious way the overhead light switched off (annoying), my resolve not to turn on the TV (harder than yoga), and I still had a hundred inane thoughts to think.

I probably would not have repeated any of these inconsequential observations to Mitchell, but while he was alive I almost always imagined him at the other end of such thoughts, as if our marriage was like the green patch of lawn beneath the maple tree in our front yard, the place where leaves fell, swirled around, and finally piled up so high and dry that we knew it was time to grab our old bamboo rakes and make big piles to burn, the thick smoke sweet with the harvest of fleeting colors, the incense of another year.

I sat at the desk and pasted the photo of Ed's biscotti palace and cracker chapels into my book. It was not quite six-thirty, and T.'s invitation to a late breakfast was working on me like a prison sentence. I checked my phone, and beneath a coupon for a used-book website and an offer of cheap drugs from a Canadian pharmacy, I found an email from Sam with a photograph attached.

O Captain! My Captain!
I hope the sailing is smooth. And while you are in foreign lands, I thought
you might enjoy this little slice of Americana—courtesy of you. Susie
and I think of it as the Colonial Corner in our Cobble Hill sublet—
and we always think of you and Dad when we're sitting in there.

The camelback sofa had long lived in Mitchell's study, but when I had a hospital bed installed for him, something had to go. That was the weekend Sam hung the flat-screen TV in the living room, so I offered the sofa to him. Mitchell didn't like the idea of it leaving the house. Maybe he still believed he would recover, or maybe he wanted me to pretend I believed he would. I know he didn't like Sam's readiness to supplement his teaching salary with hand-me-downs and handouts.

From the living room windows, Mitchell watched Sam tie the sofa to the roof of the BMW. When Sam came back into the house, triumphant, Mitchell said, "If you found a summer job, you could afford a new sofa."

Sam said, "I'll think of you whenever I am sitting down, Dad."

Before he left, I pulled Sam aside and told him to take some of the towels and sheets I'd stashed in the closet of his old bedroom.

He asked if I could spare any blankets.

I nodded and asked him to send his father a picture of the sofa once it was in place.

Sam said, "Wouldn't that be rubbing it in?"

I said, "He knows he is never going to see where you and Susie live. And so do you. You've got the sofa, and his new car. Does he get a thank-you yet? Send him the picture."

"There's an old wooden chair upstairs in the attic."

"Take it," I said. I knew if he stayed five more minutes, he'd ask if I could spare the refrigerator. And if he stayed ten more minutes, Mitchell would present him with a bill for the food he'd consumed since his arrival. They were always disappointed with each other, and time together made them both ravenous for compensation.

Until the belated arrival of the picture, I hadn't known that the chair Sam had found upstairs was the Shaker gathering chair my brother had sent me as a wedding gift, the one authentic piece of furniture in the house. Plus, one of the blankets Sam had chosen was a patchwork quilt made for me by Cambridge middle-school kids who'd successfully completed the Reading Rainbow program. The photograph of Sam and Susie's sublet was an unnerving glimpse into the future, the museum of Mom and Dad. And now Sam was shopping for a permanent home for his collection.

Susie and I spent the weekend walking around Williamsburg, poking our heads into open houses. There are a lot of new (tiny) loft spaces for sale in the old brick buildings, and we have to be out of here by December, so time to shop, right? I know you said there was more money (how much?) coming my way (when?), and if that's true maybe when you get back to Cambridge we can square away how and when I should expect it? No rush. Not trying to build Rome in a day. Love from the New World.

Mitchell was dead, but for Sam the story would never end. I understood now that he would always want more from his father. And in the sad light cast by this insight, I also saw how often I had indulged Sam because I knew the feeling.

I'd urged Mitchell to settle the inheritance issue before he died. Almost weekly, Mitchell had proposed a new scheme for managing the transfer of money to Rachel and Sam. Many of his plans were wise, most of them were designed to prevent Sam from doing what Sam would surely do with unrestricted access to a pot of money, and ultimately Mitchell left all of that money in trust. He made me the sole trustee and entrusted me with an elaborate binder of handwritten notes about investment strategies he preferred, as well as the percentage of annual interest he anticipated, and his preferred maximum whole-dollar distributions to each child, which effectively created a part-time job for me as a funnel for his largesse.

I took a shower, and every thought I had about the money, and the kids, and the trust was swept right down the drain along with the fleeting pleasure of the puffy pillows and the other dust stirred up by my solitary existence. I didn't towel off the steam on the big bathroom mirror. If Mitchell had been a better Jew, or if I had been a better wife, I would have covered all of the mirrors in my home after he died, and I would have understood sooner what I understood when I repeatedly looked for my reflection, which wasn't there. From now on, wherever I was, I would always be alone with these thoughts. I was a sentimental warehouse stuffed with old sofas, a matching pair of ancient bamboo rakes, and ironies and indignities and intimacies no one else could understand. It was a relief to know I would be at home by Wednesday evening, where I could lie still, let this stuff drift around and pile up until I was buried.

I put on the hotel bathrobe and wrapped my hair in a towel. I sat at the desk and dialed into my online investment accounts. Maybe it was the amount of money Mitchell had amassed for the two kids, not to mention how much he'd left for me, or maybe it was the soft white hotel robe, or maybe I'd tied the towel too tight around my head, but I felt momentarily like an heiress. I called down to the front desk.

"*Pronto.*"

I thought I recognized the voice. "Ricardo?"

"*Signora Berman. Come la posso aiutare?*"

I was already lost. "Breakfast? Room service? Is that possible?"

This occasioned a long, muffled pause. Eventually, a much younger man said, "*Pronto.* How may I help you?"

"Coffee? Is it possible to get some sent up to my room?"

"No. We have no room serving, *signora*. We have—. Oh, okay. Only if you did have room serving, coffee is what you prefer to enjoy?"

I said, "Yes," hypothetically speaking. I got the clear sense Ricardo was orchestrating the young man's responses.

"Which is the preferred favorite?"

"Coffee?"

"*Si, signora.*"

"Latte?"

"*Perfetto. Prego*—oh. Okay. If room serving *con succo*, which one should arrive?"

Did he mean, *with sugar?* Unclear. This indulgence was turning into a trial. "Lovely," I said.

"Lovely?"

"*Con succo*," I said, hoping I wasn't ordering a whole pineapple. "*Perfetto.*"

He said, "*Prego, prego,*" and hung up.

I reread Sam's email. Five or six times, I tapped out a few lines of response and deleted them. I couldn't quite imagine what Mitchell would have wanted me to say about the money. I could imagine what Mitchell would have said, but he wouldn't have wanted me to say that, which is why he'd left it to me to say what had to be said. In a fit of inspiration, I added Rachel's name to the address line and wrote:

Dearest you two—

I miss you, and I miss your father, and among the many hopes and wishes he harbored on your behalf, I know he most wanted you both to thrive and love your lives. And I know it pleased him to think that he could leave you both with evidence of the simple truth that he carried you with him in his mind and heart every day. Your father left you each a bequest of $425,000. My intention is to give you the full amount immediately. When I return to Cambridge, I will put you both in touch with Lawrence Macomber, a longtime friend of your father, who now is a director at the Harvard Management Company. He kindly offered to advise you both on strategies for making the most of this gift.

I know that your father left each of you with much more than a sum of money, but that material is wholly yours to tally and invest as you see fit. The money is another matter. It initially passed into my hands, and I write today to let you know it is on its way to you.

I hit "Save" because I heard a knock at the door. Or I might have hit "Save" because I realized I was about to give away almost a million dollars—and then I heard the knock.

As I opened the door, Ricardo hoisted a silver tray overhead and squeezed past me. He made a beeline for the little desk, which was crammed with my stuff, so he twirled toward the unmade bed. He said nothing. He lowered the tray and got it firmly into both of his hands. It was a full coffee service for two, with two flutes of blood-orange juice and two crème-filled pasty cornets.

"It's beautiful," I said.

He nodded dismissively, as if that should have gone without saying.

"You'll want to put it down," I said. I pointed to the bed.

He didn't love that idea. He was staring at the bathroom door.

I knew the sink counter was even less promising than the desk.

"So, so, so. You are one?"

He barked out the English words as if he had just memorized them. I said, "I am one. Why?"

"One," he said, dubiously, glancing at the two of everything on his tray. "*Uno*," he added, just so there could be no confusion.

"Yes. One." He seemed to be accusing me of something. "*Uno. Why?*" I had intended to thank him for the glue, but he was staring at the bathroom door again, as if he suspected I'd secreted in a bunch of freeloaders for breakfast. I bent down to pull the comforter halfway up the bed, and the towel fell off my head, which only heightened my sense of fraudulence. With as much authority as I could muster in a bathrobe and bare feet, I pointed to the bed again. "Here, please."

While he set down the tray, I went to the desk to dig up my wallet for a tip. I pulled out a five-euro note, but when I turned, Ricardo was backing out of the bathroom, and as he headed out of my room, he slid open the closet door—one last check for unregistered guests—and then he left without another word.

THE HOTEL RESTAURANT WAS STILL CROWDED AT EIGHT-thirty, but I spotted an open window table. I didn't sit down immediately for the same reason no one else had claimed that table—the view was blocked by a big man outside, leaning against the granite windowsill. It was T., and though I couldn't hear what he was saying out there, I recognized the timbre of his voice as he chatted with someone beside him whom I couldn't see. He was wearing his blue linen blazer, and I guessed that he had been out all night and his companion—a paramour? Ed?—had kindly led him back to the hotel. I didn't want to go out and intrude into his private nightlife, but when I sat down directly behind him, I felt like J. Edgar Hoover or the mother of a teenager who'd stayed out partying past dawn. Before I could move, T. reached out and took an espresso cup from his invisible acquaintance and noticed me. He turned, his smiling face cleanly shaved, a crisp crimson-and-white pinstripe shirt tucked into a pair of khaki trousers, an espresso cup in either hand. I was impressed that he'd persuaded someone to provide him and his companion with street-side beverage service, but I still thought my breakfast story trumped his.

By the time he appeared in the restaurant, T. had traded the espresso cups for two wood-handled black umbrellas, which he was wielding like canes. He said, "You might be expecting me to sit down."

"I was just admiring your sticks," I said.

T. said, "I was thinking a walk might be the thing." He looked ill at ease, and he was clearly hoping not to have to explain himself.

I grabbed my bag. "I ate two breakfasts earlier," I said, standing up, "so we're both done here."

T. handed me an umbrella and headed out of the hotel. He was standing too straight and taking long, purposeful strides, as if he was trying to walk off something—maybe a hangover, maybe a cranky back. Even before we reached the end of Largo Europa, his pace was taking its toll on me. With each hurried step, I could feel my feet skidding forward in my shoes, widening the little holes in my open-toed pumps. Instead of heading left past the post office, he hustled us to the right, and after we'd zigzagged through four crosswalks, the Church of the Eremitani appeared on our left, and I realized we were going to pass the café where I'd picked up a free biscotti after Ed's lecture.

I called out to T., but he was so far ahead he didn't hear me, so I yelled, "Uncle!"

He stopped but didn't turn around.

When I caught up to him, I pointed to the café. "I just want to step in here and put on a sports bra and running shoes."

T. said, "Forgive me."

I said, "Buy me something foamy," and headed inside to the bar. The young waiter had been replaced by his father or an uncle—same smile, same apron, brown mop of hair reduced to a scraggly tonsure of gray curls.

T. ordered two latte macchiatos and something else that made the bartender smile, which turned out to be a blood orange. While the milk steamed, the bartender peeled the orange and then set it on a plate with a paring knife and slid it onto the bar with our beverages.

I said, "*Grazie.*"

He said, "*Prego.*"

T. was awkwardly twisting his torso, attempting to shrug off his coat.

I said, "Are you okay?" T. stiffened. My question had registered as a violation of the terms of conduct for our peculiar friendship. I instantly regretted my breach of our policy of presumptive intimacy—no questions asked. Hoping to make it clear I didn't need an explanation, I casually reached for the collar and slid the blazer halfway down his arms.

T. said, "I had an odd night."

I was staring at a thin streak of something dark on his shirt below one of his shoulders, a run of several inches where the crimson pinstripes seemed to have leeched into the white space. It was obviously blood. I said, "I think you may have sprung a leak."

"That's nothing," he said.

The bartender disappeared into the little kitchen behind the bar.

I still had one hand on his blazer, and I saw another, darker splotch of blood, about the size of a coat button, right on his spine, and his shirt seemed to be stuck to it. With my free hand, I pinched a bit of the loose pinstripe fabric gathered at his waist, tugged lightly, and felt a release, like tape giving way.

T. said, "Much better."

I said, "How do you say Band-Aid in Italian?"

"*Grappa*," T. said and slipped on his jacket. "Thank you. I was rushing earlier so we could walk around the old arena before it rains." He sipped from his glass and picked up the knife. "During dinner last night, I was treated to a debate about Scrovegni's sincerity."

I wasn't really interested in what had been served up at a dinner to which I wasn't invited. I drank some coffee and did my best not to think about his back. I just kept telling myself, *He's a doctor, he's a doctor.*

After a few silent seconds, T. said, "Enrico Scrovegni specifically dedicated the chapel to the Virgin of Charity."

"There was only one Blessed Virgin," I said.

"There are many versions of the Virgin," T. said.

"One virgin, many virtues. And the greatest of these is charity," I added, mixing up the Virgin and the Seven Virtues. This felt like an argument in search of a topic.

T. said, "Speaking of the Virgin of Charity, she was the basis of Scrovegni's bid for salvation. Will the Virgin accept Scrovegni's gift of the chapel in exchange for forgiveness?"

Along with a newfound devotion to the Virgin of Charity, T. seemed to have picked up a note of piety during his dinner at the basilica. "It's an age-old question," I said, hoping to leaven the tone. "Can a man buy his way back into a woman's good graces?"

T. said, "Scripture says it is easier for a camel to pass through the eye of a needle than it is for a rich man to pass into heaven."

I said, "And any woman can tell you that it's easier to buy a new pair of socks than to try to thread a needle and darn them."

"Ye of little faith," T. said. He sliced the orange into six ruby-red discs and fanned them out among the bits and streams of bloody juice on the white plate. He held his hand over the plate, palm down, and piously said, "The Blessed Sacrament." The melodrama of the moment made me queasy. The whole ritual seemed to be connected to the blood on his back that we weren't talking about. And as if the weirdness quotient weren't high enough, the bartender came back bearing a crystal cruet, pulled out the faceted stopper and said, "*Miele di acacia*," and ceremoniously poured a clear viscous liquid onto the oranges.

"Now," T. said.

I said, "Now what?"

He pointed to the bartender and said, "Join us. *Si, si, si. Unisciti a noi.*"

They both took hold of a slice and looked at me, their hands still balanced at the edge of the plate, where the pool of bloody juice was glimmering. The bartender nodded, urging me to join them, as if this were some kind of initiation. I smiled and didn't move. The moment was teetering in my imagination between a dare and a Black Mass.

Two young blonde women with backpacks poked their heads in the doorway. They hovered there like hummingbirds or a couple of angels who'd flown in from a Giotto fresco. They smiled and said nothing.

To me, the bartender said, "*Si, signora. Unisciti a noi.*"

T. said, "Trust me."

I pinched the smallest slice between my fingers. I said, "What is it?"

T. and the bartender popped their slices into their mouths. I followed their lead, feeling the acid bite on my tongue.

T. staggered back a few steps and mumbled, "Jesus Christ."

The bartender nodded, gleefully chewing away, wiping the bloody juice from his chin with the back of his hand.

I smooshed the slice against the roof of my mouth. Satan didn't show up, but as I tasted the sweetness of honey, I felt an evanescent, smoky aroma filter up into my head. I said, "I can feel it more than taste it."

We all ate a second slice, and then the bartender urged the newcomers up to the bar and took their orders. T. put the glass stopper back into the cruet and explained that the magic was in the monoflora source of local honeys. This clear nectar had been produced exclusively by bees feasting on the flowers of the acacia tree. While he talked, we sipped our bitter coffee and took turns slicking our fingers across the plate and sucking up what was left of the syrup. When the bartender turned to us from his espresso machine, T. wagged a twenty-euro note.

The bartender said, "*No, no. Troppo.*"

T. said, "*No, no, perfetto,*" and slid the cash under the edge of the white plate.

The bartender smiled and said, "*Grazie.*"

T. said, "*Prego, prego.*"

I said to T., "How do you say *heaven*?"

T. said, "You're the Dante scholar."

I pointed to the plate and said, "*Paradiso*."

The bartender said something I didn't understand. As I followed T. out to the street, I asked him to translate.

"He said life is bittersweet." T. hooked his arm around mine and led us across the street. "Like an orange," he said. "And then he said you cannot change the nature of things."

"He said all that?"

"And more," T. said, leading us off the sidewalk and onto a path hemmed in by rhododendron backed by a stand of gnarly pines. "The Italians have a way of saying a lot of words per word. He also said, 'You are here now, and this is the time for honeying the bitter fruit.'"

Neither of us said anything for a while.

As the path opened up a bit, the land at either side fell away into a series of soft little hills that tipped down toward a river on one side and a dry gulley on the other, and we passed a few remnants of an ancient stone wall, crumbly granite blocks coated with lichen-like layers of powdery white lime.

T. said, "This is what remains of the old Roman Arena."

ACCORDING TO T., PADUA WAS PUT ON THE MAP BY PRINCE Antenor, who settled the place with a bunch of refugees from the Trojan War in 1183 BC. "This much of what those priests told me last night I believe," T. said, "because it comes from *The Aeneid*, and even Dante trusted Virgil."

"Not all the way," I said. It had always bugged me that Dante had turned Virgil into a functionary, his personal tour guide through the Inferno—and then ditched Virgil somewhere in Purgatory, based on the old Roman poet's being a pagan and, thus, unfit for Paradise. "An old blind man leads you safely through hell and back, and that's the thanks he gets?"

T. said, "It is unthinkable to abandon a friend in the middle of a journey."

"Enough," I said. "I'm leaving tomorrow. That decision is now ancient history." It did occur to me that I hadn't yet reserved my ride home.

T. said the Arena had survived the Roman Empire, and Attila and his Huns, who rumbled into town around 450, and even the Goths, who followed a hundred years later. It was the Lombards who destroyed most of what the Romans had bothered to build, and in the centuries that followed, Padua sort of fell off the map and eventually got absorbed into the new Holy Roman Empire. It remained a backwater until it got a constitution of its own in the 12th century, and then the commune founded the second university in Italy in 1222 and launched a century of prosperity.

All the while, T. said, the locals scavenged rock from the arena to fortify their foundations and shore up their bridges. I thought of Sam, who would have happily borrowed bricks from the chimney in my house to build himself a barbecue pit. But even in its decimated state, long before Enrico Scrovegni built his palace and chapel on the site, the Arena remained a kind of spiritual center and hosted pageants and public forums and, most importantly, an annual celebration of the Feast of the Annunciation, which involved two little boys being carried from the cathedral on chairs to commemorate the angel Gabriel flying down from heaven to tell the Virgin Mary that she was about to become a handmaiden to history.

I said, "Why boys?" I was thinking of Rachel's two little boys—how happy they'd be if they were hoisted up and paraded through town, how quickly I'd dial 911 if some priest dressed them up in heavenly robes and lipstick.

"Everyone at the table last night seemed to agree they would have been boys. Oddly, that was just about the only uncontested fact," T.

said. "Was the idea of building a chapel here original to Scrovegni, or did he replace an old church built on the Arena and dedicated to Mary? The record is unclear. For his personal digs, did he rehab an extant palace or start from scratch? No one seems to know."

I said, "What year was Dante in Padua?" I was scratching an old itch, but since I'd been in the chapel, I was feeling personally offended by Dante—especially his famous crack about Giotto's fleeting fame.

T. said, "I don't know that Dante ever was here."

"Dante would've heard about the chapel, surely. He would have wanted to see it, wouldn't he? After he got tossed out of Florence, Dante was always begging at some patron's table and then complaining about the quality of the accommodations, so you have to admit it seems likely he would have figured out how run into the richest man in Padua while he was here. And he must have been here. How else do you explain his attack on Scrovegni in *The Inferno*?"

T. said, "I think you might have me confused with the attorney representing Mr. Dante."

I said, "I'm not saying Scrovegni was a saint."

"From what I heard last night, I think the case against Scrovegni—Enrico, the son, anyway—is just that he was a rich boob," T. said. "For instance, there's apparently plenty of evidence that Enrico was a knight—almost all of it left by him. But there's absolutely no record of him ever raising his lance on behalf of the commune, and somebody wrote a sonnet about his habit of crying in public. Ed's theory is that Enrico was one of those guys who joined a civic organization devoted to fighting heresy or indecency and took his honorary title too seriously."

"Like the Knights of Columbus," I said. As a young girl, I was amazed when the fathers of my friends turned up at parish bake sales and car washes with three-foot swords swinging beneath their elaborate topcoats, big black feathers flouncing around on their fancy hats, as if they might be called up at any moment to retake Istanbul. "Did Enrico have a wife?"

"Two of them," T. said, "both from famous families, but you'll have to ask Ed about them. That was the after-dinner topic, and I had to be somewhere else."

Whenever either of our kids would bolt from the dinner table with that excuse, Mitchell would say, "But you can't be somewhere else."

Of course, he had since proved himself wrong.

As it started to rain, we were rounding the wrought-iron fence that kept the world away from the chapel, and T. said we had three minutes to join the next group. He took our official letters to the ticket desk while I checked our umbrellas and my bag, and soon we were being hustled into the dehumidifying chamber to watch the video. I took a seat in the last row, trying to catch my breath, and T. stood behind me. As the closing credits rolled on the TV screen, I felt his hands on my shoulders, and his face next to mine. I thought I felt the warmth of his face, but he whispered, "You're flushed."

"Reflected glory," I said, thinking of Giotto, though I immediately realized he might think I was flirting with him.

"Don't wait for me," T. said. "I have to explain our credentials to the guards who clear everyone out."

I FOLLOWED THE HERD OF TOURISTS INTO THE CHAPEL. I felt lost, all turned around. I stopped to locate myself on Sara's map. From where I was, I could see the original double-doored entrance at the far end, below the Last Judgment, and Enrico hoisting his chapel up to the Virgin. I headed that way and then looked up and to the left until I located the mound of murdered babies beneath their weeping mothers' outstretched arms, Sara's Number 20, the Slaughter of the Innocents, my only anchor in the sea of blue that seemed to swirl beneath the painted frames and figures as I tried to get a purchase on another image.

Instead of the sense of awe I was waiting to experience again, I was agitated by the presence of other people, impatient with my own inability to settle in one place without having my imagination fill in the blank space in every fresco with a white jet in a blue sky, or the image of my black TV against the white wall of my living room, and it didn't help that a wheezy ancient woman with a walker was trailing me, wheeling her way down the aisle and inching ever nearer, like an omen, her rosary beads clicking against her chrome handlebars.

I walked all the way back to the other end of the chapel, to start at the beginning. According to Sara's map, the first six panels, above the arched tops of the windows, were scenes from the life of Joachim and St. Anne. This was annoying. I had never heard of either of them.

I'd read the Bible. I'd suffered through more than my share of sermons on the scriptures. At the very least, I should have been able to follow the story.

T. was nowhere to be seen. I sidled my way through the crowded center aisle again and reclaimed my familiar perch in the corner and fixed my attention on the topmost panel, Number 6 on Sara's map, Meeting at the Golden Gate. This panel calmed me down or made me sad—the distinction was lost on me lately.

In the background, beneath a deep blue sky, stood a tall, white crenellated wall, the edge of a fortress or a city. At its center was a generous open arch, trimmed in gold, and on that narrow threshold was a cluster of five women—three in pastel robes smiling expectantly; one in a white peasant dress, with a blanket draped over her folded arms, her fragile face alert and delighted; and one in black, her cape pulled over her head like a shroud. These women were staring at an older couple—Joachim and Anne, I assumed—as they embraced. At the far left of the fresco, a man with a basket—a shopper? a peddler?—looked surprised to find his passage into the city blocked by the elderly couple's embrace.

Joachim's robe was pale rose, and Anne's robe was rusty orange, and as they leaned into each other, their gold-leaf halos overlapped and the generous folds of their robes came together, and they became a single figure, an intimate arch, another golden gate. Joachim gripped Anne's shoulders, drawing her nearer to him. Anne rested one hand on her husband's fulsome graying beard, and her other hand was pressed against the back of his head, pulling his face into a deep kiss.

They were old, and heavyset, and admirably oblivious to the onlookers, so it was easy to turn them into Mitchell and me. We weren't famous or fashionable, but we were together till the end.

A uniformed guard shouted, "*Pronto!*"

Had I left the chapel then, I would have left Padua grateful to Giotto for giving me a happy ending to my story, taken this image home with me to Cambridge, and pulled the stone back into place in my comfy crypt, furnished largely by Mitchell's largesse. But as the crowd filtered out, I drifted over to the opposite corner to get a look at the Seven Vices on the lowest register. Just then, the guard waved and nodded his approval for my lingering presence, and I saw T., watching me from ten feet away.

He stiffly walked my way, staring at one of the paintings on the wall. He stopped a few inches behind me and said, "You know everything."

"I don't even know why Joachim and Anne get top billing," I said, turning to face the other side of the chapel.

"Let's not be coy about this. It's not a secret, E., but it is a mystery, an intolerably resolute mystery."

He didn't sound pleased, and because I couldn't see his face, I felt unnerved by the acerbic edge in his voice. I was almost certain we were talking at cross-purposes, but I didn't know where the confusion origi-nated. I whispered, "Are you talking about one of the frescoes?" But when I turned to him, he held up his hand to silence me. We had the place to ourselves, and T. closed his eyes, as if he wished he were alone.

The chapel was empty for almost a full minute, but the air was thick with secrecy—what T. suspected I knew about him, what I suspected T. overestimated about me, not to mention the blood on his back that neither of us seemed able to discuss. It was suffocating.

Finally, a new group was ushered in.

As matter-of-factly as I could manage, I said, "I really don't understand this, T."

He turned briefly to the front of the church, as if he'd spotted a few spies among the new batch of tourists. "Surely, you don't expect me to venture an explanation right here," he said.

He seemed more confused than annoyed—or maybe that's how I was feeling. Every time I shifted my gaze, I saw someone I recognized— Lazarus, still looking a little stunned after being raised from the dead, and plainly embarrassed to be standing in front of his sisters, Mary and Martha, in nothing but his bandages. And that serene woman on the top row with Mary and the baby Jesus had to be Elizabeth, cousin of Mary, so, yes, the baby paddling around beside her was little John the Baptist, and oh!, the Wedding at Cana, and Mary Magdalene, and was that Judas in the yellow robe? It was as if I'd stumbled into an ancient and endless family reunion.

I said, "I don't understand the six panels along the top of the wall." I don't know if I thought I was talking to Giotto, or to T., or to myself, but I was apparently frustrated with one of us because I had spoken so loudly that I temporarily had the attention of everyone in the chapel. The silence was total until a woman near me hissed the word *américaine* with a pointedly French accent, and then everyone nodded knowingly and turned their attention elsewhere.

T. said, "I had been wondering about the acoustics in this place, too."

"Quite satisfactory," I said.

T. said, "Robust."

I pointed to the Meeting at the Golden Gate. "Just tell me where this kiss takes place."

T. said, "That's the gate to Jerusalem."

"Start at the beginning," I said. I tried to take his hand in mine to lead him back to the first fresco, but I caught the cuff of his blazer and almost toppled him over when I turned and tugged.

When he recovered, he stood still and flexed his shoulders back, and this made him wince. "As you would say, Uncle." But, at last, he was smiling. He hooked his arm into mine. "It begins with Joachim being turned away from the temple."

I said, "Who is he? What makes him unworthy? And why have I never heard of him?"

T. said, "You must have been a good Catholic."

"I actually was a good Catholic. I was a very good Catholic." A few nearby tourists turned to me, smiling their disapproval for my past-tense boast.

According to T., Joachim and Anne were not bit players. They were the parents of the Virgin Mary, but they had been of no interest to the young men who wrote the Gospels and the rest of the New Testament, and so their stories never made it into the Catholic Bible. T. thought Giotto would have read about them in *The Golden Legend*, a compendium of the miraculous lives of many saints that was codified and circulated in 1250 or so. "The *Who's Who of Early Christendom*," he said.

Joachim appeared in the first panel carrying a sacrificial lamb in his arms, but because he and Anne had been married for twenty years and still had no children, his sacrifice was rejected and he was cast out. Meanwhile, a rabbi half-hidden behind a wall was lavishing his attention on a much younger, presumably virile man. The baby business complicated my desire to cast Mitchell in the role of Joachim—I was clinging to my happy ending—until I realized that Joachim's failure to father a child might be Mitchell's failure to finish his book, which was the reason he was cast out of the inner sanctum of scholars into the barren field of academic administration.

In the next panel, Joachim had wandered out to a rocky wilderness to tend to his flock with a couple of young shepherds, who shifted their glances away from him and his shame while the sheep scattered—Mitchell slinking past undergrads in Harvard Yard. Only a skinny little sheepdog, its articulated ribs especially evident compared to the full-bellied sheep in the foreground, looked happy to see him, and the dog and Joachim locked eyes—comrades in indignity.

The third panel broke the narrative line. It was a picture of Anne on her knees inside a room with verdant green walls—a kind of lushness entirely absent from the stony white landscapes in the previous scenes. To the right of Anne, a red-winged angel hovered in a window high above her, its torso evident inside the room, but the rest of its heavenly body was not visible in the exterior view of that wall. The annunciating angel was apparent only to Anne.

"The angel tells Anne to go to Jerusalem," T. said. "You recognize this moment."

"Not quite," I said. I was trying to see myself in the pious posture of Anne. "But I am crazy about the color of her bedroom."

T. said, "This is the Immaculate Conception."

I said, "No, that's when Mary conceives Jesus." I was pleased to have at least one ace up my sleeve from catechism classes.

T. said, "No, Mary is a virgin when she gives birth, but that's not what makes her immaculate. At her conception, when Anne and Joachim conceived their only child, an angel swept by so Mary would not be stained with original sin—thus, immaculate."

I said, "Trust me, Catholic girls know what immaculate means."

I was certain T. was wrong, but I was also losing the thread of my version of the story. "Who is that other woman?" To the left of Anne, on a porch separated by a wall with a lancet window, a handmaiden in an unflattering peasant dress was turning wool onto a wooden spindle, face forward, her dark eyes shifting toward the green room.

T. said, "That's obviously our friend Shelby."

He was right. Only Shelby would risk that outfit. "Maybe you're here somewhere, too," I said, spinning around to try to spot a likeness of T. in one of the paintings.

T said, "We should look for each other before we leave. Everything echoes something, and everyone prefigures someone else."

"It's sort of reassuring," I said, "like a never-ending story."

T. put his arm around my shoulder and whispered, "Spoiler alert. Not everybody gets a happy ending."

The guard called time and cleared the room, and we inched on to the fourth fresco, back to the stony wilderness—Joachim on his knees, a solemn shepherd to his left, a reassuring angel to his right, and a few sheep nosing around in the foreground. At the center, on a rocky height, red flames leapt into the bruised-blue sky from a stone barbecue oven, licking and curling around the blackened skeleton of a sacrificial lamb, its eviscerated neck and cranium raised up above its burned body, pointing to a disembodied heavenly hand reaching down from unseen heights.

T. said, "Put on your peepers."

I didn't want to magnify this moment. I was eager to move on. I couldn't turn Mitchell into Joachim here. It was the carcass of the lamb that made me mindful of Mitchell, and for the first time ever I had to imagine the horrific moments in the crematorium after his flesh had vaporized in the intense heat, before his bones were reduced to ash. That was the end of his story. That was the happy ending I'd arranged for my husband. I said, "I've seen enough."

I tried to hand the binoculars to T., but he shrugged off the offer. I barely paused at the fifth panel, where Joachim was asleep while two young shepherds tended the flock. In the blue sky above, the red-winged angel who'd earlier visited Anne swooped in and urged Joachim on to Jerusalem and then sailed away, the tail end of its heavenly body evanescing in a comet stream.

T. was lingering, and to hasten him along, I said, "And, finally, they meet at the Golden Gate."

"The threshold of history," T. said. "Their story is just getting started."

"Lucky them," I said, though I didn't envy Anne a pregnancy at her age with no hope of an epidural.

T. almost said something—he turned to me expectantly, opened his mouth, and narrowed his gaze, but instead of speaking he reached around his waist and pulled his blazer and shirt away from his back.

I said, "You want to go."

T. said, "You want to stay?"

It sounded more like a request than a question. I said, "For one or two more tours."

T. said, "And then an early lunch?" His head twisted away reflexively, and he winced over his shoulder, as if something surprising was happening on his back. He said, "Lunch with Ed?"

I said, "For god's sake, let me help you. Are you bleeding again?"

T. said, "I'll find you on a bench outside."

The guard was herding the others to the exit.

T. turned and held up his hand, palm toward the Seven Vices on the opposite wall. "If ever I were able to talk about—" He moved his hand in tight little circles. "If I could talk to anyone about all of this, I'd want to talk to you." He hurried away. The tourists cleared out. I was alone.

I FELT THE PRESENCE OF THE OTHER PAINTED FIGURES AS I paced the center aisle of the chapel. I was looking for something, some explanation for the way the paintings worked on my imagination. In the café the day before with Ed and T., it was the depth and vastness of the sky that I remembered. I had recalled each painted scene as if I had been standing so close that I could see above the heads and shoulders of the human figures in the foreground. But I was not close, in fact. A railing all along the central aisle kept me at least ten feet from the chapel walls, and the lowest register of painted panels was ten feet higher than my line of sight. Anne and Joachim—they were at least another thirty feet above me. And yet, from this vantage, where I should have registered distortions in perspective, I was still inside the frame, aware of sky, or at least the sense of possibility that blue skies so reliably betoken, and my mind was reflexively adjusting for the angles and occlusions, rounding out the world around me, as if I had seen these scenes before, my point of view informed by memory.

The frames that Giotto painted for each scene appeared to have dimension—they looked like raised-stone reliefs into which paintings had been fitted, which should have heightened my awareness that I was looking at art, paint on a plaster wall. Instead, the emphatic framing turned the paintings into windows, portals with a vantage on another time. These were not isolated snapshots from the past that simply let you see how other people dressed or spent their time. I was not looking at Anne or Joachim or the shepherds. Every painted figure was a habitable space within a world I'd entered, an invitation to see beyond the familiar borders and boundaries of myself.

When I was alone in the chapel, it was not the painted people or their circumstances that drew me in. The frescoes themselves were charismatic.

Like a pulse, I sensed the presence of that blue sky not only in the background of each picture but behind the frames and under every painted pilaster and column, a blueness roiling beneath the deepest-down coat of unpainted plaster, beneath the brick and mortar of the chapel walls. I knew this was an illusion, but so is the sky itself, that luminous dome above us, the true-blue air we breathe, the impossibly expanding insubstantial depth that we call space.

A priest in a black cassock and white sneakers led a group of four young, black-suited men to my side and pointed to Joachim and the burned carcass of the lamb. "Now, look closely," he said.

The four young men raised their binoculars and focused. They looked like seniors in high school. In England. In 1940. They were extraordinarily clean-cut.

I pointed my peepers at that sacrificial lamb, as T. had suggested.

"Faintly sketched, above the charred carcass of the sacrificial lamb, almost invisible against the night sky, the plumes of smoke assume a shape." The priest paused. "Can you see it?"

One young man whispered, "An angel!"

"An angel," said the priest. "Notice its head cast up, its wings at rest, its fragile existence drawn ever higher by the loving hand of God in heaven."

"Prefiguring the Resurrection," said another of the four young ones.

"Sheep figure in all of the Joachim paintings," the priest continued. His tone was more didactic than pontifical, so I couldn't tell if the young men were prep-school students or seminarians. "We begin the cycle with the rejected sacrifice at the temple, and then the flock in the wilderness, and his holocaust, and, finally, when Joachim dreams in the desert, a single lamb sits on the highest ledge, apart from the bigger, woolly animals, its fragile legs folded, its head erect, its smooth white body shorn of its coat. Now, what do you notice about the two paintings in which St. Anne is present?"

Almost in unison, the four young men said, "No sheep."

The priest was beaming. "There are no sheep in the Anne paintings, almost as if women occupy a separate realm. Which they did. Even St. Anne would not have been allowed into the temple."

One young man said, "So you're comparing women to sheep?"

I was standing two feet away from this nitwit.

Another young man said, "Maybe Giotto is just saying women shouldn't have to work outside the house."

"Use your heads," the priest snapped. He smiled apologetically in my direction. "Think about the Lamb of God."

All four close-cropped heads bowed in unison. One of them muttered, "Jesus is the Lamb of God."

"And who is the Mother of God?"

Someone said, "Mary."

"And who is the mother of the Blessed Virgin Mary?"

"St. Anne."

The priest said, "Giotto is illustrating the promise of Jesus, the coming of the Christ Child. When he depicts St. Anne, there are no sheep—symbolic prefigurations of the Lamb of God—because from this moment forward, the presence of Jesus becomes real in the story of the salvation of history."

This all made sense if you ignored the fact that the sheep were sheep. But the boys were nodding knowingly, and the priest led them across the room toward the manger and the Magi.

When I looked again at Anne, alone in her green room, and Shelby in the peasant dress on the porch, I noted that Shelby was winding wool and, later, at the Golden Gate, among the onlookers, there was Shelby again—it was unmistakably Shelby, her small breasts getting no boost whatsoever from that peasant dress—and she had a hand-knit wool blanket folded over her arms.

In Giotto's telling of the story, you could see the sheep as symbols, or you could see the sheep as sheep—just like the angels. Were those half-seen heralds really present, or were they fond hopes to which the dreamer pinned a pair of wings? Unlike Anne and Joachim, the Shelby figure was not visited by an angel. Outside of Anne's room, the angel's body wasn't visible. And yet before the sainted couple had consummated their lifelong dream of conceiving a child, Shelby knew that Anne would soon be pregnant. Thus, the receiving blanket she had woven from the wool of that shorn sheep. This wasn't a miracle or a symbol. This was Giotto's genius, the human truth of the Golden Legend—not merely a mystical tale of divine intercession but a record of the foresight of a woman who had paid attention to the needs and longings of the people whom she loved and served. There was nothing mysterious about a woman like Shelby showing up at the Golden Gate with a receiving blanket at the ready. She was always expecting the best.

According to the soles of my feet, it was time to get off the marble floor, but according to Mitchell's watch, I had six minutes left before the next changeover. Again, I felt the presence of Jesus and his Apostles and the other familiar painted figures, but now they were hovering, staring down on me, rather like my Cambridge neighbors at their windows when I ventured out to the mailbox in my bathrobe. I ignored them. I didn't want to know what they were thinking. I didn't want to see me through their eyes.

I took a few backward steps and let my gaze drop down from the Golden Gate to the Slaughter of the Innocents, which seemed too sad a last impression, so I lowered my gaze again, and there was Jesus being beaten by a crowd of jeering men wielding metal rods. T. had warned me that this story didn't end well for everyone. The horror of the scene was compounded by humiliation. One man was pinching the face of Jesus; another was pulling his hair. I consulted Sara's map. This was Number 32, The Flagellation (Coronation with Thorns).

I thought I deserved a more uplifting final image for the morning, but instead of turning to an angel or a starry patch of sky, I looked up again at Jesus being flogged. A stream of blood ran down his face from puncture wounds in his scalp beneath the crown of thorns. Like the tears that ran down the faces of the grieving mothers above him.

Like the blood on T.'s back?

T. had been standing beneath the bloodied body of Jesus when he'd said, "You know everything."

Someone brushed against my back, and I was certain it was T. I wished he'd found me staring at the ceiling or admiring the altar—anywhere but here. I turned. There was no one near me. Most of the crowd was clotted in the middle of the aisle, staring up and over my head at the Last Judgment. But a posse of well-dressed women was headed my way, and the tallest one was smiling at me. I moved deep into the corner and consulted Sara's map so I wouldn't have to interact like a normal adult.

"Liz?"

I tried to squeeze my entire body through the open toes of my pumps so I could slither away along the marble floor.

"Liz Berman?"

I said, "Hello."

"You don't remember me."

I knew her name was Rosalie Ellenbogen. She'd ended up as vice president of Harvard Real Estate before she took a job at NYU, or maybe Columbia.

"Rosalie Ellenbogen," she said.

The other women had veered off and disappeared into a scrum of tourists. I tried to spot another tall one among them, a redhead named Rose Hips, or Rose of Lima, or some absurd variation on Rosalie. She'd also worked at Harvard until she and Rosalie ditched their respective husbands and turned themselves into the world's tallest lesbian couple. But the posse had dissipated. Rosalie was alone. I was happy to think that was a chronic condition.

Rosalie said, "I was so sorry to read of Mitchell's passing."

Suddenly, time was passing the wrong way, like a reel of film rewinding, flicking back through the years, flashing images of the illness, Rachel's wedding, Sam's college graduation, and finally uncovering a sequence of Mitchell snapping shut his briefcase while I read the morning paper, and then Mitchell warning me that he was about to lean in and kiss me good-bye, my beloved Judas, pausing long enough beside my chair for me to straighten his necktie.

How often I had wanted to tug that silk like a length of rope, bend his head toward mine, and tighten and tighten his knotted tie. But I had choked back my anger instead of choking Mitchell to death, and I wouldn't have said another word to Rosalie if she had walked away.

Instead, Rosalie said, "Remember me to your children."

"Remind me," I said. "It was you and not your tall friend Rose Petal who fucked Mitchell, right? You can imagine, he was rather confused when you came out. And a little titillated, too."

"I don't know what you mean," she said.

I said, "Then maybe you don't know that your husband—Dan? Dave? Don? He called me and let me know he had pictures."

Rosalie said, "This is ancient history."

"No, home-security footage. I remember now—it was a movie," I said. "He offered to make me a copy, but I was buried in back episodes of *Prime Suspect* at the time." At the time, Rosalie had told everyone that her husband was shocked by her self-discovery but was kind during the divorce. A few months later, Dan-Dave-Don sent me a handwritten note. According to him, his home movie had cost Rosalie half of a sizable fortune he'd inherited. He also boasted about keeping his promise to keep Mitchell's name out of the whole mess. Unless I wanted the videocassette, he intended to destroy the evidence.

Rosalie said, "I had only intended to offer my condolences." She drifted away toward the altar end of the chapel.

I had never said a word about Rosalie to Mitchell, even during the week she came out to her colleagues at Harvard and Mitchell said, "You never know about people," so often that I realized he was hoping I did know about the affair, or else hoping he might work up the nerve to tell me. I kept my silence as I kept my vow of fidelity—one of the Seven Virtues. And I learned that the flipside of that coin was a deadly vice. Like an unpopular schoolgirl with a perfect attendance record, I turned up for my marriage every day, my happiness wedded to my unhappiness.

Four, five, and even six years later, Mitchell would still occasionally toss Rosalie's name into a discussion of a news story about gay marriage. "Everybody has a right to be happy," he'd say piously, as if he was proud to have done his part in the long struggle for human rights.

When the guard finally called us to the exit, I was all turned around until I realized that the Golden Gate, the Slaughter of the Innocents, and the Flagellation were behind me. I was staring at Number 41g on Sara's map, the last fresco in the eye-level row. This was the final image in the chapel sequence, the last of Giotto's black-and-white depictions of the Seven Virtues and the Seven Vices. Its title was Despair. It was a plain and realistic painting of a woman about my age, her fleshy arms angled out from her sides as if she were falling through the air, fists clenched, her scarf twisted around a nail in the wall above her head and looped and knotted around her neck, her soft skin bunched up against her jaw by the pressure of her handmade noose, her head bent toward her shoulder, her eyes closed.

I closed my eyes. As quick as that, the features of her face were inscribed upon my mind, as if she had long lived in my memory, as if I knew her well, as if she were my old familiar.

I should have left it there, but I noticed a thin red streak of something curling across her hair to the temple of her head. It was not ornamental. It was invasive, like the antenna of a huge insect or the talon of small bird of prey. With the binoculars, I could trace that red line to the faded outline of a blood-red body, the horns and hairy torso of a furry beast with cloven hooves, a disgusting little demon diving into her forehead, claiming its prey.

This marked her as another kind of sacrificial lamb.

I marked this as the first accurate portrait of a woman ever painted by a man.

The guard yelled, "*Pronto!*"

I tilted the binoculars away from the hairy red beast and aimed my gaze at the hanged woman's face. But as I tried to magnify her features, they were not there. Where I recalled the thin bluish veil of her eyelids and the smooth pink curve of her cheek, the portrait erupted into gravelly gray patches of unpainted plaster. I dropped the binoculars and took a step closer. Her entire face had been erased. From just below her brow to the dark line of her lower lip, her painted features were blistered and eroded, her skin stripped away by time. Other frescoes had been touched up or filled in during the recent restoration, but she was so far gone that no one had even attempted to revive her. She had not been seen for centuries. I turned and walked away, and at the far end of the chapel, in the darkness near the altar, I remembered every facet of her face.

AS I HURRIED BACK TOWARD THE VISITOR CENTER, ED waved and stood up from a green bench. He was wearing blue jeans with the cuffs rolled up above a pair of penny loafers and a black raincoat with old-fashioned brass buckles, as if we had a date at the malt shop. He was also holding my red bag and black umbrella, which I would have forgotten to retrieve. I fished around in the pockets of my shirtdress and found the coat-check token and, idiotically, handed it to him as he leaned in to kiss my cheeks, so we ended up with our hands locked and his wet lips pressed against my neck.

He said, "I'm so sorry."

"My pleasure," I said. "I haven't had a hickey in years."

He looked at the coin I'd pressed into his hand. "Is this a tip?"

We both bent toward his raised palm to examine the evidence. Instead of the coat-check token, I'd dug up a two-euro coin. Set inside a thin band of brass was a portrait of a man with a noble Roman nose, etched in silver, a wreath of laurels on his head.

I said, "I'm guessing an emperor or a pope."

Ed said, "It's your friend—Dante."

"No friend of mine," I said, "He abandons his three kids and a wife to wander around writing poetry and that makes him a national hero?"

Ed said, "He didn't want to leave. He was exiled from Florence."

I said, "He was invited back several times after that disastrous trip to Rome."

Ed said, "You know it wasn't that simple."

"I know, I know," I said. I felt Ed was scolding me for simplifying history. It wasn't the first time I'd been reprimanded for reducing Dante's heroics to a domestic drama. "He was aligned with the Guelphs, and the Ghibellines controlled Florence. I know, I know." But even as I said this, I was sure I didn't know which side was which in that endless civil war. "Or was it the other way around? Who wanted to pledge allegiance to the pope? Wait a minute—which side became the Whites and which ones became the Blacks?" The history was all mixed up in my mind. I felt as if I'd crawled under my bed and got my head stuck in that suitcase stuffed with Mitchell's memorabilia. "Dante was an antipapist White, right? Anyway, all he had to do to get back into Florence was apologize."

Ed said, "Maybe he didn't think he'd done anything wrong."

I said, "Ever met a man who did?"

Ed said, "Do you mind if I ask a question about your husband?"

For a brief moment, I wanted to confess the affair with Rosalie on Mitchell's behalf. Instead, I said, "Of course not."

Ed said, "I'm sure he loved you."

I said, "That requires a very long answer, but it isn't really a question." I wasn't sure if Ed was speaking in his pastoral role as comforter or preparing to propose himself as a fill-in for my absent, loving husband.

He said, "I'm sure he wanted you to be happy," compounding my confusion.

"You can say anything to me, Ed," I said.

To his shiny shoes, Ed said, "That's my point. That's the conundrum. I feel I can say anything to you." And then he didn't say anything else. He stood stock still, hands hanging at his sides, like a young boy who found himself on the threshold of a declaration of something and could not figure out how to go forward or retreat. He sat down on the bench and then stood right up, as if we were going to start again from my entrance, take it from the top. "T. said your husband was writing a book about Dante," Ed said.

I was game. "My husband had a lot of little projects on the side," I said, trying to keep the door open for Ed to slip in whatever was really on his mind. But he walked a few paces away from me, leading us slowly forward, and I figured he wanted to leave behind whatever he hadn't said. "Mitchell wanted to call his book *Who Stole Dante?* He thought Giotto and Scrovegni were two of the thieves."

"Which explains why Dante immortalized the Scrovegnis in the Seventh Circle of Hell? To avenge the theft?"

"Maybe," I said. Ed seemed to be a chapter or two ahead of me. "The truth is, I haven't read every little note on every page." Suddenly, everything I said sounded like a confession, a bid for absolution.

"He might have been on to something—something original," Ed said. "The pope who orchestrated Dante's exile—Boniface VIII— he and his successor, Benedict IX, were deeply connected to Enrico Scrovegni through a Dominican priest, Altegrado de' Cattanei. Altegrado was given several papal assignments—in Padua and in Rome." He paused, as if to say, Get it? One of Ed's most endearing qualities was his baseless conviction that I was his intellectual equal.

I nodded instead of admitting that I just wanted to prove Mitchell wrong.

"Altegrado probably designed the entire scheme for the chapel— which scenes were to be painted by Giotto." Ed looked at me expectantly, but without any encouragement he sallied forth. "Most scholars identify him as the priest who appears with Enrico in the bottom of the Last Judgment fresco, hoisting the chapel up to the Virgin Mary, securing their salvation and—"

"But who was Dante mad at?" I think I broke his train of thought.

I also may have yelled. I know I had taken hold of Ed's crinkly black sleeves and tugged too hard because he sounded sort of unnerved when he said, "I don't know, I don't know," and backed away a few steps.

I was as surprised as he was by my agitation, but instead of letting go, I tugged again and said, "Just give me your best guess."

"I don't know, but running through them all—I mean the lifeblood of the popes, Altegrado, and Giotto—the lifeblood is Scrovegni's money." He paused, but he seemed to recognize I was not satisfied. "I think Dante's damnation of Scrovegni must be a response to that image of Altegrado and Scrovegni—the picture of them giving the chapel to the Virgin Mary."

"So Dante was here, in Padua!" I was triumphant, though I couldn't have explained why. "Did Dante see the chapel?"

"I don't know," Ed said, and for a few seconds he closed his eyes, and I could see he was retreating into his ponderous, priestly mode, as if I had asked him a challenging moral question. "I also don't know why I never thought to ask myself that question. Is that something your husband figured out—that Dante was here while Giotto painted the chapel?"

"Like most men, my husband was a genius," I said, instead of throttling him. "Let's just stipulate that every thought I have is appended by a footnote to him."

Ed looked appropriately chastened. "Sorry about that," he said.

As if I'd known Ed for two decades, not two days, I said, "I'm just in a bad mood about my marriage this morning."

"I'm married to the Catholic Church," he said. "We're even."

"So was Dante here?"

"Dubious," Ed said. "We have a better record about Dante than almost any of his contemporaries, and there is no mention of his seeing the chapel. But I wish you would stay for a month and talk to me every day about this stuff. I might actually end up with a book. Why does it matter to you that Dante was here?"

I said, "I'm just trying to understand why Dante condemned Giotto's patron. Dante and Giotto were friends."

"Acquaintances, anyway, early on," Ed said. "But he was constantly reinventing himself. Dante was never really who he appeared to be." Ed held out the coin in his palm and placed a finger over Dante's chin.

"When you do that," I said, "he looks a lot like T."

Ed said, "Spitting image."

I didn't say anything.

Ed said, "He's all yours," and handed me the coin. Quick as that, we were dealing in a different currency.

I said, "As long as T. isn't here, is there something we should be talking about behind his back?"

"I really wish you weren't leaving Italy," Ed said.

"I'm here now," I said.

Ed said, "That's a very T.-ish thing to say." He handed me my bag and stuck the umbrella under his arm. "We were supposed to meet him ten minutes ago at a little restaurant just past your hotel." He held out his free arm, and I hooked mine into his as we set off.

"Speaking of things T. says, I want to clear up something about the Immaculate Conception."

"T. has it right," Ed said wearily.

"You don't even know what he said."

Ed said, "I'm guessing T. said the Immaculate Conception occurred a generation before the birth of Jesus, an instance of divine intercession at the moment St. Anne conceived the child who would become the Virgin Mary. It wasn't codified into doctrine until 1854, but the idea that Mary was free from original sin by a singular grace and privilege granted by Almighty God at the moment of her conception—that was in circulation by the 11th century. I gave T. this same lecture yesterday."

I said, "Am I the only Catholic who didn't know this?"

Ed said, "Are you still a Catholic?"

That stung. Plus, T. being right made me petulant, which is why I sounded whiny when I said, "At least I was baptized. T. was never a Catholic, was he?"

"What do you really want to know?" Ed stopped walking. We were fifty feet shy of the next intersection.

I said, "Now, I'm sorry, Ed." He had correctly guessed that my interest in the Virgin was not as profound as my curiosity about T. "I honestly forget I've only known T. for three days. You've known him for almost twenty-five years. Forgive me."

"Knowing T." He smiled wryly. "That's the immaculate misconception." He didn't explain that doctrine. He led us across several streets and right past my hotel. "Do you know what Dante said about Giotto's kids?"

Apparently, conception was our theme for the day. I said, "I'm not sure I knew Giotto had kids."

"Eight or nine," Ed said.

"You know everything," I said.

"I'm trying desperately to impress you," he said.

"I'm serious," I said.

He didn't say anything, which made it clear that he was, too. I stopped for a moment, hoping to come up with a reasonable response.

Graciously, Ed just carried on. "Dante asked Giotto why his paintings were so beautiful but his kids were so ugly."

This is only deepened my resentment of Dante.

"Come on. There's more to the story," Ed said, urging me along. "Giotto told Dante there was an explanation for the discrepancy. He said he made his paintings during the day, but he made his children in the dark of night."

I said, "Man enough not to defend what didn't need defending."

Ed stopped suddenly and swung open a red steel door. "I don't want to come between you and T." He was holding open the door, releasing a stream of garlicky air from the café. "But that is why T. invited me along today, as his interlocutor. I'm sure he won't be pleased that we wasted all of our time talking about Dante. And now we're late, so he'll assume I've told you everything." Ed let the red door swing shut and backed away a few steps. He looked down the street as if he wanted to sprint away. "He's convinced I told you about his daughter yesterday at the café."

"I didn't even know T. had a daughter."

"She's dead," Ed said. "She hanged herself. She was twenty-four years old. Forgive me for telling you like this." Two business-suited men and an older woman had line up behind us, so Ed opened the door and impatiently swept them past us and into the restaurant. He let the door close again.

All I could see was the tilted head and open arms of the faceless woman Giotto had named Despair. *You know everything.* I had been standing right in front of her, where Giotto had painted her, right where she had hanged herself, when T. had said, "You know everything."

But I knew nothing. I said, "When?"

"At the end of last year," Ed said. "Christmas Eve—not to put too fine a point on it. She had gone home for the holidays. She was staying with T. in his loft in Houston, and he was called in for an emergency of some kind, and when he got home, he found her. The thing is, she was wearing a pair of his scrubs." He pulled open that red door.

I said, "And now we're going to have lunch?"

"He doesn't talk about her," Ed said. "This trip—it's the first time he's been out of his house in six months."

"What made him come here?"

"Lily—that was her name," Ed said. "My niece, Lily. She had been studying in Florence. She was supposed to be there for two years. I think that's why he's going to Florence. He thinks he owes it to her? Oh, E., I really don't know why any of us is here."

T. HAD ORDERED LUNCH, AND BY THE TIME ED AND I WERE seated a waiter came by with a platter of translucent white fish floating on a stew of bitter greens and sweet fennel, which he ceremoniously dowsed with olive oil. We each decanted masses of this stuff into hand-painted yellow bowls and ripped our way through two loaves of bread for dunking. Twice, T. told me the name of the fish, but all I remembered was that the word had a bravura quality when he pronounced it, like *Bonanza!* or *Papa Gino!*

Ed and T. could not decide if the stew was spiked with

something—maybe grappa, maybe limoncello—or if the fish was undercooked or perfect, or if it was going to rain again this afternoon. They were not really talking to each other, they were sparring, and I told myself again and again, *We're just eating lunch. We're just eating lunch.* And because I didn't trust myself not to burst into tears on the sidelines, for the remainder of our meal we talked almost exclusively about sheep, thanks to no small effort on my part.

I launched into a long-winded version of the story I'd invented about Shelby and the wool in the Anne and Joachim paintings, and Ed said that Giotto had been a shepherd as a boy in Vicchio, a small village twenty miles outside of Florence. Ed tried to turn this into another reason for me to rejoin the tour, but T. assured me that the museum billed as Giotto's house probably never was Giotto's house. Then T. said most of Giotto's frescoes probably weren't even painted by Giotto but by apprentices in his workshop. Ed suggested that T. might be leaning too heavily on guidebook descriptions of Renaissance workshops and that the guilds and studios of artisans were not nearly so well organized in 1300. T. conceded that he hadn't squandered the last two decades of his life cross-referencing footnotes about the Jubilee Year, but he believed it was widely understood that Giotto hadn't painted every inch of the chapel. Ed said the stuff by other hands was obvious to anyone with a discerning eye, like the big portrait of God the Father above the altar. I confessed that I hadn't really investigated the altar area thoroughly, but could we all agree the sheep were by Giotto? Ed said Giotto's whole career was launched because the great master painter Cimabue ran into him on his way to Florence and saw a bunch of sheep Giotto had drawn on bits of slate with a hunk of granite and recognized Giotto's genius.

T. said, "When was this?"

Ed said, "Giotto was eight, so 1275 or so. He was born a year or two after Dante."

T. said, "But Dante was born in Florence," as if someone had said he wasn't. For the first time, I noticed he was wearing a fresh blue-and-white pinstripe shirt.

"Which is where Cimabue had his studio," Ed said.

"His workshop," T. said.

"In a manner of speaking," Ed said. "And Giotto lived there, and started his family there, and then we're back to your wool, E., because Giotto eventually acquired looms and spinning wheels and leased them out to supplement his income as a painter. It's weird, but no one talks about the sheep or wool in relation to the chapel frescoes."

"They're so prominent," I said.

T. was preparing to say something contradictory—his smile gave him away—and Ed was peering at T.—pleadingly? pityingly?—but by then we'd mopped the fish platter dry, and the waiter had tried and failed to gin up interest in the contents of the pastry case, and half an hour earlier, midway through my first glass of pinot grigio, I'd realized I'd had enough to feel vaguely drunk, so when T. wagged his hand to indicate we wanted our bill and tipped the remains of our second bottle of wine into my glass, I drunkenly suggested that the three of us should go back to my hotel room and lie on the bed to continue the conversation.

T. said, "I get to be Scrovegni. Ed is Giotto. E. is Dante."

I said, "There are never any good parts for women." I was sick of being saddled with Mitchell's business.

T. said, "Maybe Ed should be Altegrado."

"That's better," I said. "That way you two have the weight of the chapel on your shoulders." I wanted to be Giotto.

But Ed said, "E. can be the Virgin Mary."

T. said, "That really changes the game."

"Anyway," Ed said, "I have to get back to the Eremitani archives."

T. snagged the check and gave the waiter a credit card. "Let's not argue about the bill," he said.

Ed said, "Still playing Scrovegni."

T. said, "Buying the necessary indulgences."

T. OFFERED TO WALK ME BACK TO THE HOTEL ON HIS WAY
to an appointment of an unspecified nature with a nameless person,
but Ed said he was going my way, and I said I was actually going his
way because I wanted to take a few more turns around the chapel. I
also wanted to get far enough away from T. so I could let out my breath
and think of some way to be of some comfort to him. T. raised his hand
to his head, thumb and pinky finger extended as if he were talking on
a telephone, and I nodded enthusiastically, even though I didn't know
if that meant he was going to call me or I should call him.

Ed waited until we were well away from T. to tell me that the
chapel was closed to the public for the afternoon to clear the way for a
delegation from the World Heritage Center.

"I'll never see the rest of it," I said. Ed's news had registered like a
punishment. "I looked at all the wrong things. I didn't even see the big
version of the Gardner Giotto."

Ed said, "You're still planning to leave tomorrow?" He sounded
genuinely astonished.

It hadn't occurred to me until that moment that Ed might think
he had passed T. from his care into mine by telling me about Lily, that
Ed might have been eager to find a substitute caretaker for T. "I've
given away my place on the tour," I said.

"Fine," Ed said. "You can always come back some other time."

But I knew I never would, as surely as I would never take up knitting, or plant a vegetable garden, or get a cat, or remarry. I knew I
would end up buying a book of photographs of the frescoes and paging
through it on the plane so I could pass any test administered by Rachel.
I figured Ed was waiting for me to say something about his revelation

at the doorway, but I was already gone, already feeling frantic about whether I should buy the little paperback guidebook to the chapel that would be easy to carry on the plane or one of the handsome, oversized hardback tomes I'd noticed in the gift shop, which I'd have to shove into the suitcase with Mitchell's Dante debacle, and then what? When I got home I could set that suitcase full of Padua paraphernalia on the mantel as a memorial to our mutual failures or, even better, stick it in the front yard under the maple tree like a gravestone, a monument to everything unfinished. In a fit of inspiration, I said, "I have something I would like to give you."

Ed said, "Are you thinking we will never meet again?" He pressed his hand to my back and led me around a corner, and the Hotel Arena sign appeared a few hundred yards ahead of us.

I said, "No." I was actually thinking I might never see T. again. "The manuscript—my husband's notes and speculations—I don't know what else to do with them."

Ed said, "You could read them."

"I could also clothe the hungry and feed the naked," I said.

"Or vice versa," Ed said.

"The point is you'd be doing me a favor."

"I don't think now's the best moment for making big decisions," Ed said. This was precisely what people said whenever I threatened to sell my too-big house. I didn't admire how easily he seemed to slip into his preachy tone. A little more cheerily, he added, "I'm thinking we will meet again. You have a house in Cambridge. If you can't be bothered to read it, stick the manuscript in a closet and save it for me. You never know when I might turn up. Harvard has a library or two a person might want to consult."

Harvard had ninety libraries, and I was surprised at how much self-discipline was required to prevent me from repeating this boast. "You'll be welcome any time," I said. I knew I owed Ed something more than a promise of clean sheets, but I was a little loopy from the wine, and more than once I almost asked him straight out about the crazy hand-rolled cuffs on his blue jeans. Finally, I said, "T. will be all right on his own, right?" I felt myself tearing up, so I pretended I'd dropped something. "Without you, I mean. Won't you miss him?"

"He'll be back. Caroline is arriving later this week."

"The ex-wife?" It was spontaneous combustion—my interest was ignited. This was why I hadn't allowed myself to turn on the television. Ten minutes of any soap opera, even in a language I didn't understand, and I was in. "Caroline," I said calmly, hoping to tamp down my prurient reflexes. "Your sister."

"The first ex-wife," Ed said. "T. and Caroline both married again, and both divorced again, and soon they will meet again, though they are both pretending that this won't happen, as if no one has yet invented a train to connect Padua and Florence, and I cannot begin to tell you how desperately I need a friend." Ed pulled me across the street to a bench on the tiny slice of greenery across from the hotel. "There is something I should tell you, something T. should have told you—oh, E., if you would just stay, we'd have time for everything. And T. would happily foot the bill for you to go to Florence—in case he hasn't mentioned this, he's rich as Croesus—and then you and I could go back to the chapel while T. and Caroline lick each other's self-inflicted wounds."

I didn't sit beside Ed on the bench. I said, "I don't want to know about T.'s marriage," which surprised me as much as it seemed to surprise Ed. I wanted to say more, but I honestly couldn't remember exactly what Ed had just said. I just knew I felt suddenly defensive, not of T. but of my fondness for him, the comfort of knowing he had recognized my sadness and confusion and wrapped it all up in his protective nonchalance, so instead of having to explain it, or apologize for it, or pretend it wasn't there, I could safely stuff it into Rachel's red bag and carry it with me, even occasionally check it at the door and spend an hour or two without it. I hoped maybe I had done as much for him. I surely didn't think he wanted me to do much more. I said, "You know, I don't even know his first name."

Ed calmly said, "So ask him."

He had a point. "Apparently, I don't want to know."

Ed said, "It's rewarding to mystify the obvious. It's called religion."

I didn't say anything. I was adrift, in danger of drowning in the stew of affection and confusion T. and Ed had served up for lunch.

Ed looked exasperated by my silence, or deeply bored. He stood up. "Sermon over," he said, handing me my umbrella as we headed across the street. "The chapel opens at nine o'clock tomorrow morning," he said.

I didn't know if this was an invitation or a point of information. I said, "This lamb is headed home tomorrow." With the handle of the umbrella hung over my arm, I felt like Little Bo Peep.

Ed suddenly grabbed my arm and pulled me back toward him. "Don't wander away just yet."

"Oh, Ed." I didn't want to hurt his feelings, but I really didn't want a tearful good-bye. "You'll be fine."

"It's you I'm worried about," he said, tugging me back toward him again.

"I'm going to be fine, just fine," I assured him, struggling to escape his grip. "So fine I will surprise everyone."

"Okay, okay," he said, but he would not let me move forward. "Right now, though, you're sailing past your hotel. I think you might be drunk."

A few typically fixed items—the hotel sign, the parked cars, the cobblestones—were spinning.

Ed steered me back ten feet and opened the door to the lobby. He held on to my arm until I was inside. I steadied myself on the stairs, using the umbrella as a cane. By the time I was in the elevator, I was sober enough to know I hadn't even said good-bye.

AS I OPENED THE DOOR TO MY ROOM, MY PHONE RANG, AND by the time I found it, most of the rest of the contents of my red bag were scattered on the carpet. I said, "If I drank that much at lunch every day, I'd probably have more friends." I was relieved T. had kept his promise to call. It had seemed just as likely we would never speak again. "I think Ed might have just confessed to me, but I already forgot his sins."

"Mom?" Rachel sounded unnervingly nearby. "Hello? Is this Elizabeth Berman's phone?"

I didn't want to say anything because I couldn't remember where in Italy I was supposed to be according to her itinerary.

Rachel said, "Hello?" This was not a question. It was a demand.

Finally, I said, "Rachel? You'll never guess where I am."

"Mom? I know you're in Vicenza today, but who were you just talking to?"

It took me a few seconds to realize I had international immunity— I didn't have to answer every question she asked. "Are you at the office already?"

Rachel said, "It seems like you've been gone for ages, and your trip is barely under way." I heard birds singing in the background. "Still having a good time? Still happy to be there?"

I said, "Are you in the woods somewhere?"

"We're in Mohonk. At the lake house. With David's parents." She sounded like someone dictating a telegram, holding back the bad news. "We drove up last night. The boys and I. They're going to stay. Just for a week. Or two."

The other grandparents were a little younger, a little richer, and a little sloppier than Mitchell and I, which were unfair advantages in the long-standing competition for the affection of the two young boys. Just the mention of David's parents made me want to buy a couple of new bikes or a pup tent for camping out in the backyard. They had a deepwater lake with a dock and diving board, for god's sake. I said, "Was this your idea or David's?"

Rachel said, "It's just for a few days. I'm staying through the weekend, and we can see how long after that. I just woke up and realized I hadn't told you about this before you left—or did I?"

If Sam was this vague, I'd figure he was high. "Is everything okay, sweetie?"

"Exhausted from the drive last night," Rachel said. "The birds woke us. There's something else."

It had just occurred to me that Rachel didn't know I was flying home tomorrow. When I woke up in Cambridge on Thursday morning, I would really be alone. I heard one of the boys yelling from far away.

"Willy says hello. I have an interview in the city next Monday."

"In New York?"

"It's actually a second interview. I think they're serious about me. I'm not really talking about it yet. David's parents think I'm here on a business trip." Rachel had moved to within a few feet of Willy. I heard him say, "Grandpa says I'm allowed," and then Rachel said, "Not out of the box. Get a bowl and a spoon."

This was a typical breakfast at the lake house. Surely, no one had thought to buy milk, so if Willy got lucky, he might find some crème fraîche to dump onto his dry cereal. I said, "New York."

Rachel said, "New York, New York."

I said, "Sam will be happy to be near you and the boys."

Rachel said, "He's already asking if the firm has season tickets for the Yankees."

So Sam knew.

Rachel said, "It's all still up in the air. For starters, I don't even have an offer. I haven't told the boys, of course. Nothing is settled. David and I would have to figure out what this means for his time with the boys, for starters." Other voices filtered through the long silence. "I'll call again soon so we can talk more. It might all come to nothing, but I really want to know what you think."

I said, "New York!"

Above a rising din of voices, the last I heard from Rachel was, "Is that chicken skin he's eating?"

WHEN I WOKE, MY FACE WAS PRESSED AGAINST RACHEL'S red bag at the wrong end of the bed, my head was throbbing, and my feet were propped up on the pillows. The evening sky had cleared, and the last light of day angled up from somewhere well below the tile rooftops in the streets beyond my window. By the time I managed to leverage the lower half of my body off the mattress to send some blood to my legs, I could see my bedside alarm, and after a few seconds of immense concentration, I could make out the illuminated dial. It was almost eight-thirty PM. My mouth seemed to be lined with glue and sand, but I didn't trust my balance enough to venture forth for a glass of water. From my perch, I could see that I hadn't even bothered to collect the spill of coins and brochures and pens on the carpet before I'd passed out from my drunken lunch. I found my phone underneath my thigh and listened to two messages, both of them from T.

He had recorded the first at five. "Matteo tells me that the group that went to Vicenza today is eating a last supper in Padua under his yellow awning tonight, so if you are not feeling like a member of that club, find me in front of the Church of San Clemente at seven-fifteen. I'll be the one dressed in sheep's clothing."

This instantly ignited a panicky sense of despair (I was already an hour late) and hope (I was only an hour late).

At seven-thirty, T. had recorded a second message: "So, I think Enrico Scrovegni was entirely in earnest when he built the chapel. Surely, he was hoping for forgiveness. Who isn't? But I think he got more than he paid for, maybe more than he wanted. You know he had a spiritual advisor, Altegrado de Something? Sort of Enrico's own personal Ed. This priest was some kind of bookkeeper for Boniface VIII, the pope who ruined Dante's life and then up and died. And then Altegrado became a papal notary to Pope Benedict IX. That priest probably dictated what scenes Giotto had to paint, but he couldn't have imagined what Giotto would make of that assignment, right? I mean, Judas kissing Jesus—why is that moment memorialized right beside the altar at the front of the church? Isn't it out of sequence? What was Giotto really up to in that chapel? I have a lot of questions, and I had intended to lean on you for the answers. For instance, what am I doing right now? Why am I not standing in front of San Clemente? Oh, forgive me, E. I am nowhere near enough to where I promised I would be to rectify my error. Where are you? Don't answer that. In my imagination, neither of us is where we wanted to be, where we intended to be, where we wish we were. We're lost lambs. It's enough for me—more than I deserve—that you know I cannot speak about what I've lost. All I can do is return that singular favor. So, let's not talk about everything one more time. Please wander over to the Metro café tomorrow morning at nine o'clock and let me buy you something foamy."

I was not prepared to think about breakfast. T.'s first call had raised my hopes and resurrected my appetite. But every time I thought about dinner, my hunger was mixed up with humiliation. I had managed to get stood up in absentia.

It was just like being married to a dead man.

I PACKED UP EVERYTHING BUT THE LAVENDER SHIRTDRESS, the espadrilles, and the odds and ends I figured I could jam into Rachel's red bag in the morning. I called Air France. A woman with a growly voice refused to sell me a twenty-dollar reservation for a plane that departed in less than twenty-four hours. I persuaded her to check the available flights, and she ticked off my options, one by incomprehensible one, each time stating a takeoff time in French, followed by "Zees cannot be," or "Zees one *oui*." There seemed to be a lot of *oui*s in the afternoon and early evening. I hung up. My intrepid resolve to take a train to Venice was flagging, so I decided I would hire a taxi in the morning and take the earliest available flight. It did occur to me that the additional cost could easily be deducted from Sam's inheritance. The Shaker chair was worth that much, at least, plus an in-flight movie with a little bottle of wine.

I paged through my abortive *Journal of Discovery* and then sorted through the mess on the desk, hoping to turn up something worth pasting in. I took a picture with my phone of the two-euro Dante coin, which seemed better than having no record of T. at all. Beneath my folded-up copy of the itinerary for the rest of the EurWay tour, I found the three packs of postcards Pietro had purchased for me at the Venice train station. They seemed promising, but after I had torn apart the three pleated sets along the perforations and separated them into piles, I discovered that the sets were identical, somebody's idea of ten iconic Italian images arranged in three different sequences—somebody else's scheme for stretching the truth.

I opened the desk drawer and pulled out the printed labels Mitchell had prepared. I tagged ten cards with ready-made addresses for Rachel & The Boys, ten with Sam & Susie labels, and though I thought of sending the other set to Mitchell at his former home in Cambridge, even by my miserable standards that seemed just too maudlin, so I left them blank, hoping I could come up with ten living people who might want to know where I had been.

The top of each pile was a postcard of a solitary sheep standing at an odd angle on a verdant hill. Above the crest of that delicious meadow, unseen by the happily grazing sheep, lay the red-tile roofs and noble domes of Florence. That was as close as either of us would get. I turned over all the sheep, and on those three cards I wrote, "Padua seems perfect to me. Much love. E."

The rest, if I ever sent them, would all be postmarked at the Venice airport, or else in Cambridge, but maybe Sam and Rachel wouldn't notice; maybe I could really hide out in my house until July and get used to life alone while the boys jumped off that diving board, and Sam shopped for real estate, and Rachel commuted between her once and future homes. In any case, the challenge of matching the remaining postcards to my imagined destinations seemed more promising than dragging Mitchell's Dante business from underneath the bed.

I wrote single-sentence greetings from Florence, Pisa, Sienna, Rome, Naples, Pompeii, Assisi, Rimini, and Ravenna. Some matches were easy—the Colosseum and the Leaning Tower. Others required a little more imagination. Which city was southerly enough to merit a photograph of meatballs and spaghetti?

By ten-thirty, I was wide awake and ravenous. The restaurant downstairs closed at ten, but I was hoping someone washing dishes might be willing to slip me a salami sandwich or direct me to a nearby store where I could buy a bag of something salty.

When I made it to the lobby, the glass door to the dim restaurant was open. The dining room was empty, but I spotted Sara sitting at the little bar. She was wearing an oversized violet V-neck sweater, skin-tight white jeans, and a pair of navy blue sandals with high heels so spiky that just staring at them almost gave me stigmata. Her long pink fingernails were spread out along the wide rim of an old-fashioned martini glass. And then I noticed the crisp blue linen blazer hanging from the back of the empty barstool beside her. I backed away.

For a few minutes, I got marooned in the lobby, where an over-sized gilt-framed mirror made me look even more pathetic than I felt. I didn't know if it was the unnecessarily bright light in the lobby, or if the rough canvas of Rachel's bag had impressed itself on my skin, but the contours of my face were unfamiliar, washed out and wrinkly. I thought, *She has started to drink in the middle of the day. I hope she soon has the good sense to put a noose around her neck.* Then the elevator dinged down, so instead of killing myself, I made a beeline for the front door.

I wandered in widening circles around the almost empty piaz-zas, smiling at the couples who stood aside to let me pass in the nar-row alleys, young people huddling close to each other, unmindful of my admiring gaze, of my turning around to watch them amble down into darkness, envying them their immediate and far futures. When I turned into a long and unfamiliar alley, I spotted a reas-suring brightness at the other end and two-way traffic zipping back and forth along a main street. I paused because something in front of one of the dark doorways near the other end started moving, and as I stood there, a group of several men, maybe six or seven, disag-gregated themselves, spreading out like a squid in the darkness. Each of them was dragging a little suitcase on wheels. From the far end of the alley, a much taller man approached the others, and then he bent toward the door and, a moment later, led the men inside. Before I moved, the latecomer reappeared and bent again to lock the door, and then he walked right toward me.

I recognized his head, backlit and shiny. It was the pizza man who'd lent me his eyeglasses. I remembered from T.'s message that his name was Matteo, and I had the absurd idea that he might think I had been following him, but instead of backing away or simply walking past him, I stood right where I was, where nobody but a stalker would stand alone in the middle of the night.

He was holding his black eyeglasses in one of his hands. When he was near enough for me to see him smile, he said, "Are you following me?" He sort of purred when he spoke, as if he'd studied English by watching American movies with Dean Martin and Tony Franciosa playing Latin lovers.

I said, "Is that against the law?"

He said, "I will maybe have to arrest you."

I said, "I'm lost."

He said, "I know," but I wasn't sure if he understood exactly what I meant. "I want to show you somewhere," he said. He slipped out of his blazer, and as we headed toward the light, he arranged it over my shoulders.

I said, "I'm not cold."

He said, "For me, then." The buttoned-up front of his white shirt was shimmering, as if it were new-spun silk. Plus, I hadn't noticed when I was sitting in his restaurant that he was just a few inches shy in all directions of being a giant. He walked so close to me that my back was cradled in his torso. "This is the chapel of my family," he said. He put his arm around my shoulder. "In honor to the very special Madonna della Misericordia."

Through the wavy glass panels in an ancient wooden door, I could see a statue of the Virgin Mary surrounded by dozens of pink roses. The room was only slightly bigger than a phone booth. It was a mystery where those men were hiding. I said, "What does her name mean?"

He said, "Mother of Mercy."

"The chapel is so small," I said. "Are those men tourists?"

"These are working men with love for the Madonna," he said.

"It looks tiny in there," I said. I still wasn't sure he'd understood, so I said, "Very little."

He said, "One morning, I will show you a painting also in our very little tiny chapel. For now, we lock her up in the nights and turn the—" This was the first time he seemed to be reaching for a word.

I said, "Key?"

He said, "Bells?"

I said, "Alarm?"

He said, "You are safe with me."

My eyes welled up. I was so confused by this reflex, so certain that something other than sadness had occasioned it, that I actually said, "You could make a woman swoon."

He smiled and said, "Soon." He lightly turned me with his hand and led us toward the bright corner.

I said, "You are from an old family?"

He said, "Everybody is, no?"

I said, "I am going home tomorrow." I was thinking of my old family, which was disappearing. I was also regretting my swoon comment, so I said, "I really am lost," as if that might clear things up.

He said, "T. is telling me your name is E."

I was sure he'd meant that as a question, but I said, "He told me your name is Matteo."

He slowed us down and stretched his arm around my shoulders. "*Permesso*," he said. He reached down into the interior breast pocket of his blazer, a space occupied by my breast, and tucked away his eyeglasses. He must have also found a mint, which he popped into his mouth.

I felt lightheaded, and either I fell back against his chest and hip or he just sort of scooped me up as he resumed our earlier pace. I managed to stay upright.

He said, "Cool air coming to us."

At the moment, thin streams of sweat were speeding down my arms and legs. He smelled like wood smoke, an occupational hazard, I guessed. We turned onto the well-lit street, and I recognized the big stone buildings from my walk with Ed and T. after the lecture at the Church of the Eremitani. The hotel was only blocks away. Maybe it was the proximity of my bedroom, or maybe it was the heat of his chest against my back, or maybe it was the lingering memory of those seven shadowy men and their seven suitcases, but I had a clear and miserable vision of Matteo on top of me on top of the bed on top of Mitchell and all of the Dante memorabilia I'd stuffed into his suitcase, so I said, "I have some work to do tonight," which made no impression on Matteo, so I added, "Piles and piles of paper I have to deal with before I leave Padua."

He said, "We say *Padova*."

I said, "*Padova*."

He said, "Almost. *Padova*. Like you mean it."

I said it very slowly. "*Pa. Do. Va.*"

"*Suona come uno di noi*." He leaned into me, delighted. "Like one of us. Now, what are these papers that make you busy this night?"

"Bad memories, mostly," I said. I couldn't tell if Matteo really believed I had work to do, or if he was just being gracious about letting me retreat to my room alone. Either way, it was a relief. "I wish I could just burn it all," I said. "Start fresh."

Near the hotel, he stepped in front of me and grabbed the brass handle of the plate-glass door. When he tugged, the glass whinnied and wavered. The door was locked, and he'd almost pulled it off its hinges. Before we could locate an intercom or bell, a buzzer sounded, and he ushered me into the lobby.

Ricardo was standing at his post, leaning forward, hands pressed against the desk, looking like a stoic steward on the deck of the *Titanic*.

When I turned to say good-bye, Matteo said, "I take the papers now for burning." He put a hand against my back—his blazer, my back—and led me to the elevator. "This is my best time."

Ricardo said, "*Buona notte*."

Matteo said, "*Notte.*"

I said nothing. Since I'd felt the press of his big hand against my back, I had been practicing my Pranayama, deep yogic breathing. This kept me upright in the elevator, and my hand didn't even shake when I stuck the key into the electronic lock and led Matteo into my room. But when I got as far as the bed, I stopped—walking, breathing, thinking, being.

He slipped his coat off my shoulders, tossed it back toward the red chair near the door, and stood behind me, inching in until I could feel the soft press of his chest and belly, my hips against his thighs. He ran his hands down my sides beneath my arms.

To steady myself, I said, "I am leaving tomorrow."

He said, "I have been following you in my heart." His hands had reached my waist. He pressed in closer, wrapped his arms around me, and starting at my waist, he undid the buttons of my dress, which were as compliant as a zipper. He worked his way swiftly up to my neck, and then he gently pulled the dress apart until it slipped off my shoulders. He kissed my neck. He said, "Mmm."

The aroma of wood smoke was more profound than ever, tinged with yeast and garlic. I had a brief flirtation with the possibility of passing out, overcome with desire—but for him or a pizza? I could already imagine how my sheets and hair would smell when I woke the next morning. The moment reeked of aftermath. I was suddenly wide awake. I clumsily pulled up the sleeves of my dress.

Matteo said, "What?"

If he'd had an arugula pie in his pocket, I might have let him finish what he came to do. My appetites were all mixed up at the moment. "I really am going home tomorrow," I said, doing up a few buttons, hoping he understood that I was pretending we had agreed this was a mistake.

He said, "We are here now."

A very T.-ish thing to say, I thought. I could feel him towering over me.

Graciously, ungrudgingly, he said, "What do you need to burn?"

This provoked a grade-school memory of Joan of Arc, flames flying up her body, head tilted toward the sky. I said, "It's just some paper."

"Okay," he said. "Paper burns."

Handing over that suitcase seemed more intimate than anything that had happened yet between us. But if I left it under the bed, I knew the idea of it would haunt me, as if I had abandoned a lame animal in a wooded darkness, or bolted the door behind me as I walked out of the home of a dying man. Or maybe I knew a maid would discover it, and Ricardo would call me in Cambridge, and I would begrudgingly pay the exorbitant price of shipping Mitchell's unfinished business to my doorstep—thus preserving Mitchell's greatest failure and my status as the aggrieved widow, burdened by his losses and mine.

I bent down beside the bed and reached in under the sideboard. By the time I got the suitcase out and had its handle in the air, Matteo was pulling something from the inside pocket of his blazer, as if he might have to put on his glasses and examine the documents to be sure I was not involving him in a crime. I rolled the suitcase to him. He bent down and kissed me, which totally surprised me. His tongue was huge. He reached around my back, but I stiffened when I realized the suitcase had become a currency, and he now felt I owed him something for his willingness to do my bidding, that I was in his debt.

He propped his two hands on the suitcase handle, and I saw that he was wearing a wedding band. He said, "This is not looking as you think."

I pointed to his hand and said, "Did you just put that on?"

He let go of the suitcase and tossed something onto the bed. "You don't understand," he said.

But I did. On my bed was a perforated strand of three black condom packets. I was flattered by his overestimation of my stamina, but I said, "I am going home."

"I must have something to say," he said.

"Trust me," I said, "you said it."

He said, "You must let me—"

"No," I said. "I got it."

He reached up and held my face in his huge hands. Urgently, beseechingly, he said, "You are knowing nothing."

I said, "That is not exactly a compliment."

Maybe he wasn't listening, or maybe he didn't understand, but his ardor was undiminished. He said, "When we will ever meet again?"

"I'm not even here," I said. I took a step away from him. The suitcase handle tilted back against his belly, and I saw that he was hard already, so maybe that breath mint was actually a Viagra, and though his size would not have been a deal breaker, it was breathtaking, probably better suited to a yogi with a more rigorous Pranayama practice. I said, "In my mind, I am not here."

"I know," he said ardently, as if everything I'd said so far had made perfect sense. "You must let me speak to heal your losses."

Someone had told him I was a widow. I didn't want him to say anything about Mitchell, so I said, "I was actually lost," as if an adverb might tip the balance back toward my side. "Mixed up," I added, pointing a finger at my head and twirling it around, indicating a possible mental illness.

"I know all about this," he said. His tone wasn't threatening, but it was impatient, as if his walking me back to the hotel entitled him to spew something before he retreated back into the night. I really wished I could slip a condom over his head. "You must let me speak."

"In Italian," I said.

"*Si, si, si,*" he said proudly, "*Italia.*" He seemed to think I was conceding home-field advantage.

"No, no, no," I said. "In Italian. You understand? You can say everything, anything at all, but just say it in Italian."

And astonishingly, he did. His brushed back my hair, and then withdrew his hands and leaned so far forward on the suitcase handle, I was sure it would soon break. He spoke softly, sometimes smiling, sometimes purposefully shifting his gaze away from mine and whispering. It was mesmerizing. At one point, he slapped his hand right against his heart and heaved out a huge blast of air, and then he shrugged and held up one finger, to assure me there was just one more thing, the last thing, and he smiled broadly while he explained something that seemed to involve the buttons on my dress, his bald head, somebody sleeping peacefully, the Madonna della Misericordia, and a bird or a plane or an angel—something with wings.

I didn't say anything.

Matteo looked genuinely confused. He said, "No? No?"

The light above our heads flicked off.

He said something else in Italian, not a compliment as far as I could judge his tone, and then I heard the whir of the suitcase rolling away and the door swinging open and shut. I didn't move for several seconds. I heard nothing, but I knew he was standing just outside my door. I felt I owed him something—not a triple-header, but an apology or an explanation or a rain check, maybe. And then I heard him knock—just once. I took a deep breath, and I stepped toward the door. I took the handle in my hand, and as I pulled the door wide open, Mitchell's suitcase fell against my shins. I stepped out into the hallway. It was bright and empty.

I RIGHTED THE SUITCASE, AND WHEN I TRIED TO COLLAPSE the long telescoping handle, it wouldn't budge. I didn't know if Matteo had bent it out of whack while he was delivering his Italian aria, or if the bang against the door had jammed the handle so it wouldn't collapse. Either way, I took it as a sign. That suitcase was an unfit traveling companion. I grabbed my nail scissors and cut away the tag with Mitchell's name. I'd never noticed it before, but instead of our telephone and street address, he'd printed his Harvard information in the blank spaces beneath "Home."

I wheeled the suitcase to the elevator, and in the lobby, I found Ricardo at the front desk with an open book.

I said, "I found this in my room. It was under the bed. It isn't mine."

Ricardo said, "*Signora Berman.*" He checked his watch, as if he considered this an inappropriate hour for conducting business with a single woman.

"The handle is broken," I said.

He said, "You broke this?"

I said, "No."

Ricardo said, "He broke this?" I noted a slight change in tone, as if he might feel he had to come to my rescue if Matteo had wronged me, but that seemed to open the door to my room yet again, so I said, "It was broken. Perhaps that is why it was left under my bed."

Ricardo said, "We are on the end of his English."

I said, "I'm tired, too. It is late. Please, take this." I wanted to turn and leave him with the problem, but I was certain it would end up at my door again.

Ricardo said, "You want safekeeping?"

"*Perfetto,*" I said. "Safekeeping."

He ducked down and came back with a tag for me to fill out.

I said, "It is not mine."

He said, "*Non il mio.*"

I really wasn't sure if he was translating what I'd said into Italian or issuing a disclaimer. I was just determined not to let him or Matteo write the end of this story. On the tag, I wrote, "Owner Unknown." I could feel Ricardo was waiting for me to fill in the rest of the blanks, so I copied the phone number from a tour agency brochure hanging beside the front desk, invented an illegible email address, and handed him the ticket.

"You are safe with me," he said.

I didn't say anything.

VI

✳

I didn't sleep. I watched a little bit of news with British accents, and several long commercials for a colorful array of headbands and adhesive tape that seemed to be an at-home facelift kit. At eight-thirty, I finally got out of bed, and I surprised myself by feeling momentarily excited about what had almost happened with Matteo, as if his kiss and his embrace had almost awakened me, or some part of myself that had been asleep for years. However, during a very brief consult with Mirror, Mirror on the bathroom wall, I decided I looked less like Snow White and more like poor Lazarus, dragged out of his cozy tomb, trying to pass as a normal, live person.

I slipped into the linen shirtdress, which was so wrinkled it looked like lavender aluminum foil. My hair was staticky, flying up after each brushstroke, as if by ignoring all the firing synapses that were trying to form thoughts in my head I had caused an electrical storm up there. Even by my shamelessly low fashion standard for the day, the red bag with the lavender dress was a no-go, so I emptied it out and plucked my phone and room key from the mess. As a bonus, I found Pietro's business card, printed in Italian and English on opposite sides: *From Venice? To Venice? Picking you up every times!* There was my ride to the airport. And the prospect of seeing Pietro reminded me of those postcards I'd written, and I didn't think, I just grabbed the two stacks for Sam and Rachel.

As I got out of the elevator, the young tux at the front desk said, "*Signora Berman?*"

I said, "Yes."

He said, "*Momento,*" and hustled into the restaurant.

I braced myself for a final encounter with Anna, or maybe Anna and Francesca both wanted to berate me for my generosity. Instead, Shelby appeared in the doorway and yelled, "I thought I'd missed you!"

I said, "Shelby!"

She said, "Are you okay?"

"I'm fine," I said, following her to her table. "I look a mess, I know, but I'm really fine."

"I love those shirtdresses of yours," Shelby said. "They look good no matter how many times you wear them."

Shelby had shimmied into her white jumpsuit, as if she had decided to skip the train ride to Venice and hop on her rocket instead. I thought this, but I said, "I'm happy to have a chance to say good-bye," which was just as true.

She handed me something small and cool. "It fell right off my knitting needle on the bus to Vicenza," she said. "Like a sign or something. It was only thanks to you I was able to take that side-trip, after all."

It was a little disk of lapis lazuli, like a fragment of a comet that had fallen through Giotto's painted sky. I didn't believe it had fallen out of its own accord. I knew Shelby had pried it free for me. "This is a sign of how sweet you are, Shelby," I said.

She said, "Are you really going home today?"

I said, "Right after I mail these postcards."

Shelby was so impressed with my literary output and the number of friends I had back in Cambridge that I felt obliged to tell her the truth.

"But they'll get all ten postcards at once," she said.

"No," I said. "You see, I'll mail one here, and maybe one or two from the airport, and then the rest from Cambridge—every few days."

Shelby furrowed her brow. "With Italian stamps?"

She had a point. I said, "That won't work, will it?" If she'd asked, I couldn't have re-created the logic of writing the postcards in the first place.

Instead, she said, "Everybody loves a postcard, no matter what."

I didn't say anything.

Shelby said, "Are you sure you're okay?"

I said, "Nothing a pot of coffee won't clear up." There wasn't a waiter in sight.

Shelby put her hands on mine. "You know what might be fun?" She had shifted her voice into that higher register usually reserved for babies and the elderly. She even tilted her head, so I could see she was thinking very hard. "What if I mailed them for you? Right in order?"

"They're not worth the trouble." I was talking about the postcards, but it occurred to me that Shelby might think I was referring to my children. "They'll be happy even if I hand-deliver them."

"I insist," she said, and she pulled the two piles to her side of the table. "It will make me think of you. Please. Maybe it will even inspire me to send a few to you! What do you say?"

"I'm just going to say thank you," I said. I was saved from having to say more because Shelby's phone began to blast a brass-band version of "Close to You."

Shelby said, "That's Allen!"

I stood and blew her a kiss. Every patron in the restaurant was staring at her, all but begging her to answer that phone.

Shelby was in no hurry. She held up the little boom box and said, "This is our away-from-home theme."

"It's perfect," I said.

Shelby said, "I know," and then turned her attention to her far-away husband.

T. WAS WAITING FOR ME AT A TABLE AT THE METRO WITH two tall latte macchiatos and a heaping plate of eight little pressed sandwiches—prosciutto and Gruyère, salami and something green and garlicky, mozzarella and roasted red peppers, and chocolate-hazelnut spread—each about the size of a ladyfinger. We were silent for a long while.

Finally, he said, "I thought you might be hungry."

I said, "Apology accepted." As usual, I had no idea exactly how much he knew or precisely what he meant. He might have been referring to our botched dinner date or my late-night run-in with Matteo. Either way, he was right. I was hungry. I was already selecting my second sandwich. He was wearing a fresh white shirt and his blue linen blazer, wrinkle-free. I said, "I have to make a telephone call to an Italian man, and I was hoping you would make it for me." I fished Pietro's car-service card out of my pocket.

T. picked up the card and turned it over several times, as if he were examining the facets of a gemstone. "Illiterate in two languages," he said.

"Umberto Eco was all booked up," I said. I handed him my phone.

"If you had come to Florence, do you suppose we might have run out of things to not talk about?" He checked under the hood of his second sandwich. He seemed pleased by what he found.

I said, "There's always my hair." I could tell the situation up there had not calmed down.

T. said, "Speaks for itself." He made the call. After a while, he held the phone away from his ear, and I could hear a woman screeching. Finally, T. said, *"Mille grazie. Ciao—si, si, si, ciao."* He handed me my phone. "If you locate Pietro, please let him know someone at home is hoping to castrate him."

I said, "At least he has an answering service."

T. said, "I think that was his wife and maybe his mother, too—in Italy, they operate as tag teams."

"I love the train," I said, "but I will need another coffee."

T. stuck his hand in the air and whirled it around. The bartender nodded.

T. slid Petro's taxi-service card back to my side of the table and said, "This was a sign from God. You are not supposed to leave today."

But he was leaving today, and I knew he was going to Florence for the same reason I was going to Cambridge—to touch the wound, to press the tender, swollen tissue of the past until the dull but steady sadness throbbed and throbbed, almost like a pulse. I said, "What were we not talking about? Just before you made the phone call?"

T. said, "Had you asked me to recommend a dry cleaner in the neighborhood?"

He was right. My dress looked like a topographical map. "I'll tell you a secret about linen shirtdresses," I said.

He said, "If it has something to do with the problem of having so many buttons, word is out."

I was going to repeat Shelby's false claim about linen dresses looking good in any condition, but I looked down and saw that the two halves of the front of me were misaligned. "I must have missed a button," I said.

"Or two," T. said.

I said, "I can see something is off at the hemline, but is it wrong all the way to the top?"

T. said, "Your collar is occupying two different time zones. Maybe it will sort itself out on the plane."

"I can't walk back to the hotel like this." I felt my eyes well up, and as foolish as I felt for that unbidden burst of melodrama, I knew I couldn't speak without bawling.

T. stood up, leaned over the table, and said, "*Permesso.*" He undid and redid one button just above my sternum, behind which I kept my heart. He sat back in his chair. "Now you can work your way down."

I bent my head and began the long descent. I was still on the verge of tears, so I said, "I do wish you would hum something vulgar. This show may take a while." It was not as tedious as I'd imagined—Matteo had considerably widened the buttonholes with his big fingers—but it did require concentration.

T. said, "What did you do for dinner last night?"

I said, "Matteo." I looked up.

T. nodded.

I said, "And you?"

"Sara."

I nodded. This almost made sense. She had fingernails that could draw blood.

Our coffees arrived, and when I attempted to pay for everything on our table with my room key, the young waiter said, "No problem," and backed away.

Maybe T. had prepaid, or he had a running tab, or else I looked like a charity case.

T. said, "Are you all packed?"

I nodded. My phone buzzed with a message alert from somebody.

T. said, "The future is calling."

"We're not on speaking terms," I said. But since T. and I had a policy of never speaking about the past, this didn't leave us with much to say.

T. said, "You don't want to take the train. Trust me." He pulled his phone from his blazer pocket. "You'll have to negotiate a transfer from the train station in Venice to the airport with those two suitcases."

"I got rid of one," I said.

He looked genuinely surprised, as if he had heard Matteo's version of the suitcase story.

I was momentarily delighted, but the pleasure was short-lived, like a shooting star you see when you are alone.

T. made a call, and in the midst of an impressive barrage of Italian, he turned to me. "Soon? The airport, I mean."

I said, "Soon as we're done here," daring him to say that we would never be done.

T. nodded.

When we were fully caffeinated, my phone buzzed again, and I turned it off, but T. took this as a cue. He stood up and led me back to the door of the hotel. A black Limousine Venice town car was already idling at the curb.

T. stuck his head into the passenger-seat window and said something to the driver, and then he turned to me and said, "You have an hour if you need it. He'll wait. His tip depends on it." He backed away a few steps from the door of the hotel and said, "I have to pay a visit to a virgin. Did we ever decide if it is the Scrovegni Chapel or the Arena Chapel?"

In that moment, all I could remember of the chapel was a blue blur that slowly came into focus as a patch of sky I could see through a windowpane from my sofa in Cambridge, and even that little square got smaller and smaller, farther and farther away, as I realized that T. and I were not standing still on that sidewalk, that we were moving away from each other, that I was already gone, and all I could see was the little disk of lapis lazuli Shelby had plucked from her knitting needle, something compact and dense, something I could hold in the palm of my hand, the essence of it all. I wanted to be sure we were prepared to leave it right there—everything unasked, everything unsaid. I said, "Shouldn't we say something?"

"Annunciation time?" T. said.

"Okay," I said.

But neither of us spoke. Eventually, the limo engine raced, and as I turned, the driver shrugged apologetically, and then he slid the passenger window smoothly up and turned off his engine. Even he seemed to know this was not going well.

I looked up at T.

"Uncle," he whispered. He was weeping.

"Oh, T."

"You mustn't," he said, shaking his head, *no, no, no*. He turned his shoulder to me and raised one hand defensively, keeping me in place. "I can't. It will do me in."

I was already bawling, and I couldn't catch a breath to say his name.

He wiped his shiny face and said, "You know I have to—I need to be in Florence," and then he bent his head and heaved out a terrible breath. He raised his gaze to mine, tears still streaming down his face. "Home," he said. "You want to go, I know."

I said, "I know you know," and then I just sobbed until I could get ahead of my sadness long enough to explain why I was going home, why I was not going on to Florence, why I still hadn't spoken his daughter's name, but all I managed was to stammeringly say, "I can't just do the next thing and the next thing every day."

T. said, "Your work is done here." He wiped his face and smiled.

It was a few seconds before I could see clearly enough to see that he was offering me his handkerchief. I took it. "That bad?"

He nodded and said, "We've made a mess of each other."

I didn't bother to wipe my eyes because I could already feel him pulling away, pulling his sadness and some of mine back into himself, leaving me with a little puddle of our mixed-up sorrows and regrets to absorb, and then a tour bus slid in behind the limo and flung its door open with an exhausted sigh, and I just kept telling myself it had only been three days, barely three days since T. and I had met, and before the first passenger emerged, T. nodded, and I nodded, and we turned away from each other.

WHEN I GOT TO MY ROOM, I FOUND AN IVORY ENVELOPE addressed to *E.* leaning against the door. Once inside, I opened it and found a delicate silver strand of rosary beads. It was at least two feet long, and at the juncture of the loop, where a few additional beads and a small cross were attached to the strand, there was an embossed medallion of St. Somebody, though I soon realized I would need a desk lamp, and a magnifier, and probably Wikipedia to identify her.

Sunlight was streaming in through the window, illuminating a wedge of dusty air and cutting a shiny swath through the tangle of sheets where I had slept. And then I saw my little solitary black suitcase on the red chair beside the door, and I saw just how small my life was, how little there was left of me. *Three days*, I thought.

I looked at the envelope again. Only three people knew me as E. I tipped it upside down, and out slid a business card with an address and telephone number I didn't recognize, but a printed sketch of a yellow awning that I did. On the back, Matteo had written instructions for making the most of his present.

She is Madonna della Misericordia. Hang on the neck, keeping the Holy Cross on the backbone, to be curing the lonely nights.

I really didn't know if the rosary was a parting gift or a parting shot. I also didn't know if I was sad because I was already missing T., or if missing T. was my hedge against some deeper sadness ahead of me.

I didn't know what to feel. I had not felt like myself for three days. I was astonished by my readiness to watch my children slip away into their far-off futures, a little appalled that not a single neighbor or former colleague had called to ask how I was faring, a little more embarrassed to admit that no one in my fading constellation of friends in Cambridge had crossed my mind, and genuinely bewildered by the attention and interest and amusement I had stirred up with strangers, especially men, which was especially delightful and entirely unfamiliar.

But those three strange days were over. And I didn't know who I would be if I walked out of the tomb. Mitchell was dead. My marriage was done. I had no reason to be anywhere. There was no one left to take attendance, no one to mark me present.

Most people came to Italy and came to life. I had come to Italy to die.

PART II: PADOVA

I

There is, for each of us, an afterlife. The problem is, we're not dead enough to enjoy it. I think that Mitchell's afterlife began long before he died, sometime soon after we returned from Paris, when he gave up on his idea of himself as an academic, a man of letters, and settled into the long twilight of his fondest hopes and unfulfilled ambitions. My own sense of possibility, what might become of me, was much less well defined, and so it survived as long as the marriage was intact, as dust survives in even a well-kept house, momentarily roused from overlooked corners and spun into the air from uninspected ledges when a window is flung open or someone unexpected rushes into a room. But when Mitchell died and my marriage ended, there was nowhere for the bits and pieces of that nebulousness to cling, nothing to contain the scattered sense of what I might have been.

I had not come to life in Italy. I had come into the afterlife in Italy. I knew it when Matteo's hands could not hold me. I knew it when Ed's overtures did not persuade me to stay. I knew it each time I conspired with T. to keep the past at bay, to sweep our conversations clean of what had really brought us together, to be sure that we had between us none of the dust that living people gather into their cupped palms, breathe warmly on, and try to shape into the selves they had always meant to be.

T. had rolled the stone away from the entrance of my tomb and awakened something in me, but it was not a desire for life. He had looked inside and recognized my situation. He countenanced my sadness. He made no effort to deflect or discount my disappointments. He offered me a way back into the world that required nothing of me.

I had not returned the favor. His former life was chasing him down, chasing him to Florence, where he had only his dead daughter before him and his ex-wife hot on his trail. He needed nothing but the company of someone who wanted nothing from him, someone who could tolerate his being out of reach.

I could do that. And there was nowhere else I had to be. So I decided I was not going to Cambridge. I was going to Florence.

Admittedly, I had a few moments of difficulty deciding whether the resurrected me would call T. and tell him to expect me for dinner in Florence, or if I should just turn up and offer to buy him something fizzy. I was also not sure about the rules of the afterlife. For instance, was the new me allowed or not allowed to call Shelby and ask for help navigating the Italian trains? I was breathing way too rapidly, excited to the point of exhaustion at the prospect of moving forward, and so I decided the new me would definitely need some open floor space for yoga every morning. I dug out the EurWay itinerary to call the hotel in Florence and book myself a double room.

When I turned it on, my phone yipped in its maddeningly indiscriminate way, as excited by a hang-up or an ad for anti-aging cream as it would be by a message from the dead. The text that popped up was from my ex-son-in-law, Poor David—the name inadvertently bestowed upon him by Rachel. After the divorce, she prefaced every response to a question about David's work or well-being from Mitchell or me with a sigh—Poor David. He'd been hired as a line cook by one of Boston's celebrity chefs, who then closed her new waterfront restaurant after six months, and though one of the principal investors offered Poor David the helm in the kitchen of a small bistro meant to be the first of a franchised chain, that venture went bust about a month before opening night, so Rachel fronted Poor David the down payment on a refurbished mail van, which he intended to launch as a stew-themed food truck as soon as he could get the cold storage areas to stay cold. These days, Poor David was microwaving nachos and jalapeño poppers for late-night room-service customers in an extended-stay hotel ten miles south of Boston. This rotten job had only one real benefit—he was available for chauffeuring his two boys to their many afternoon arts and athletic programs and cooking dinner for them in the van, which he and the boys had taken to calling their clubhouse.

mrs b! was at yr house sunday hoped to say hello etc but no you!! hows rome?! yr roses r MAJOR this yr but 2 days of rain since this pic so maybe this was best day of season?? can we talk soon or sometime? call when yr in mood anytime fine no pressure!!

I was sure Poor David hadn't dropped by to admire my garden. I figured he was looking to commiserate with someone about Rachel's career move. I pecked out a response:

Beautiful. So sorry to miss the blossoming—but nothing compared to how we will miss those 2 sweet boys if Rachel takes that new job in NYC.

I also had several unread emails, and at least two were from human beings, so I cracked open the complimentary bottle of mineral water on my bedside table and read Rachel's latest missive.

Dear You—
The idea of being in New York is not the same as being in Midtown on a humid day.
Grueling three-hour interview today. I did manage to make them do most of the talking (Daddy's rule). More surprising: they think they have to woo me. Evidence: Insanely expensive lunch with one partner and three associates from the firm and one woman (paralegal with hair extensions). Her only contribution came in the powder room (her term): "Two kids? What are you going to do with two kids and no husband when you're working every weekend?" (She nannies on weekends, btw.)
I checked the Florence hotel website and saw this:

Do you have a view of the Arno from that balcony? (If not, complain—
it was promised.) Mostly, I'm worried that you are stuck in a closet
with a tiny bed just because we changed you to a single room.

On the home front: I had a text from David with a question about
parking his food truck in your driveway for a couple of weeks while you
are gone. I think he might be trying to sell it (my only hope of a return
on that investment). But do not feel obliged. He has a parking space
(rental) and I can tell him to keep the truck where it is—not a problem,
especially compared to telling him I am moving with the boys to NYC.
Maybe we can talk this weekend?
Love from me to you.

And then my phone dinged with a new text from Poor David:

??? What new job? NYC trip not pharma biz?

That settled it. I was definitely going to Florence. A food truck
parked in my driveway would not be a perfect welcome home, but that
was nothing compared to the prospect of Rachel parked on my sofa,
ledger in her lap, forcing me to account for myself.

The other email was an apologetic note from one of my only neighbors in Cambridge with whom I exchanged more than nods and waves.
Anandi Roy and her podiatrist husband, Samir, had moved to Falcon
Place a few months before Mitchell and I had purchased an almost
identical Greek Revival across the street. The other homes on the small
dead end were mostly tiny mansard-roofed cottages that attracted single women and a roundelay of childless couples who stayed as long
as it took their noisy, round-the-clock contractors to knock down a
couple of interior walls, replace the butcher-block counters with granite, and run an incessantly beeping back hoe through the old garden
and lay down strips of golf-course-green sod. And then a sign would go

up, advertising the availability of another overpriced, updated, open-concept bungalow for sale on a quiet street in Cambridge.

Dearest Elizabeth,

This note brings you my affection and the oddest of questions. Do you know someone who operates a mobile canteen? Hours after you departed, a most unlikely truck with the word "Stewed" painted on each side appeared in your driveway. It is outfitted with a stainless kitchenette. (Samir had a look inside after dark last night.) This morning, Melanie Monterosso stopped me in the street with concerns that someone is operating a business illegally from your home. She showed me something from Facebook that did look like an ad for that Stewed truck with a menu and a promise of "Cambridge Locations— Check Back Daily." And now Samir claims he might have noticed a cot in the truck, and he worries we have a squatter in the neighborhood. I was hoping you might forward this to the truck's owner as fair warning before Melanie takes action. Also, dear friend, I am afraid Samir will soon insist on my calling someone in City Hall.

On a so much sweeter note, Samir and I heard the Bartok on Sunday at the Gardner Museum. Thank you for the kind gift of those tickets—magical and melancholy to occupy your seat and Mitchell's.

We miss you both.

Yours, Anandi

Melanie Monterosso was seeking revenge. She still blamed me for the raid on her unlicensed in-home hot-yoga studio a few years ago, just because I had dropped out after two classes. I should've turned her in for attempted murder—she was a tyrant on the mat—but I hadn't reported her to the authorities, even after Mitchell's umpteenth admiring comment about Melanie's entrepreneurial spirit as she went power-walking by in a leotard.

I knew it was Anandi who'd called the zoning board about Melanie's unlicensed yoga studio, and before that, Public Works about neighbors dumping yard waste into storm drains on Falcon Place, and before that, Animal Control about a roving pack of coyotes, which, when captured, turned out to be a skittish mother fox and her two whimpering kits. Each time she lodged an official complaint, Anandi identified herself as Elizabeth Berman. Her rationale for this charade was both personal and historical.

Anandi's husband, Samir, was a tireless snoop, and an affable but unrepentant chauvinist, so whenever he spotted something amiss in the neighborhood, he commissioned his wife to contact the appropriate government agency. Anandi was compliant until September 11, 2001, after which she was convinced that she and all other Hindus in America were effectively Muslims, who were de facto terrorists, so soliciting public scrutiny terrified her, and she begged me to allow her to use my name. I suggested she should also probably use my home phone, in case such calls were traced. As her true friend, I considered it my duty to confirm her paranoia. It was only when Anandi suggested I might just as well lodge the complaints myself that I balked.

I said, "Samir is not *my* husband."

Anandi said, "But I am pretending that Mitchell is my husband."

I said, "Who isn't?"

Anandi laughed.

I'd made a joke, but it was inadvertent. This was just a few days after Dan-Dave-Don Ellenbogen had called to offer me filmed evidence of the affair between his wife, Rosalie, and Mitchell, and when Anandi knocked on my front door that day, I had resolved to tell her about the affair.

I never did expose Mitchell. And, thus, I never exposed myself. Mitchell and I had a long history of being disappointed in ourselves and in each other, and early in the marriage that stabbing sense of what each other might have been, what we could have become, seemed to us both a genuine and poignant intimacy, and eventually became a substitute for it. Anandi made her call that day. Samir got Melanie's yoga studio shut down, as he had got the storm drains flushed out. I didn't regret any of these results any more than I regretted the idea of affable Samir and elegant Anandi replacing Mitchell and me at the Bartók and the upcoming Schubert and Mozart concerts.

Instead of responding to the Stewed controversy, I Googled the Gardner Museum website. I clicked on a photo of the courtyard, and after several failed attempts to compose a message that I would not regret, I just texted the picture to T. under the subject heading, "Thinking of you, here and there."

T. didn't respond immediately. I hoped he was in the chapel—he'd told me he was off to see the Virgin when we'd parted. I imagined he was disconnected from everything but Giotto, whose name I then appended to my original Google search of the museum's website. I waited while my phone downloaded the gem of gems from the Gardner's collection.

This was *The Presentation of the Infant Jesus in the Temple*—or, it would be when my balky Internet connection completed the transfer. It was my favorite painting in the Gardner, and it would have been easy to imagine T. staring up at the original, frescoed version of this very painting, Number 18 on Sara's map, if only I had seen it. But I hadn't seen the original.

I had not yet checked out of the Hotel Arena, and I already regretted having left Padua without seeing the Presentation fresco. This was pure Old Me—an expert in emotional deficit financing, wallowing in my losses before they even occurred.

Before the baby Jesus and the rest of the temple scene materialized, my phone dinged with a text. I ditched the download. I was certain T. was writing to invite me to join him in the chapel.

Wrong again.

I'm on the train. You're on a plane? God spare us both!
Love, Shelby

I felt a familiar sense of something rising precipitously—something like my blood pressure. I should have done a few minutes of Pranayama to steady myself, but I was too busy telepathically sending myself a batch of alarming text messages.

Shelby is gone. This means you will be traveling solo to Florence.

Probably at night, even if you race through the chapel on your way out of Padua.

Arriving in an unlaundered pastel shirtdress wrinkled as badly as balled-up wrapping paper.

With no assurance that T. will be registered at the standard hotel and not one of the EurWay upgrade options.

No one is waiting for you.

No one even knows where you are.

Florence suddenly seemed very far away. I knew that if I did nothing, my panic would quickly peak, and soon I would be rolling downhill toward a deep depression, gathering regrets and anxieties and self-recriminations until the avalanche was over and I landed on my couch in Cambridge to await the next thaw. Or I could lighten up, tell myself I had been resurrected for a reason.

I wasn't expecting any miracles. I didn't try to fly or pass through the door without opening it. But I did have a free pass for the chapel. And I had a generous refund coming from EurWay Travel. So I decided to book myself one more night in Padua, spend the afternoon with Giotto, and then invite Ed to dinner to iron out all of the other wrinkles in my plan to join T. in Florence.

AN UNFAMILIAR TUXEDOED MAN AT THE FRONT DESK NOD-ded as I approached, and then turned his attention to the front door and the street beyond.

I said, "*Pronto.*" I wasn't sure that was a polite opening.

His face swiveled my way. He said, *"Pronto?"* He wasn't thrilled. He tilted his head. *"Prego?"*

"Okay," I said. *"Prego.* I would like to stay one more night."

He said, "Just one night in Padua? Is too little!" He smiled and tore off a reservation form from the pad near the telephone. "Please sign all over the places required and see to me your passport, *signora.*"

I said, "But I have a room already."

"We can see," he said. He picked up the receiver, but before he dialed, he uttered a string of incomprehensible sentences, and for the first time, my inability to translate a single word of Italian registered as a character flaw, a moral deficiency, as if he couldn't believe I had spent four months on my sofa watching soap operas and home-improvement shows instead of memorizing a few useful phrases. He shoved a pen toward me and pointed at the registration card. "And her passport is needed." He dialed and spoke to someone in sharp, demanding sentences.

Instead of risking his turning that voice on me, I filled out another reservation form. "I do have a room," I said.

"*Si, si, si,*" he said. "We have room for you."

I tried and failed to locate the key in Rachel's bag. "Room 414," I said.

"*Si, si, si.* Room 707," he said, and slammed down the phone. He checked a box on the reservation form and asked me to sign the form again. "And how will she like to pay?"

Through the nose, I thought, looking at the price for my new room, which was exactly twice the rate for 414. "Is it a bigger room?"

He said, *"Bellissimo."* Even I knew he meant, *Basta!*

I handed him my credit card and passport. After he disappeared into the back room, a mother and her very young daughter, dressed in matching lime-green sundresses and white sandals, strolled out of the elevator. I smiled at them both. As the desk man returned, the little girl said, "Is that her nightgown, Mommy?"

"Ah! *Pronto, Signora Berman!*" The desk man handed me my credit card and a key for 707 and said, "We will take your bag to your room."

I didn't trust this offer. A minute earlier, he hadn't known I had a bag or a room. "I will get my bag," I said. "I have a few other things to get together. And I would like to have something dry-cleaned. Is that possible?"

He nodded.

I was certain he had not understood. I said, "My dress."

"This dress needs help," he said. "We can do this for you, *signora.* You will see. The ticket comes to your room with your bag."

A few minutes later, after I'd cleared out of 414, I wheeled my suitcase and Rachel's bag into Room 707. I was delighted by the size—there was plenty of floor space for me to stretch out—and daylight was pouring in through two large sliding-glass doors on the far wall. And then a little boy ran into view, slapped the cement cap of the balcony wall, stuck out his tongue, ran away, and then reappeared a few seconds later and ricocheted out of sight again. When I finally figured out how to open the slider, I watched him do the balcony circuit once more, and then I stepped outside. He had run to the far end, and when he turned and spotted me, he stopped. I walked into my room, dragged the desk chair out to the balcony, and by then his father was standing beside the boy, pulling him into his thigh protectively.

The father yelled, "Sorry." He had on a khaki-green military uniform—American army, a captain, I guessed, only because I wasn't sure I was up to squaring off with a general. But I didn't want to spend the rest of the day with that kid poking his nose into my business.

I walked halfway down the balcony. "It's a strange arrangement," I said. "No walls to separate us from each other."

"Very," the father said. "The wife and daughter are having a girls' day out on the town. I'm hoping if this one gets some exercise, he'll conk out so I can get some work done. He thinks it's his private runway out here."

"I understand. He's just a child," I said. "How old is he?"

The boy looked my way.

"Just turned four," the father said.

"And you?" I said.

The father didn't say anything.

"So," I said, "when I am in the room, I'll put the chair out so we don't bother each other. Otherwise, he can have the run of the place."

The father didn't say anything.

I said, "Does that sound fair?"

The boy said, "Yes."

The father said, "Yes."

I placed the chair between my slider and the room next door, its back to the boy, and then I latched the door and drew the curtains. I pulled off the lavender shirtdress and tossed it on the bed. I rummaged through my suitcase. I didn't remember balling up the other two shirt-dresses when I'd packed, but they were unfit for human habitation and went straight to the bed for dry-cleaning, along with the Marimekko, in which I had felt rather smartly turned out. Had everyone else noticed that the black-and-white block print was embellished with a couple of big red blobs of soaked-in pizza sauce?

A knock at the door was followed by an Irish brogue. I found a bathrobe in the closet, and as I tied the sash, a young man in a green vest wheeled in a suitcase and handed me a yellow slip of paper. "I can take the dry-cleaning now, missus, or you can call down to the front desk when you have it sorted. Where shall I put the case for you?" He had mounds of jet-black hair that had to be pushed out of his eyes constantly, giving off fleeting glimpses of his wide-open pale face. He couldn't have been twenty-one.

"That's not my suitcase," I said, honestly hoping he might accept this as a fact and take the Dante book away.

He bent and read the tag. "Signora Berman. That's you, right?

And it says here, *Complimenti di Ricardo*." He stood up. "That's Italian. Compliments from Ricardo," he said.

"It is my husband's suitcase," I said, but I was thinking of Dante and his juvenile imagination of himself as a solo traveler with no luggage. How much truer and funnier *The Comedy* might have been if Dante had understood he was doomed to navigate his way through the circles of hell with the baggage of his failed marriage.

The valet rolled the case to the bed and stood it beside mine, where they appeared to be identical. "A matched pair," he said, evidently pleased by his role in this reunion.

"We were never very well matched," I said.

"Either way," he said, unfazed by my indiscretion. He probably stumbled into a lot of intimacies in his line of work, and most of them were probably a lot more intriguing than an unpleasant old woman in a borrowed bathrobe.

"Should I fill this dry-cleaning form out while you wait, or just call down later?"

"Either way," he said. His hand was working like a windshield wiper on that hair. "But if you want them to go out today, we have to act quickly."

I glanced at the form. "I can't read Italian," I said.

"You will find an English form in here." He slid open the closet, pulled out a laundry bag, and held it open. "But leave it to me."

I grabbed the pile of dresses. "Four," I said. "Three are linen."

He nodded at the open bag. "In they go, then," he said.

"One—the cotton one—it might have a spot or two," I said, stuffing that one inside the others. It now seemed obvious that T., and maybe Shelby, too, must have noticed the stains and refrained from pointing them out. Out of pity? I deposited the clump into the bag. "Should all this be noted somewhere?"

"Three badly wrinkled linens, one spotted cotton," he said. "So noted. Anything else I can do to familiarize you with the room?"

"I've stayed here before," I said.

"Welcome back, then," he said. He backed up and opened the door. "To you and your husband," he added, letting me know his professionalism made him impartial. He let the door slam behind him.

I collapsed the handle on Mitchell's suitcase and slid it across the floor to the queen-size bed, which was set into a cozy alcove painted silvery blue and outfitted with built-in bedside tables—and a white-painted platform frame that prevented any under-bed stowage. I crawled across the room, shoving that suitcase ahead of me until it was nestled under the desk, in the space where a normal person might want to keep a desk chair.

I rummaged through the closet and my suitcase, hoping I might turn up an alternative to my stretchy jeans, which seemed wrong for a long afternoon visit with Giotto—almost sacrilegious. I even searched the side pockets of Rachel's bag, hoping she might have hidden something in there for emergencies, but all I uncovered was the blinking red message flag on my phone. I had missed two calls. I was certain at least one of them was from T. This almost merited a treat from the minibar, but when I saw the price of the tiny bottle of wine, I opted for a glass of water and then sat on the bed.

My only voicemail was from Simon Allerby, the oncologist who'd diagnosed and treated Mitchell. He'd called twice and left one brief, cheery greeting, letting me know he had been at the hospital all night and asking me to call him back any time before midnight—"my time, of course, not Italian time," he'd added with a laugh, though his knowing my whereabouts unnerved me. Simon had rarely been the bearer of good news.

I drifted toward the sliding-glass doors as I dialed. In the time it took to walk those ten steps and pull back the curtains, I'd invented the discovery of a heritable genetic basis for Mitchell's cancer, which had likely been passed on to Sam and Rachel, and maybe her two boys, too.

I could have come up with something even worse, but Simon picked up on the first ring.

I was so numb I could barely speak, which was precisely how Simon, like most doctors, preferred laypeople to behave during conversations.

Simon was very grateful I had returned his call, and he hoped Italy was—well, Italy—and, frankly, at the moment, he was hoping I could do him a small favor and get a message to his colleague, Toby Harrington, assuming, of course, that by now Toby had made the connection, as promised, the prospect of which had so pleased Mitchell, who had wanted to show me the treasures of Italy himself but understood that his illness might mean I would be alone among strangers and unable to permit myself to fully embrace the—

I said, "Toby with a T.—a doctor?"

Toby with a T. yes, of course, and silver hair and, let's admit it, a silver tongue—plus, a sterling reputation, to say the very least. Toby had been a longtime colleague of Simon's at the University of Texas Medical Center in Houston before Simon had moved to Boston. Simon had consulted Toby on Mitchell's initial diagnosis, and it was only after the terrible tragedy with Toby's daughter—Simon remembered her as a black-haired beauty, even as a little girl, and happy, he would say if he were called to testify in court, truly happy as a child—well, it was after that when Toby announced he would be taking some time off in Italy, and Simon eventually put two and two together and realized Toby would be traveling with the same group Mitchell had picked out, and that's when Mitchell had Simon put him in contact with Toby, who, gracious as ever, had kept in touch with Mitchell until, well, right through the winter and till the end, and what occasioned this call was, well, Toby seemed not to be returning calls, which was entirely reasonable under the circumstances, but Simon had received a rather urgent request from an old mutual friend.

I scrolled down through my recent calls and recited T.'s cell-phone number, and for no good reason, I tugged the curtains closed, as if someone who wandered down my way would be able to see me as I was now seeing myself. I knelt down and pressed my forehead against the cool plaster wall next to the curtain pulls.

Yes, Simon did have that mobile-phone number, and he had left a few messages, but he was hoping I might be willing to pass on a more personal message to Toby, as their mutual friend was involved in something of a legal nature best not inscribed or recorded on the public record, so perhaps I could get a pen and paper and copy down the name of the mutual friend?

"I won't see him—not for days, at least, maybe weeks. Maybe never, really," I said. That much was true. It was also true that I had been the object of pity, and not just because my dress was a mess. For T., and surely for Ed and Matteo, too, I had been a charity case. "I'm afraid the doctor and I have opted for different forks in the road," I said. What a relief it must have been for T. to get my text and think of me at the Gardner, back on the other side of the world, freeing him at last from his obligation. "I wish I could tell you where he's headed, Simon, but I am not certain he hasn't opted out of the tour entirely, set off on his own."

Simon was not surprised. He didn't want to be indiscreet and wouldn't say more.

"The doctor has been remarkably solicitous," I said, "just like a real friend." I pressed my forehead hard against the wall until I could feel the imprint of the rough plaster surface on my skin. "This legal business with your mutual acquaintance—did someone die?" I regretted the slightly hopeful note in my voice.

No, no, no—complicated, counterclaims, confidentiality. No concern of mine from this moment forward, Simon assured me. *Ciao!*

Ciao, indeed.

Ciao, Simon. *Ciao*, Florence. *Ciao*, Toby.

THE ONLY HALFWAY REASONABLE THOUGHT I COULD MUS-ter for half an hour was the impossibility of explaining to Rachel why I had ditched not only the tour but my entire wardrobe in Padua. I had no luck at the front desk when I tried to get an estimated date for the return of my four dresses, so I headed for the chapel. I had nowhere else to be.

A sharp, dry breeze was blowing down Largo Europa when I stepped out of the hotel, and Rachel's red bag nearly got away from me. That wind flew right up under the cuffs of my jeans, inflating my thighs and almost lifting me out of my shoes, as if I were filling up with helium. A man's gray felt hat blew by on the sidewalk, but no man followed. My limo had also been blown away, saving me the bother of trying to translate my change of plan into Italian for the driver.

As I turned to venture forth, the young valet who'd stopped me earlier that morning, when I was on my way out to meet T., swung open the lobby door and asked if I needed a cab.

I told him I had been looking for a limousine.

He asked me if I was checking out.

I told him I was staying until tomorrow.

He asked if I was checking in.

I would have sworn we were both speaking English. I reminded him that I was staying at the hotel with the EurWay tour.

He assured me that all of the EurWay guests had checked out, and they were taking the train to Florence this morning.

This probably explained why my limo driver had disappeared, but not why all memory of me had blown down the street with that stray hat. I assured the young man that he must remember me, Signora Berman, and my friend Shelby, who had been waiting for me at the buffet breakfast this morning.

He nodded enthusiastically and said, Shelby! *Si, si, si,* Signora

Shelby sadly was gone with the rest of the EurWay guests, and was I checking in? He pointed to the reception desk.

I walked away, and ten minutes later I found my access to the chapel blocked by a motley assortment of day-trippers. Dozens of tourists were milling around the paved path outside the visitor center, jockeying for seats on the oversubscribed green benches, consulting their guidebooks and phones, and evidently wishing they had made advance reservations—or, at least, wishing they had attempted to book a time slot so they would have known in advance that the chapel was again closed to the public for the afternoon. This information was posted, in very small type, in several languages, on several pages taped to the inside of the glass double doors, so I found myself waiting in line to confirm what was painfully evident every time someone turned away from those doors and uttered her disappointment or his rage or something about Mussolini making the trains run on time.

When I made it to the front of the line and bent to read the fine print, the news did not get better, but the view did. Inside the empty visitor center, marooned in the middle of the white space and seated at a table with a stack of folders and a big sign that read CPOCH, was Sara, looking as beautiful and bored as ever. This made sense. The English on the signage was clearly her work—the diction and syntax impeccably imperfect, and absurdly lucid. I tried to get her attention by wagging my gold-sealed letter of approval from the Commune di Padova, but she didn't respond. Despite the complaints muttered behind me by tourists eager to confirm their bad luck, I held my ground long enough to pull out my phone and take a photograph of a particularly delightful patch of Sara's prose.

> *Chapel access not possible to you Wednesday post noon. On the days*
> *of this week Thursday including Sunday, you may like to see many*
> *Inspectors and experticians and world famous scholastics of the widest*

possible stature present on the grounds and interiors of the Cappella Scrovegni. These are saving this masterpiece of all-time for generations that come. Promising by Saturday, the chapel can be accessible to the public in areas between the antechamber and the altar (seen as the middle portion of the nave). A global view of the famous fresco cycle shall be enjoyed by all visitors on these days.

As my camera clicked, I realized there was no one left to share the joke, but the flash of my camera had brought Sara to her feet and quickly to the door. She was saying something—quite a lot of it—in Italian, and I waved my letter and assured her I was not planning to photograph any of the frescoes, and she opened the door, locked it behind me, and hustled me over to her little table.

I said, "I don't want to put you out or get you into trouble."

She said, "*Si, si, si, professore*, you are no trouble."

She was wearing a little white cotton blouse—a teddy, really, with some simple eyelets at the neckline, which traced a teasingly chaste line just above her breasts. Her long hair was tumbling around one of her shoulders. I said, "You look especially beautiful today."

She pretended to examine my letter, and that's when I noticed two uniformed guards milling around the gift shop. She said, "*Inglese?*"

I said, "Yes. Am I the only one here?"

"No, no," Sara said, sliding her finger down a long list of names. "Many have come before and for sure some come even after you." She didn't sound thrilled by my timing.

"I really don't have to go into the chapel today if it's a bother," I said. "Really, it's okay."

"The chapel is closed, of course." Sara handed me a heavy white folder labeled Centre for the Preservation of Cultural Heritage (CPOCH). She said, "This folder I am handing you now has for you a name tag and agenda in the chosen language for your benefit."

The guards were slowly drawing nearer, but Sara didn't seem to notice. I'm sure she thought men drifting toward her was the law of gravity. I said, "Sara—" I stopped because she did not look up. "Sara? This folder must belong to someone."

"*Sì, sì, sì*," she said. She looked a little confused, and more than a little annoyed.

I blamed my outfit. From her seat, Sara was forced to stare at the expandable waist of my stretchy jeans, which, with a navy cardigan and a trench coat, constituted my only outdoor option while my dresses were laundered. I said, "My name is Elizabeth." I heard the crepe soles of my comfortable walking shoes squeak against the marble floor. "Berman."

Sara said, "*Prego, Professore Berman.*" She had no idea who I was. She did give my footwear a disapproving glance.

I said, "From the Hotel Arena?"

Sara's nostrils flared and her eyes widened. "In the folder I am handing over to you, *professore*, is the map needed for the short walk to any hotel you have selected and the ceremonial dinner as sponsored by the Centre this night." She stopped to answer a phone call and then quickly ordered one of the guards to go to the front door and let in a group of three middle-aged men standing at the entrance, who then lined up directly behind me. Sara said, "We are done with you, I think?" and dismissed me with a wave.

I shoved my way through the scrum of disappointed tourists at the front door. It didn't please me that I hadn't made a lasting impression on Sara, but, frankly, neither had much of what she'd been taught about English grammar. In truth, with the notable exception of T., Sara had treated all of the EurWay tourists with the kind of diffidence often feigned by service workers who consider themselves superior to the people who are paying their wages. Maybe I would have been worth remembering if I had tipped her? But as I walked the now familiar route back to the Hotel Arena, it occurred to me that maybe Sara had remembered me but refused to admit it. Maybe she had meant to snub me. Surely, she had noticed how much time I spent with T. Even when they were enjoying a clandestine dinner, I probably featured prominently in his stories about his day's adventures in Padua. How annoying for her. How confounding.

By the time I walked up the marble steps into the hotel lobby, the initial sting of being snubbed by Sara had softened into something else, something like compassion. Or pity. The long-haired Irish kid was at the desk, and in my new spirit of generosity, I stopped and asked if he could change a ten-euro note for me. I realized I hadn't tipped him, either.

He said, "Coins or two fives?"

"Five coins and a five," I said. When he handed me the change, I slid two coins back toward him. "I forgot to tip you."

He said, "No charge for making change, ma'am."

"No, earlier—in my room, this morning—I didn't have a tip prepared," I said.

"This is for housekeeping, then?" He placed his index and middle finger on the two coins. This made the tip seem mingy.

"No," I said, though I realized I had not tipped the maid for cleaning 414 before I moved out. "That's for the laundry."

"We haven't any coin-op machines," he said, "but I can arrange to have laundry collected from your room." Either he had no memory of me or he was blinded by his hair, which was hanging well below both eyes. He seemed content to keep his gaze hidden. "You are staying with us?" He pointed to the white folder I was holding under one arm. "For the conference?"

If I denied this, I knew it was likely that I would end up being checked in for the third time and moved to yet another room, so I nodded, accepted the two coins he slid my way, and rode the elevator back to my new, spacious quarters with the balcony designed to accommodate burglars and Peeping Toms. I put the chair out to signal my desire not to be disturbed, and after an unpleasant encounter with myself in the floor-length mirror, I traded my stretchy jeans for the white robe. I turned on my phone, and while I waited for it to come back to life, I debated whether I should text Ed a summary of my sad story or just call him with a surprise invitation to dinner. Like so many of my choices lately, this one was made for me. Ed had never called or emailed me, so I had no way of contacting him, short of banging on the door of the basilica.

THE DEAD—I MEAN, THE REALLY DEAD ONES—CAN'T TELL you anything you don't know. It took me several hours, a lot of furious pacing, more than a few bouts of tearful self-recrimination, plus two extraordinarily pricey little bottles of white wine to understand this. But the message I had received from Mitchell from beyond the grave, courtesy of Dr. Simon Allerby, was not news. Mitchell almost never knew what I wanted, what would please me, because I almost never wanted exactly what he wanted, which registered with him as indecisiveness, or diffidence, or vindictiveness, or clinical depression. As a result, most of his gifts, and almost all of the plans he made on our behalf, were basically prescriptions.

Typically, my discovery of Mitchell's elaborate scheme to orchestrate my Grand Tour would have occasioned several days of depression and reflection, a lot of reverse engineering, and then damage control. This time was different. Although I was humiliated, I was also very hungry, and one of the unadvertised benefits of the afterlife seemed to be a kind of reverse polarity that made me more attentive to me and less interested in the impression I made on others. Plus, while reviewing my dining options, I realized that as long as I avoided Matteo's pizzeria, there was little chance of my encountering anyone I knew, which took the sting out of the public aspect of my shame. And, frankly, after I'd shimmied back into the stretchy jeans and hazarded a glance in the mirror on the back of the closet door, it was hard to maintain a sense of indignation about anyone else injuring my pride. The damage was done.

My phone dinged, and I couldn't think of anyone who wouldn't feel alarmed or betrayed if I admitted I was still in Padua, so I dug into my suitcase for a dining companion and pulled out the paperback of *The Name of the Rose*, which I had yet to even pretend to read. Mitchell had put that book in my Christmas stocking—"Background reading for the layperson in anticipation of the Italian Journey." He had nestled it in with a collection of mind-numbing herbal teas and a tiny halogen Don't Wake Your Neighbor bedtime reading light. When my phone dinged yet again, I ditched Umberto Eco, grabbed the CPOCH folder, and headed for the hotel dining room.

The restaurant was almost empty, but there were only a few spots for me to choose from, as most of the tables had been reserved, strung together in front of the windows and set with gold chargers, red napkins, and green bottles of prosecco tilting in silver ice buckets. As a waiter approached, I shuffled through the folder to be sure I wasn't accidentally inviting myself to the CPOCH dinner Sara had mentioned. I was relieved to discover the conference dinner was scheduled for eight in a restaurant near the basilica, so I was safe on that score, but I did turn up a blue-and-white ID badge with Mitchell's name printed in bold italic script, and after I was seated next to the only other solo diner, I also found a copy of a registration form completed by Mitchell in November with details of his Harvard affiliation, his status as a "Scholar/Sustaining Member" of the Centre, and the time and location of lectures and panel presentations he had elected to attend.

Mitchell had never mentioned CPOCH or the conference. Had he hoped I would travel ahead to Florence while he indulged the fiction of himself as a Dante scholar? I looked through the other stapled papers, but I didn't find any more evidence of his intentions. What surfaced instead was the memory of watching T. lean in toward Ed as I approached from the café down the street on the afternoon of Ed's disastrous lecture. They hadn't wanted me to know what they'd been discussing, and I guessed now that Ed had tried to persuade T. to tell me the truth about Mitchell's role in our meeting. When I thought about our conversations on Tuesday, before and after our lunch with T., I was sure that Ed had wanted to confess but couldn't bring himself to betray T.'s confidence. That was hardly a sin. It simply meant he was a better friend than T. deserved or a better priest than I understood. These memories gave way to Matteo and our chance meeting in the alley. It was easy to imagine Matteo's version of that event, his thinking he had stumbled into an opportunity to do exactly what T. had asked him to do—be kind to the old girl. I couldn't fault Matteo for seizing his chance to bestow on me his biggest favor.

It was T. who mystified me. Not his secrecy—he hadn't told me his name, so I wasn't surprised that he'd kept quiet about his private arrangement with Mitchell. But I just could not imagine what Mitchell and T. had found to say to each other for four months.

A man said, "Skipping the dinner?"

I fumbled for the menu and said, "I'd like pasta. Is there a special?" When I looked up, I caught the glance of a waiter far across the room, and he smiled and came swiftly to my side, blocking my view of the diner at the next table, who must have asked the question that startled me.

The invisible man said, "The tagliatelle is supposed to be great."

The waiter nodded his agreement.

I nodded.

The waiter said, "*Tagliatelle al ragù.*" He was eyeing two younger waiters fussing with the flatware on the banquet table, obviously envying them their assignment. "*Vino?*"

That I understood. "No. Water is fine."

The man said, "It's Bolognese."

I said, "The tagliatelle?"

The waiter said, "*Si, si, si. Tagliatelle.* You get these flat spaghettis with meat sauce. You like. Everybody like all the time. *Insalata?*"

I nodded.

The waiter said, "*Castelfranco, finocchio, caprese?*"

I said, "*Si?*"

The waiter said, "No."

The mystery diner at the next table leaned forward so we could see each other. He was the army captain, out of uniform. He said, "The three salads are explained in English on the other side of your menu."

I nodded and leaned toward the waiter and whispered so the captain wouldn't hear me. "Capistrano?"

The waiter said, "*Si, si, si. Castelfranco. Bellisimo.*" He walked away.

The captain said, "I hope I haven't misled both of us with the Bolognese. It got raves on TripAdvisor." He seemed to think we were meeting for the first time. "I noticed your folder. My wife is attending the conference, as well. I hope my pasta gets here soon, because I am on kid duty at nineteen-forty-five. You're skipping the conference dinner, I see."

"Guilty as charged," I said. "Convene the court-martial, Captain."

"How did you know I'm army?" He rubbed his close-cropped gray hair as if he were petting a dog. He was more pleased than surprised. He was older than he'd looked on the balcony, and I figured the four-year-old boy was a part of the deal he'd made with a second wife. The brand-new jeans and yellow polo shirt he was wearing were definitely her idea. Baseball might be the national pastime, but a surprising number of American women want their husbands to dress like caddies on the junior varsity golf team. "Was it my head or the shiny shoes?" This was the last question he asked me. "Usually, it's one end or the other that gives me away. Sometimes the fingernails." He showed me his manicured hands, holding them up like a surgeon who'd just scrubbed.

Once our dinners arrived, he told me that his wife—he referred to her as "the new wife"—had put her teaching career on hold for their two kids. He was stationed in Germany at the Conn Barracks, just outside of Schweinfurt.

I told him I didn't know the map of Germany very well.

He said, "A hundred miles east of Frankfurt."

I said I'd never been to Germany.

"About two hundred miles southwest of Leipzig." He just couldn't believe I didn't have any useful coordinates for locating his base camp. A little heatedly he added, "Seventy-five miles northwest of Nuremberg."

"The Nuremberg trials," I said, hoping to shift the subject from geography to history. I felt a kind of camaraderie with his first wife. When had she understood that she had fallen off his map? I said, "It's amazing to me how many marriages fail when you consider that we managed to patch things up with the Germans."

He didn't say anything. He was examining his cuticles. I couldn't tell if he was pouting or if he had actually forgotten that I existed.

For a few minutes, we concentrated on the Bolognese, which tasted like bits of veal and tomato stewed in something illicit, like duck fat. It was not a generous portion, and I wanted to savor it, and my only other entertainment option was a folder full of scheduled events that represented Mitchell's dying wish to spend a few days without me in Italy, so I said, "Was it the Germans who bombed Padua?"

The captain snapped to attention. "In World War I, it was the Austrians bombarding the place," he said. "During World War II, it was the Allies."

I said, "Napoleon's troops tore down a lot of the better buildings in town, as well." I hoped I was quoting Ed nearly correctly. "They tore down Enrico Scrovegni's palace."

The captain said, "It's a miracle your little chapel is standing. That's what I said to Cheryl this afternoon. Look at what happened to the cathedrals at Coventry and Dresden." I could tell he was gauging my reaction, and whatever he saw encouraged him to keep going. "That church right next door to Giotto's chapel was blown to bits," he said.

"The Church of the Eremitani," I said.

"I don't know the name of it," he said. "But most of this town from there to the old train station was leveled. Once Mussolini lost control in 1943, Padua hosted the Nazis, so the Allies bombed this whole sector nearly out of existence." He seemed pleased by these facts, or maybe I was more receptive than his young wife to his history lesson. "I see I didn't lead you wrong with the pasta."

My plate was almost as clean as it had been before I'd been served. "I'm glad I ordered that salad."

"You should look for Cheryl tomorrow. You can't miss her. She's blonde, and I'm biased, but she'll be on everybody's radar." He stood up. He was done with me—almost. "Thing is, she probably won't approach you." This was what he had wanted to say since he'd spotted my CPOCH folder. This was why I was worth talking to. "She's feeling of out of her league. She didn't even want to go to the dinner tonight."

I said, "Neither did I."

He said, "That's different." He didn't bother to explain how.

I took a guess. "I'm old."

"Yeah," he said, glancing at his watch, "for you it's just another dinner. She's not a professor of anything, but she is teaching an art appreciation course for wives at the barracks, so you might ask her about that. Or maybe don't let on that we met and see if you can get her talking about her art class. That's it. That's better. Just do me a favor and seek her out. Cheryl Stamford. I'll get them to rush that salad to you."

The captain collared a waiter on his way out, and my salad arrived within seconds. That was a genuine favor, as several elegantly dressed young couples were taking their places at the big table by the window, and I was beginning to think the only way to avoid looking like a party pooper in my droopy old cardigan was to pull a Shelby and wrap myself in the tablecloth. Instead, I tucked into the salad. It looked like a plate of pale Boston lettuce, the creamy white leaves streaked and spotted with the blood redness of radicchio. It tasted like a hybrid, too, the mild tang of the unidentifiable greens offset by salty shards of Parmesan and maybe some anchovy in the dressing. It was the perfect aperitif. It made me happy, and it made me sad. It reminded me of all the bad salads I'd eaten instead of pasta, hoping I might be worth looking at if there was less of me, all those heaps of aspiring compost dressed in ascorbic acid, the bitter diet of the disappeared.

BACK IN MY BIG ROOM, I FOUND THREE HANG-UPS FROM Rachel and two new emails. I drew the curtains and crawled into bed before I read them. I'd left *The Name of the Rose* on the white bedside table, and I set Mitchell's Swiss Army watch on the cover. That little shrine didn't lift my spirits, so I turned on the TV and muted the commentary on the soccer game. After a few dizzying minutes, all that running around and the sudden close-ups of sweaty shirts made me feel guilty, so I forced myself to sit up and do at least ten forward bends. The idea of this self-torture was to renew the spine and hamstrings by leaning over your outstretched legs and grasping the soles of your feet. Even at the height of my yogic powers, this wasn't pretty. I took a couple of deep breaths, and I stayed still until I recalled the proper name for this exercise. It dignified the project to tell myself I was performing paschimottanasana.

After the tenth forward bend, my spine didn't seem much

improved, but it didn't hurt. My hamstrings never got involved, probably because I couldn't extend my outstretched hands past my knees. The soles of my feet might as well have been in Schweinfurt.

I grabbed my phone and scrolled down to an email from Anna.

Mrs. Berman: Per your request for a daily photograph, my sister sends you this very accurate view of the exterior of the hotel in Florence, where we are temporarily residing. Sincerely, Anna

Anna was a woman of her word—minced as it was. Fortunately, Shelby was next in my lineup.

I mailed the first set of postcards to your children in the Padova train station and that made me miss you like crazy. You are probably in Cambridge already but I am still wishing you were here. Everyone else is already complaining about the crowds in Florence as if they thought they'd rented the whole city for a private party. I was here for all of half an hour before I had to run out and see Himself. I hope you admire a six-pack as much as I do! Mailed the Firenze postcards on my way to dinner. Missed you even more. XOXOXOXO

Shelby's sweet note soured the pleasure of my secret exile, and after a few minutes it was clear that I was on my way to spending the entire night awake, trying to formulate a genuine response that was not a lie but did not blow my cover. I shopped the minibar for a sedative, but the tininess of those rows of little nips of gin and scotch and rum did me in. It looked like a drunk's dollhouse. I emptied my suitcase and Rachel's bag, looking for one of the magazines or newspapers I had read on the airplane. All I came up with was the envelope from Matteo. Then my phone dinged with a new text. It was from T. I didn't read it. I climbed back into bed. I stuck Matteo's note into Umberto Eco, as if I might need a bookmark, and I coiled the rosary beads on the nightstand next to Mitchell's watch. That seemed all wrong. I flicked on the bedside lamp.

Suddenly, everything seemed to be out of place.

I pulled Matteo's note out of the book and read his instructions.

Hang on the neck, keeping the Holy Cross on the backbone, to be curing the lonely nights.

I turned off the light, hung the rosary around my neck, and gave the Virgin of Misericordia permission to work her magic. The beads didn't cure my loneliness, but as I lay in the darkness, they did feel cool against my skin. After a few minutes, I reached out and finally located Mitchell's watch and slipped it back on my wrist. I was starting to feel like a medium conducting a séance, a gathering of everyone who was not there. It seemed mean not to invite T. to the party. I slapped around the duvet until I found my phone. Doing all of this in pitch blackness preserved the supernatural aspect. And then I read T.'s text.

I see Florence from the balcony
and Cambridge in the beyond.

I could clearly see something. For starters, I had seen that balcony before. I knew it came with a little single bed. T. and I were apparently sharing a room in a city where we weren't. He hadn't gone to Florence. He had downloaded the same photo that Rachel had forwarded to me from the hotel website.

T. was here.

II

✵

I skipped the buffet breakfast at the hotel on Thursday morning so I wouldn't run into Cheryl and feel responsible for her and the future of the NATO alliance all day long. The bar at Café Metro was jammed, but almost all of the tables were unoccupied. I sat in my dark corner near the arcade and waited for a waitress. Apparently, someone had put out a casting call for elegant middle-aged men in expensive blue blazers. There were so many plausible T.s among the comers and goers that he'd have to have worn his stethoscope for me to make a positive identification.

A young woman with a big beehive hairdo planted herself behind the crowd at the bar and started sweeping her way toward me with a fury that made me think she was often stuck doing the dirty work. She was backing up swiftly, so I stood to clear a path for her. When she felt me looming, she stopped and smiled.

She said, "*Vuoi qualcosa?*" She was dressed in a shiny black blouse, black tights, and teal-blue high heels—more Ronnie Spector than Cinderella.

I said, "*Latte macchiato?*"

She said, "*Grande?*"

I said, "*Sì.*" This was going so well, I added, "*Panini?*"

She said, "*Panino?*"

I said, "*Pane?*"

She said, "*Tramezzino?*"

That made me worry we'd left snacks and headed into the entrées. I tried, "Pastry?" I pointed at the display case, hoping I wouldn't end up with a punch bowl full of tiramisu.

She said, "*Sì, sì. Cornetti.*"

It was roulette, but this sounded smallish. I said, "*Sì, cornetti.*"

She said, "*Con crema?*"

I said, "*No, grazie.*"

She said, "*Marmellata?*"

I didn't want marmalade, but she was looking so hopeful that I nodded my assent and went back to my table. Instead of looking for T. at the bar while I waited, I scrolled through my camera's memory and found the picture of the two-euro coin Ed and I had exchanged. Two days ago, Dante had looked like a ringer for T. But the image didn't tally with my memory of him now, even when I covered up the peculiar chin. I didn't know if I should delete it or save it. Would it appreciate in value if I never saw him again?

My coffee arrived with two little knots of brioche and a pot of red-currant jam. I gave the sweet server a twenty-euro note and never saw that beehive again.

I had no new email, but I did owe a few, and as I dunked the pastry into the jam and poked around in my mailbox, it occurred to me that I was rather rich in the currency of confusion. Why not spend it?

Sweet Shelby—

How lucky I am to have met you. I will think of you every year at

this time, just when these beauties bloom in my Cambridge backyard.
Grateful forever.

Rachel, my dear, dear girl—
I would rather dunk my head in the Arno than get into the middle
of your business. A thousand apologies from this old girl, with love
as ever.

Oh, David—

I wish I could say the right thing. Be brave like your namesake? (And might you be able to squeeze the truck into my garage? Rachel knows where I keep my car keys, and you can park me in the driveway.)

My best to you.

Anna—

Thank you for the lovely note and photo. Now, please accept this coin as a token of my assurance that the photographic debt is paid. I will be

happy to think that you and your sister are enjoying yourselves too much to bother taking pictures for me.

Fondly—

Elizabeth Berman

BY TEN-THIRTY, A SERIOUS TEENAGE BOY WITH A CPOCH TAG pinned to his chest was escorting me down a hall in the Arena Chapel visitor center, hushing me all the way. He opened the door to a conference room and pointed to an empty aisle seat. I scooted in, and he disappeared.

"But I simply cannot agree with my two eloquent colleagues about the chapel bestowing fame upon Giotto. The oft-repeated anecdote characterizing his response to an envoy sent by Pope Boniface VIII might serve as evidence in this informal setting." The speaker was a big woman with a British accent and a brutish bouffant of white hair. She wasn't that old, but she looked aggressively old-fashioned in her floral print dress and pink kitten heels, which were standing at either side of her stockinged feet under the table on the dais, where she and two anemic men in pale summer suits constituted the panel of experts for Mitchell's first chosen event on the CPOCH schedule, *In and Out of Favor: Forensic Architecture in Scrovegni's Chapel*.

"By the age of thirty, although his major commissions had come to him at the favor of his master, Cimabue, Giotto was already being sought out by the Vatican for its renewal plans in advance of first celebration of the Jubilee Year in 1300." I spun around in my seat, hoping I might spot Ed among the small crowd scattered around me. The woman cleared her throat, as if she'd noted my inattention, and then continued. "The envoy of the pope requested samples of Giotto's recent work. Giotto demurred. He secured a piece of, let us imagine, vellum, upon an easel, dipped a paintbrush into a pot of red paint, placed one of his hands on his hip, and leaned forward— he was, in effect, turning his body into a drafting compass. Giotto then painted a perfect circle in one go. This, he told the aston- ished envoy, was his application to the pope. Giotto was granted the Lateran commission, as surely we all recall. But my point is this: Giotto at that moment conferred fame upon himself. He asserted, with that circle, that he was above his competition. He knew it. For heaven's sake, even the pope knew it. Giotto was famous when he arrived in Padua and surely would have demanded more control over the architectural program for the chapel than has so far been alleged by my colleagues."

"A nod to the inestimable critic John Ruskin might be in order here." The slope-shouldered man to her left tilted his head forward and surprised everyone when, in a basso profundo, he continued. "'I think it unnecessary,' Ruskin wrote, 'to repeat here any other of the anecdotes commonly related of Giotto, as, separately taken, they are quite valueless.'"

"Um—all right, okay." This was the other little man on the panel. He had leaned way back in his chair. "Maybe now is the right time for the ten-minute break we promised everyone earlier."

The white-haired woman would not leave it there. "'Yet much may be gathered from the general tone of these anecdotes,' Ruskin went on to say, if I recall his words correctly." She slid back into her shoes, stood up, and soliloquized:

> It is remarkable that they are, almost without exception, records of good-humoured jests, involving or illustrating some point of practical good sense; and by comparing this general colour of the reputation of Giotto with the actual character of his designs, there cannot remain the smallest doubt that his mind was one of the most healthy, kind, and active, that ever informed a human frame. His love of beauty was entirely free from weakness; his love of truth untinged by severity; his industry constant, without impatience; his workmanship accurate, without formalism; his temper serene, and yet playful; his imagination exhaustless, without extravagance; and his faith firm, without superstition. I do not know, in the annals of art, such another example of happy, practical, unerring, and benevolent power.

She had recited this from memory, or else she had a teleprompter in her shoes. While she waited for the enthusiastic applause to die down, she tilted her head toward the panelist who had attempted to discredit her. It wasn't clear if she was bowing triumphantly or threatening to ram him with her helmet of hair the next time he challenged her authority. "In short," she added, "almost from the moment he took up a paintbrush, Giotto di Bondone was secure in his genius and confident of his acclaim. When we reconvene, we shall have the opportunity to examine the physical evidence of the control he exerted over the architectural arrangement of the chapel." She left the stage.

As most of the audience filtered out, the two other panelists eyed each other wearily and then disappeared out a side exit. I was one of four people left in the auditorium. I didn't need a break yet. I'd missed most of the first thirty minutes because I'd stopped at my hotel room on the way back from the café. I wanted to pick up my copy of Sara's map to orient myself in the chapel. And the day had gone hot and humid, and my saggy cardigan was sticking to my blouse, making my back furiously itchy, as if blue dye were leaching into my skin. I found my Marimekko shift waiting for me in the closet, spot-free. And the belt fit. My three linen shirtdresses were still missing, but that barely dimmed my delight. Despite the Bolognese and brioche, I'd lost at least five pounds.

Eventually, the three other audience members deserted me. I was content to have the place to myself, imagining that the white walls of the little room were the white plaster walls of the chapel before Giotto got his hands on it. Had Scrovegni paired up with another painter, I would not have been there, and maybe no one but a few neighbors and a few friends of Scrovegni would ever have known or cared that the place existed. This seemed to me a kind of illumination of my marriage and so many others—which, like most churches and chapels, were not

particularly well made or uplifting, but ordinary and serviceable are-
nas for the sustaining rituals of a few hopeful people. I didn't have to
denigrate the hard work Mitchell and I did to make a marriage and to
make it work to admit that it was a disappointment—not inspiring, not
especially imaginative, not even much of a model for our unmarried
son and our divorced daughter.

I finally checked my program and discovered that no one was
coming back to join me. Everyone else had reconvened outside, on
the chapel grounds. By the time I found my group, the basso profundo was finishing up his description of the chapel's strange little
apse, a polygonal tower that housed both the altar and Scrovegni's
tomb. From the outside, the apse looked like a brick rocket ship
pasted onto the end of the chapel's barrel vault. He promised we
would soon go inside and see that its frescoed walls were unrelated to
the panels Giotto had painted in the body of the church and could be
confidently attributed to much lesser artisans. "In my reading of the
arrangement, the apse indicates that Giotto was not the sole or even
the lead architect on this project. The hastily painted wooden panel
above the altar—I will point out the ersatz image of God the Father
stuck into that obvious hole near the top of Giotto's work—rather
seals the case." He set off down the paved path.

The white-haired woman did not budge. "Perhaps the original
wood panel was lost."

The basso profundo said, "I can't imagine Giotto instructed the
workmen to cut a hole in the middle of the plaster wall he had just frescoed to make room for a piece of wood."

The woman nodded. "But there is reason to imagine that Giotto
had always intended for there to be a hole high up in that wall at the
apse end of the barrel vault, a kind of trapdoor used for freeing doves
or shining a dramatic bit of candlelight during the liturgical pageants
hosted by Scrovegni and his family."

The basso profundo smiled. Most of the rest of us were caught between him and his adversary. He said, "I rather agree with the more informed speculation that we lost a stained-glass window in that spot, possibly designed by Giotto before the architecture was revised—without his participation. There is evidence that Scrovegni had hoped to build a genuine transept with two side chapels, which would have made sense of Giotto's original stained-glass window. A window above the chancel arch would have admitted much-needed additional light. Surely it was a window that had to be patched up with a panel of wood. "

The third panelist meekly suggested we move directly inside as we had already devoted more time than anticipated to the apse.

The basso profundo agreed.

The white-haired woman followed for a few paces and then planted her little heels directly in front of a bricked-up indentation in the chapel's exterior. This peculiar niche was a six-foot-high arch of no apparent use, not deep enough to have held a statue or any ornament. "This is where we encounter incontrovertible evidence of Giotto's alteration of the architectural plan of the chapel."

We all stared at the blank space, as if we expected the Virgin to appear and fill us in on the details.

The basso profundo snaked through the crowd to find his meek colleague and, in a very effective stage whisper, said, "I cannot listen for another minute to that migraine of a woman," and then headed toward the dehumidifying chamber.

The meek man said, "I think many of us are overheated. Perhaps the significance of the brick indentation can be explained while we are all seated in the cool antechamber."

I had developed a deep loyalty to the pushy woman on the panel, but my back was getting furiously itchy again, so I followed the others into the air-conditioning. We dried out, but the debate about who designed the chapel building did not dry up, both sides fueled by questions and speculation from members of the audience. Once we were herded into the chapel, the crowd gathered in the front half of the nave to study the controversial painted wood panel.

I was more puzzled by Mitchell's interest in this topic. There were several other morning lectures whose titles looked more promising, and one was devoted exclusively to circular and cyclical elements in the work of Giotto and Dante. His choices for later in the day didn't make any more sense. If I stuck it out, I would be learning everything I never wanted to know about moneybags and sacred animation. I drifted to the back, trying to locate where that odd niche in the brick outside showed up inside the chapel. I visited briefly with my faceless friend with the noose, Despair, and when I turned around, the little meek man waved from the other side of the aisle.

"It was over here," he whispered, "behind the figure of Charity." He looked exhausted, his dark eyes set in dark circles on his round face, and when I got closer, I saw that someone had shaved away a small patch of the thinning brown hair just above one of his ears. An infection? A bite? He had the demeanor of a sad sack, the guy in a crowd who would be singled out by a nasty crow or an angry hornet. He said, "Is your name really Mitchell, or is it Michelle? The Italians aren't champion spellers."

"Neither," I said. "My husband's name was Mitchell."

"My partner's name was Michael," he said, as if this gave us something in common. "He left me a few months ago." He looked up into the deep blue sky above us. "Which I have recently taken to telling strangers," he added. "Maybe I'm hoping people who didn't know us will act surprised. Or we can debate the significance of this Charity panel."

I said, "I'm not a scholar."

He said, "Welcome to the club."

I said, "I'm not sure what I think I'm doing here."

"Everyone else is doing their best imitation of a scholar," he said.

I said, "I don't even know what CPOCH does."

"Plans expensive guided tours of significant artistic sites for people who are willing to pay $5,000 and up annually to be treated like VIPs and lectured at by college professors from the provinces." His affect had not changed since he'd waved to me.

"So my husband must have been a paying member," I said.

"Sustaining member—that's what the blue-and-white badge means. I think that's the $10,000 level," he said.

He must have noticed the strain in my facial muscles.

"Or maybe he got a discounted membership. They do offer come-ons. Was this his first year as a member?" He eventually filled in my silence. "You should be receiving a biannual copy of the Centre's bulletin. You'll find your husband's name among the Centre's Panel of Scholars."

Maybe it was reflexive loyalty, or maybe it was a genuine hope that Mitchell had got something for his money, but I said, "I suppose the Centre has more standing in Britain and on the Continent than it does in the States."

"I doubt it," he said. "It's mostly Americans who sign up. And a few Canadians from the mainland. The three of us are based in Halifax. At the College of Art & Design."

"All of these experts teach in Nova Scotia?" I had meant to make that sound like a point of interest, but my dismissive tone echoed right up to the heavens. I sounded like a typical Harvard wife. In an effort to muffle the insult, I said, "That arch of brick we saw outside is on the other side of Charity?"

She was one of the Virtues, and like the other Seven Virtues and the Seven Vices, she was painted all in gray tones, as if she were a statue of herself, a beatific young woman with plaited hair holding a basket laden with fruit and nuts in one hand, and either a giant fig or a small artichoke in the other, which she had raised up toward a tiny haloed figure who had popped into the top of the painted frame to accept her gift. On the ground beside her feet were two sacks of coins, apparently ready for distribution to the needy.

He nodded.

I said, "These are as unlike the rest of the frescoes as that God the Father they're all debating." The crowd had moved right into the sanctuary, spread out around the altar as if readying a lamb for sacrifice. "Are we sure Giotto did these strange, gray paintings?"

"About ten years later, he used variations on these very figures for an even bigger commission—the Palace of Reason. He made a vast fresco on the ceiling and walls, an astonishingly accurate astronomical map of the heavens decorated with figures of astrological significance, inspired by the ancients and contemporary science. I really think it was his secular response to all of this Christian folderol Scrovegni had paid for."

It had never occurred to me that the chapel might not reflect Giotto's beliefs and convictions, that he had applied his genius to please his patron, not for the glory of God. I said, "Isn't the Palace of Reason right here in Padua?"

"Yes, but the original burned to the ground in 1440-something," he said, saving me the bother of venturing beyond the tiny sector of town that was all I knew of Padua or Padova, or Italy for that matter. "So much of what Giotto painted has been lost or destroyed. Even in here. For centuries, moisture in the air drew salts in the plaster to the surface and popped paint off the walls." He reflexively touched his bald spot, as if he was hoping to find a few bristles of new growth. "And about fifty years ago, all of the frescoes were restored and covered with a resin, which kept the salts in place but so effectively sealed the surface that the entire painted surface started to dry up and peel away, like dead skin."

I said, "The road to hell is paved with good intentions." The horrors of hell were looming above us in Giotto's superb rendering of the Last Judgment, but he didn't crack a smile.

"We'll never know even the half of who Giotto was," he said. "The paintings we do have—the ones that weren't lost or destroyed—acquire a disproportionate significance. It's like discovering one stupid thing someone did one night and judging him on that mistake, imagining he spent all of his free nights like that."

I think we both realized he had shifted the topic from painters to partners. Nonetheless, he had a point. I couldn't tell if he'd been the cheater or the cheated, but I had devoted a disproportionate amount of my Mitchell scholarship to exegesis of his brief affair with Rosalie.

"I love these panels," he said. "For all of the Virtues and Vices, to set them apart from the living characters, Giotto used this bravura technique—as if to announce he was moving on to something new—this almost monochromatic approach to painting that puts more emphasis on the precision of line and shape than the bright colors and depth of field that had made him famous." He looked at his shoes. "I'm lecturing you."

"Don't stop now," I said. "I've got a $10,000 credit to spend down."

He may have smiled, or maybe he winced. He seemed determined not to express any more emotions, as if he were practicing to become a statue of himself. "Look at Charity. It's as if you are reading an etching, but the drawing is done here with a paintbrush in fresco—an almost impossible show of mastery. It's called grisaille. It turns up later, notably in work by van Eyck and Brueghel and the other true master drawers among the Dutch, and, of course, in the Sistine Chapel. But Giotto invented the technique. Or so say those who actually know about these things. I'm just paraphrasing a couple of journal articles I read last week by way of preparation."

I said, "I think you know more than you let on."

He said, "I know I was lying when I said I've been telling strangers about my partner leaving me. You're the first. Even my colleagues on the panel don't know yet."

I tucked away that confession. If you have a tomb you're not using anymore, you can always find someplace to stick another secret or sadness. "Is that a crack in the plaster I'm seeing or something Giotto painted?" I was staring at a white line that bisected Charity. It looked like a fissure in the wall that extended from beneath the bottom of the painted frame, through an incomprehensible Latin inscription, and right up between her legs into her high-waisted gown, across her profile, and on up into the wall above her.

"It's a crack. That brick alcove outside was originally a public entrance to the chapel."

I said, "An exit."

"Yes," he said, "a door."

"But you can't get out," I said. "You can't get out unless you can slip through that crack. It's like the eye of the needle."

"Easier for a rich man to pass through the eye of the needle than to enter the gates of heaven?" He sounded genuinely interested and genuinely confused. "You mean Scrovegni? I don't get it."

I was thinking of those moneybags at Charity's feet, the money Mitchell had left for me to distribute to Sam and Rachel, which I was still withholding. I said, "There used to be an exit behind her?"

"Yes, there was a door," he said. "Probably it was Giotto who demanded it be sealed up and plastered over to preserve the geometry and symmetry of this grisaille border of opposing Virtues and Vices. Over time, the building settled and the open space that was originally a portal caused the stress fracture. It does indicate Giotto had some sway over the final design of the building." He tilted his head toward the altar. "She's right about that much, though it's hardly her idea. We all read the same journal articles. Am I being petty?"

I said, "Not a model of charity."

"I should go up there and call that contest a draw," he said, staring at the crowded altar. "It's almost time for lunch." He didn't move.

"I had a huge breakfast," I said.

He said, "I have to meet with the volunteers during lunch."

We shared a talent for fending off invitations that hadn't been issued. We let a couple of silent seconds pass before we went our separate ways. I think we both registered the awkward intimacy of that long last moment.

BY THE TIME I FOUND THE DESIGNATED LUNCHROOM, THE unappetizing spread of tiny pressed sandwiches, cookies, and a tub of ice with a few little splits of wine and sparkling fruit drinks was littered with rejected scraps and empties. I assembled two towers of panini, or panino, or *tramezzi*-somethings on a plastic plate and stuck a yellow can of fizzy lemonade in the pocket of my dress. Most of the empty chairs I spotted were hung with blazers or purses, or else they were located at tables where the conversation was too convivial for my taste.

I headed for the exit, and just before I got away, a woman said, "This food you are eating is not able to leave the room." It was Sara, who had apparently been demoted from translator to hall monitor. She was seated next to another woman, and their respective lunch plates were balanced on a chair between them, one untouched sandwich and one cookie on each plate. Sara was wearing an unusually demure navy blue turtleneck dress.

"You can join us, if you like." The other woman turned my way and flounced her blonde hair, as if I might want to photograph her.

"I think you are Cheryl," I said.

"Now, how did you know that?" She turned to me briefly and then turned away and checked to be sure her purse was still below her chair.

"I know your husband," I said.

"You do not!" She looked at Sara and shrugged.

"And I saw you yesterday at the Arena Hotel with your daughter," I said. It was her daughter who thought my wrinkly dress was a nightgown.

Sara stood up for no apparent reason, though she did stifle all conversation at nearby tables. Her dress fit her like a tattoo.

Cheryl also stood, and she stared at me intently. "No, I would remember if we met," she said.

I said, "It doesn't matter."

Cheryl said, "I never forget a face," as if I didn't have one. "It's one of the things about me, I'd say. Anyway, take our chairs. Don't tell my husband, but Sara and I are going to skip out this afternoon for a little shopping."

Very loudly, and very slowly, Sara said, "Shoe shopping— shopping for shoes," as if I didn't speak English.

Cheryl said, "Did you just say you know the captain? No way!"

I said, "I must have been mistaken."

Cheryl said, "Well, maybe so, but thanks for stopping by anyway," as if we were standing in the foyer of her home and I was a confused delivery person.

I did take their chairs, and I was pleasantly surprised by my selection of little sandwiches, especially the melon and prosciutto, and a combo of an unfamiliar soft white cheese and thin slices of fennel. The lemonade tasted tinny. Evidently, you didn't get a glass or a little cup for your beverages unless you pledged $25,000.

I joined the first wave out of the lunchroom. My next lecture started in the dehumidifying chamber, and I wanted a good seat. The topic was moneybags. I split off from the crowd and ended up alone on a bench, forced to wait for the rest of my cohort before the guard would open the airtight chamber. The delay was just long enough for the heat of the day to bring my back to a boil again, and my scratching effectively spread the problem from my shoulders right down my spine. Eventually, I was admitted to the cool dehumidifier, along with three elderly priests.

Two short young women, both wearing dark pantsuits, their wavy hair parted in the middle, were standing beside the video monitor at the front of the room. They looked like flight attendants for a bargain airline. One of them had tied on a white neckerchief, which didn't really jazz up her outfit but did make it possible to tell them apart. The priests stood in the aisle until I chose a seat in the middle of the many empty rows and then parked themselves directly behind me.

One of them said, "We ought to spread out and make them feel better."

"My name is Lisa Sorretino-Balfour, assistant professor of rhetoric, composition, and modern communications at the College of St. Benedict, where I also serve as codirector of the Art History Is Our History program for returning scholars with my copresenter today, Margaret LaChappelle, associate professor of world religions and spiritual traditions and codirector of the Art History Is Our History program for returning scholars, as well as acting chairperson of the Humanities Department at St. Benedict." Lisa was reading all of this from a thick packet of typed notes. She turned the page. "Today's lecture is entitled *Moneybags*—" Here, she paused and looked up, as if she'd anticipated a roar of approving laughter from a big crowd when she'd prepared her talk. She glanced at Margaret, who was running a finger around the inside of her neckerchief. Lisa ducked back toward her notes. "The full title is actually a little longer. Here it is. I'll just start that sentence again. Okay. Today's lecture is entitled *Moneybags: Symbols of Ill-Gotten Gain in Giotto's Arena Chapel Fresco Cycle.*"

Lisa read for fifteen minutes. Except when she was interrupted by a wisecrack from one of the priests, which she never failed to mistake for a question from an interested audience member—pausing each time to look up hopefully, and then okay-okay-okaying until she had relocated herself in her text and resumed reading—she delivered a fairly steady stream of facts that occasionally threatened to cohere into an idea, if you had Sara's map in your lap. Judas figured prominently in the early pages of her notes, as he figured prominently on three of the four chapel walls, most peculiarly on the front wall above the altar, where Giotto painted him receiving the silver coins for his promise to betray Jesus (Number 27). Judas also turned up in the famous scene in which he embraced Jesus and identified him for the waiting soldiers with a kiss (Number 30), and in the Last Judgment (Number 39), after he'd hanged himself, "his guts pouring forth from his abdomen, like a broken purse," Lisa said, raising some groans from the clerical chorus. Judas, she said, was notably absent from the fourth wall.

One of the priests held up a book of photographic reproductions of the frescoes. "Envy," he said, his finger under Giotto's gray portrait of a man in flames, a snake emerging from his mouth to eat his face. "Isn't that a fat moneybag in his left hand? Or did he pack a bag lunch for his trip to hell?"

Envy was Number 41f, facing Charity, Number 40f, on the opposite wall, and I mentioned the moneybags at Charity's feet, hoping to bolster Lisa's argument that the moneybags weren't strictly associated with Judas.

Lisa ignored my contribution. "Envy does broadly represent Judas's sin of Avarice," Lisa said, "but it's not a portrait of a single man."

The priest said, "It is a picture of just one man."

Lisa said, "These are very good questions we can all discuss later."

Margaret spoke for the first time. "The moneybag is not singularly associated with Judas. It is also a symbol of fertility. You know, both a virtue and a vice." She nodded my way. "Avarice holds on to the money. Charity is prepared to give it away."

I nodded enthusiastically.

"At the front of the chapel, paired with Judas and his silver coins, is the Visitation," Margaret said, "when the pregnant Elizabeth visits the pregnant Virgin. You see, vice and virtue."

The priest lowered his book. "Judas and the Virgin Mary are two sides of the same coin?"

Margaret said, "It's not quite that literal."

The priest said, "What does money have to do with the Visitation? Was Mary charging her cousin admission to see her belly?"

Margaret said, "Many scholars see an intentional juxtaposition in the swelling stomach of the expectant mothers and the moneybag swollen with ill-gotten gains." She had almost managed to turn the corner and lead us back to the topic.

But Lisa said, "Fornication, too."

The priest said, "Fornication is associated with the Virgin?"

"Oh, no. She's a virgin." Perhaps when she was promoted to associate professor of rhetoric Lisa would recognize a rhetorical question. But she pressed on. "I'm saying that the moneybag is a symbol of fornicators, too. And sodomy." This was the first time she'd gone off script, and she should have grabbed a hold of Margaret's neckerchief because she was in free fall. "Of course, sodomy wasn't so simple back then. Sodomy wasn't just sodomy in the Middle Ages."

"Yeah," said one of the holy fathers, "you had to buy him dinner first."

There was a long silence. Finally, Margaret said, "We will enter the chapel in just about two minutes. Perhaps we should wrap up this segment by acknowledging that the medieval mind was profoundly affected by the reflective and refractive relationships among opposing ideas and qualities. The virtues and vices were not singular or solitary sins and ideals. Each one covered a lot of territory. Giotto's mirroring here in the chapel is part of a tradition that informed Church doctrine and the great artists of the age, notably Dante's depiction of hell. As you all surely recall, in the Seventh Circle, forced to exist on the infertile, burning plains of the Abominable Sands, we find blasphemers, sodomites, and usurers."

"But not the Virgin," said one of the priests.

"She was not infertile," Margaret said slowly, patronizingly. "The Virgin is in heaven, the opposite of hell. Get it?"

"But Scrovegni is there, in hell, I mean, in Dante," I said.

The doors to the chapel whooshed open, and the three wise men immediately headed in. Lisa scooted right after them. As I stood, Margaret said, "Is Mitchell Berman your husband?" She raised her hand and waved to someone I didn't see, and the glass doors behind her sighed and closed.

I sat down and didn't speak.

"You're wearing his name tag," she said.

I didn't say anything.

She said, "He wrote to me about his book, his theory about Dante."

"And then he died," I said. "Mitchell is dead, though he doesn't seem to be very good at it."

"Oh." Margaret welled up suddenly. "I'm so sorry."

This seemed more an apology for her tears than a condolence, and I didn't know how to respond. Finally, I said, "He was quite ill," which somehow made it sound like Mitchell had been determined to die, so I added, "But thank you. Now, about his book."

"You mentioned Scrovegni." She adjusted her neckerchief. For the first time, I wondered if she was hiding something—a scar, or a birthmark, or some other little demon from her past.

I said, "Did you read Mitchell's book?"

She said, "Did he finish it?"

"No, but I would like to find a way to be done with it," I said. "Why did Dante identify Scrovegni among all of the nameless money-lenders in hell? Had he seen the chapel? Had he come to Padua?"

She smiled. "You mean, did your husband have it backward? Did Dante steal Giotto?"

I nodded. "That's the book I'm not writing."

"Originality is a peculiarly modern obsession," she said. "It's a quantifiable aspect of art that can be asserted and disproved and debated by scholars and appraisers and collectors who treat art as a commodity or a currency. It would not have been a concern for Giotto. It is unrelated to beauty or truth, although it has become a substitute for those qualities. Thus, modern art. I mean, Giotto or Jackson Pollock? Seriously?" She bent her arm and dabbed her fore-head several times with the sleeve of her blazer. "I'm getting myself all hot and bothered," she said. Her sleeve had raised a knotty bump of hair on one side of her part. "Dante had his own reasons to hate Reginaldo Scrovegni because of his deep and endlessly profitable ties to the pope, who'd got Dante exiled from Florence. And the next pope was only too happy to sell Enrico Scrovegni indulgences for his own sins, his father's, and those of half a dozen relatives, whose money would otherwise have been tainted, compromising Enrico's social status and his economic prospects. This was not uncommon. It was the Vatican's means of assuring itself a share in inherited wealth. It was a kind of papal death tax, really."

"Or an early version of money laundering," I said. "No connection to Giotto or the chapel?"

"It's not unlikely that by the time Dante was writing *The Inferno* he had heard about the chapel and Scrovegni's fleeting triumph. And probably it pleased Dante to know his poem was in wide cir-culation in the Veneto when Scrovegni ran out of town and headed north to Venice instead of sticking around to defend Padua or his own honor," Margaret said. "Instead of being famous by association with the chapel, Scrovegni spent his final years associated with the Seventh Circle of Hell. But that was just good luck for Dante, a coincidence."

I said, "An ironic juxtaposition."

"Typical of the Middle Ages." Margaret smiled. Big drops of sweat were beaded up on her forehead again, occasionally running down her temple to the neckerchief. "For the record, Giotto did not steal Dante. The dates alone make it impossible, but I think maybe your husband was not aware of the recent scholarship. It was long unclear if Giotto painted here in 1300, 1310, or even 1320. We now know he had completed the fresco cycle before Dante began writing *The Comedy* in 1306. And the notion of a layered hell was not his invention or Dante's. It was present in paintings as early as the 11th century. Not to mention the Passion Cycle and the long-standing fascination with time's circularity and spirals, which was an established element of sacred ritual and art long before Dante and Giotto were born. I'd guess Giotto was more specifically inspired by the statuary he saw in Rome, and panel after panel of monumental friezes encircling the facades of temples and churches, the columns of carved figures stacked on top of each other."

"I get it," I said. "Giotto didn't—but did anyone steal Dante?"

"It's a catchy title," Margaret said.

"Actually, it's a suitcase full of bibliographic references, annotated manuscript pages, and handwritten notes I have been dragging around the world. Would any of it ever be of any use to you?"

"I won't be teaching next year," she said, and before I could ask, she added, "a sort of sabbatical. I'm supposed to be writing, but I really would like to do something more . . . more—"

I said, "Collaborative? Rewarding? Lucrative?" I stopped when I realized I was cataloging everything writing hadn't been for Mitchell.

"Fun," Margaret said. "I'd like to have some more fun. Not very original of me."

"Originality is overrated," I said.

She said, "I'm sorry to say I just didn't understand your husband's thesis—why, say, Rodin should be accused of stealing when he clearly intended to pay homage to Dante."

"Like Blake," I said.

She nodded.

I said, "We're on the same page."

She said, "You brought the manuscript to Italy?"

"More cryptic scribbling than manuscript," I said, "but I do have a suitcase full of something that I seem unable to give away."

Margaret said, "You could scan it all and copy it to one of those little memory sticks. It would be easier to get through customs. Or you could float it out on the Web."

It was a logical solution to my problem, which simply proved that my problem wasn't logical. I said, "Memory sticks." Digitizing Mitchell's overwrought pages and consigning the book to the ethers felt like burning down the chapel.

"Maybe I can do something with it," she said.

I said, "What would you do with it?"

She didn't say anything.

I didn't say anything.

She said, "Is it easily portable?"

I said, "The suitcase has wheels."

She pulled a sheet from the pile of Lisa's notes and wrote her name quickly on the back. "I'm staying at the Hotel Arena, Room 104," she said, handing me the slip of paper. "Leave it at the desk for me before Sunday." She pointed to the guard outside, and a waiting crowd lined up behind him. The doors slid open.

Just before we left, I saw the pile of Lisa's lecture notes, minus one page, stacked up on the table next to the video monitor. Margaret never looked back. This didn't bode well for the Dante book. As we slid past the crowd lining the path to the visitor center, she said, "Do you need any help getting to your next session?"

From behind, I could see another odd bump where a lot of hair had gotten stuck above the black elastic band of a wig. I said, "I'll find my way. Are you okay?" We had reached a patch of empty benches.

"I'm headed to the Church of the Eremitani for a panel about— oh." She smiled sadly. She raised a hand to her head and patted around. She eventually identified both problem areas.

I said, "There is one of those hand-blowers in the ladies' room. I think you can get your wig back into shape if you just give it a good shake under there."

She said, "Vanity, your name is woman."

I said, "Actually, my name is Elizabeth."

Margaret smiled.

I teared up.

So did Margaret.

I didn't say *cancer*, and neither did she, as if the word would stick to her like a label, turn her into an anonymous victim, a lifeless portrait of that deadly sin.

She said, "Don't you cry. That won't help."

I said, "What will?"

She didn't say anything.

I said, "What you don't need is a suitcase full of my woes."

Margaret pulled her wig down above both ears, making matters worse, but she was smiling. "Oh, just give it to me. Please. Everybody's been doing everything for me for the last year. Give me a chance to do something for somebody else for a change. It'll be fun." She checked her watch.

I checked Mitchell's watch.

She said, "I guess we both have somewhere else to be."

I nodded as she backed away, and I waved when she turned and headed quickly down the path, momentarily haloed by sunlight.

I had time enough before my final session to retrieve my phone from the coat check and find some coffee. The visitor center was empty, and I did find a huge urn of hot coffee, but I opted for a little can of espresso floating in an ice-water bath and then two more, one for each pocket. I found an empty room and ignored the one email I had received—after I confirmed that it was not from T.—and clicked into my folder of saved mail. I found the email I had written to Sam and Rachel about the money they were to inherit. I didn't read it. I did down a second espresso, wondering what it would be like to be young and rich, but that was a different soap opera, so I hit send. I didn't want to hold on to that money any longer. I didn't want to hold on to Mitchell's affair, or his book, or the other disappointments that had become so disproportionately large in my imagination of my marriage that they made it impossible for me to move forward.

I was feeling virtuous, in general, and particularly charitable, but I did drink the third espresso, just in case it was the caffeine making me feel so good about myself. I turned in my phone, headed outside, and I saw Ed. He was passing the visitor center, walking quickly out toward the street. I called his name. He was with two other Roman collars and a squat woman with a deeply hennaed pageboy do. He didn't stop, so this time I yelled, "Ed! Ed!"

The woman stopped. She was wearing a blue-and-white-striped jersey and white capri pants. Ed turned and looked right at me. He said something to the woman.

I said, "Ed. It's me. E."

He looked befuddled. Both he and the woman inspected the faces of the people nearer them and behind me and waved tentatively, as if they didn't want to hurt the feelings of whoever had called out his name, as if there were not a woman in a block-print dress standing in the middle of the path fifty feet away holding her hand above her head like a signal flag, and then they rushed away to catch up with the other two priests.

I had some experience with being invisible—at cocktail parties where I had to be introduced to associates of Mitchell's for the fourth or fifth time; at public schools when I worked as a substitute, where teachers would come into the library for the second or third research lesson with their classes and ask if I was waiting for someone; at Sam's college graduation, where his roommate, who'd stayed at our home many times, passed me in the hallway of their dorm and asked if I knew somebody in the graduating class. It happened. And it got worse with age—a sort of dementia-by-proxy that inflicted people who got near me. But never with true friends. Which made me think maybe Ed didn't want to know me, didn't want me to approach him for some reason. Or else I was actually not there.

MY LAST SESSION WAS SCHEDULED TO BEGIN IN THE DEHU-midifier, so I didn't have to go far. I claimed an empty bench. My back was erupting in itches, and though I didn't blame Ed directly, I did think of him every time I bore down and scratched, which I did often enough to keep the gathering crowd at bay, even after four and some-times five people had shoved their way onto the other green benches. No one came anywhere near me, and when we moved inside and I attempted to claim a seat in the middle of the last row, everyone shifted toward the middle, away from me, clearing the aisle seat for me, as if I were contagious.

At the front of the room, a young black man in a blue blazer, white shirt, and jeans was paging through his notes. I'd already learned from bits of gossip and speculation being traded around me that his name was Andre Williams, he was on his way to a tenured position at Stanford next year, and his topic for today—*Sacred Animation: How Giotto Made Space for Humanity in the Arena Chapel*—was based on a book that was coming out in the fall.

"Brave you," he began. "I didn't think anyone would be crazy enough to sign up for three days of me." He beamed a big smile around the room.

I fished out the CPOCH schedule. *NB: Registration requires attendance on three consecutive days. Registrants for this special series will not be allowed to attend alternative seminars. Enrollment is limited, and Professor Williams will not be able to accommodate newcomers for the Friday or Saturday session. Therefore, please do not reserve a place for this series if you are unable to take full advantage of this opportunity.* Every seat in the room was filled. I couldn't think of any place I'd gone three days in a row without the promise of a paycheck since high school.

"I thank all of you for turning up today. I beg your pardon for not giving each of you a chance to introduce yourself, but I trust you will nevertheless feel free to shout out questions when you're confused, or when you sense I am, but we do have a lot of ground to cover, and I reckon if I don't start in soon I'm going to miss my flight to California in August." This raised laughter and applause, which he spoke right over. "And after five years at a university in northernmost North America, I am ready to chuck my snowshoes, so I will begin after I ask you—not now, but when we move into the chapel—to please reach under your chairs, where you will find a packet of illustrations and some little notes I hope you will find helpful as supplementary reading, and here we go."

He asked us to imagine the front of the chapel, its center cut away to form the chancel arch, the entrance to the sanctuary. He started at the top of that wall, ignoring the controversial wooden panel when he asked us to think of God the Father, sitting in heaven, sending an angel out on a mission, "the start of the story of the birth of Our Lord and Savior," he said. On either side of that open arch, he reminded us, below the heavens, were two framed frescoes of kneeling figures—the angel Gabriel, on the left of the open arch, and the Virgin, on the right, "enacting the Annunciation of the birth of the christ, conquering space, the divide between heaven and earth, with the word of God."

I knew he meant all of this as a tribute to the power of art, but I thought God was getting more credit than Giotto so far.

A woman said, "Is there a reproduction in the packet we could use as you describe the pictures?"

Andre said, "There is no accurate reproduction of these frescoes. Which is why we are here and not staring at the screens of our laptops. I'm not asking you to recall the frescoes themselves. We will soon go inside to enjoy them. I'm asking you right now to imagine space." He then instructed us to skip right past the pair of framed frescoes at the next level down—Judas betraying Jesus on the left, and Elizabeth visiting Mary on the right—"which are part of the larger sequential story that spirals around the chapel, which we will take up soon enough," he promised. "At the next level down, at about the height of a choir in an ordinary church, is a pair of fictive chapels of uncommon interest to—"

A man near me yelled, "Fictive?"

A man near the front turned and yelled, "Fictional."

A woman said, "Trompe l'oeil."

As if this were an auction, another woman put in a bid. "Made to deceive the eye. It's a trick-of-perspective painting."

"Not a trick," Andre said. "It is perspective painting. Indeed, it is two perspective paintings made more than a century before the Renaissance painters worked out the proportions that made it possible to do with a mathematical formula what Giotto did with his inspired gaze and his bare hands. We see into those two chapels as we see into the sanctuary and altar through the open space of the chancel arch. But when we look into those fictive chapels, we are seeing through a painted wall. We are creating space where there is none. And what do we see but windows on the back walls of those chapels, and the blueness beyond, and once we register that blue as sky, we accept the actuality of that window and we acknowledge the transparency of that painted window glass, as well as the depth of space in the chapels that contain those windows, and our eyes repeatedly tell our brains that the sky is beyond those windows, and in that moment there is no distinction between the real and the fictive sky, no observable boundary between us and the painted figures, and so we enter the fullness of time, we participate in the creation of sacred space in which there is no separation of the human and the divine, the then and now, the here and hereafter."

A woman said, "This is brilliant."

Another woman said, "I'm applying to Stanford."

"So, you see, it is not a trick," Andre said. "Those chapels are miraculous. They really are. You see the hand of a genius in them, but you also see the hand of God."

A woman a few rows ahead of me said, "What about those of us who don't believe in God?"

A man yelled, "Go to Disney World."

I sat up straight, hoping to show my allegiance to the other atheist in the room, but the tall men around me deflected my effort.

The woman said, "But I'm here, not at Disney World."

Andre said, "Exactly," as if maybe it was the hand of God and not a $5,000 check that had reserved her a place among us. This generated a hum of approval.

I wondered if Giotto hadn't painted those two chapels as a gift to his benefactor, something no one else in Padua would have, a bravura flourish sure to make the monks next door mad, compensation for the bell tower and the transept with two chapels Enrico Scrovegni was not allowed to build.

"What does it mean to you if I hold my hands like this?" Andre raised his long, thin arms and extended them toward us, the palms of his hands turned up.

A man said, "Welcome."

A woman said, "I need a hug."

Andre said, "And if I do this?" He turned to the side, bent his extended arm, and held the back of his cupped hand to us.

A man said, "Follow me."

A woman said, "Come with me."

Another woman said, "Don't be afraid."

Andre bent one knee so his hip jutted toward us, lowered his arm to a forty-five-degree angle from his waist, and held up the palm of his hand, as if he was signaling someone to stop. "And this?"

A man said, "Keep your distance."

"Don't hurt me," a woman said.

"Stay away," another woman said.

Andre said, "*Noli mi tangere*." He didn't move. He didn't say anything. I couldn't translate the words precisely, but I knew what they meant. T. had struck that very pose when we parted. "*Noli mi tangere*. Do not touch me. In Giotto's rendering of the scene, which is where we will begin our time in the chapel this afternoon, Jesus adopts this pose I have adopted. He is dressed in a white robe. He stands at the far right of the frame. He is alone, in an entirely uninhabited space. At the far left, below a sloping run of hills, two angels sit on the wall of his tomb, also robed in white. These are not the little *putti* who zip and zoom like comets through the skies above the other frescoes, expressing their delight at the Nativity, their anguish at the Crucifixion—"

"I read that Giotto saw Halley's Comet." The woman stood, and then she raised her hand, as if she had not already spoken. She was two rows ahead of me, wearing a handsome ivory blazer. She was tall, and she had shoulder-length auburn hair. "I read that he used it as his inspiration for the Star of Bethlehem. Which makes me wonder if he was implying that there was a rational explanation for the wonders his contemporaries attributed to the hand of God. Which would explain his affixing comet tails on those little angels, maybe."

She was the atheist. From behind, she was plausible friend material. I was shuffling in my chair, hoping she might turn around.

Andre said, "Halley's Comet did appear in 1301, and we have Italian records of the event. Not in Giotto's hand, but it is not unlikely he knew of the observations and studied the scientific renderings. But Giotto was not a secular humanist, I'm afraid. What you want to see as a repudiation of the Scripture is interpreted by scholars and art historians as attribution—Giotto linking observable phenomena to the details recorded in the Gospels. Unlike you, Giotto did not consider science a counterargument to the divine story unfolded in Genesis."

I thought he was laying it on pretty thick, even for the holy rollers in the crowd, but a man did say, "Amen." I could have stood and asked Andre about the Palace of Reason that burned down, and how he accounted for Giotto's secular version of the heavens, but the atheist was still standing, and I was hoping she might have a few more unpleasant things to say.

Andre said, "For now, let's say it was in the air, and when we are in the chapel, we can decide for ourselves whether that is a comet or a star above the manger—or both. We have a few more ideas to discuss before we move inside."

The standing woman didn't take the hint. "I guess I do just take a more humanist approach to the paintings."

"Now, you are simply talking about yourself, not Giotto," Andre said. "Your approach will alter your perspective, but it won't alter what is on the walls."

Among the murmured approval for this rebuke, I heard one man say, "Good for him."

The woman didn't say anything. She didn't move. I thought she might try to leave the room, but she just stood there.

Andre said, "The angels seated on the wall of the tomb in Giotto's *Noli Mi Tangere* are not comet-tailed *putti*. They are angels of a higher order." He stopped and smiled patronizingly.

Everyone turned to the secular humanist, willing her to sit down and stay down.

Andre raised and lowered his hand slowly.

The woman obeyed, grasping for the back of her chair to steady herself. As she turned to sit, she saw me.

Rosalie Ellenbogen recognized me, and I recognized her.

We were both wearing blue-and-white badges over our hearts, as if we were members of the same club. But unlike Rosalie, I did not belong. She was supposed to be here, Mitchell was not supposed to be dead, and I was supposed to be in Florence. When she sat down, Rosalie straightened her back and flexed her shoulders back, accentuating her greater stature. After that, neither of us moved.

Either Mitchell's dying wish had been a three-day reunion with Rosalie, or I had yet to inflate the affair to its proper proportions, which I quickly calculated to be the better part of the last six years. I instantly regretted the silly, simpering, sympathetic email about their loving father that I had just launched across the Atlantic to my children, along with a reputation-burnishing bonus from Mr. Moneybags.

I regretted every day of the last six years. I wanted a lot back that I would never get back.

Andre said, "Below the angels sleeps a small band of soldiers, unaware that the stone covering the entrance to the tomb has been rolled back and Jesus has risen from the dead. To the right of them, on her knees, Mary Magdalene extends her arms across the empty space toward Jesus. She recognizes him. She is the first living person who recognizes the resurrected Christ. But even she cannot believe her eyes—she has fallen to her knees in shock—yet she reaches for him, to touch him, to make her vision real." Andre paused for several seconds. "*Noli Mi Tangere.* This is the first time in the entire fresco cycle where we see Jesus in an independent space."

The space between Rosalie and me was unsteady, or maybe I was dizzy from my efforts to read her mind.

"We will examine the use of space, as well as color and gesture, in every other scene from the life of Jesus to understand how Giotto anchored Jesus in the human realm, repeatedly locating him in the midst of crowds where he is swaddled and cuddled, embraced, kissed, anointed, baptized, and later pinched, beaten, and slapped by human hands. After the resurrection, though, no human hand can reach him. He is there and not there, with them and beyond them, Jesus and Christ." Andre picked up a pile of paper from beside the video monitor.

I looked at Mitchell's watch. We had at least ten more minutes in this room, plenty of time for me to plan and execute a brutal surprise attack.

Rosalie bent forward, balanced her elbows on her thighs, cradling her head in her hands. She looked ill.

I said a quick prayer on her behalf. *Let it be a stroke.*

Andre said, "Now, if you will permit me to move from the sublime to the ridiculous, I have a little cartoon for you."

A man said, "What is a cartoon?"

Another man said, "Beetle Bailey."

A woman said, "Charlie Brown."

The original man said, "Everybody's a comedian."

"It's a term of art for preliminary drawings," Andre said. "Giotto drew cartoons—*sinopie*—of the entire cycle and its fictive borders and architecture before the final surface for the fresco was applied so his patron could review and approve the work."

I could hear my own rapid intake of air, little gasps, and so could two of the men in front of me, who repeatedly turned around to register their disapproval for my insistence on breathing.

"Giotto would have made these cartoons—perfectly delineated and proportioned figures and landscapes—in red ocher, which would be visible when the final layer of fine white plaster—the *intonaco*—was applied to the wall, so it could be seen beneath as the final fresco was painted. I am not an artist, however, and I made you a little stick-figure cartoon." He handed out two piles for distribution. "I want to use this to prepare you for the other scene we will concentrate on this afternoon, which gives us a clear and simple introduction to the use of color, shape, and geometry in the fresco cycle, and a charming illustration of Giotto's use of space."

"Oh, man." One of the men in the front held up the page he'd received and said, "Don't quit your day job." Laughter spread my way as the pages were passed back.

And just like that, I welled up, tears streaming down my face. At last, my true companion was at hand.

I could fill in the lines, flesh out those people. I knew them well. I recognized every detail except the angel, which I was certain did not appear in the panel painting of this scene, which I had memorized during my many hours on my own in the Gardner Museum while Mitchell pined and pondered over one of Mrs. Gardner's exquisite editions of Dante.

I was here, and I was there. But I wanted to be there and there

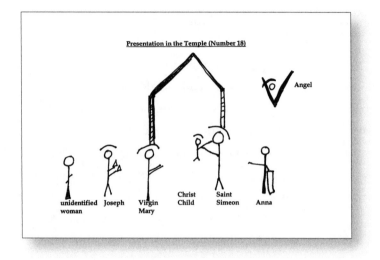

alone, there in the museum before I knew what it meant to be here. I also wanted the hand of God to reach down through the ceiling and pluck me out of that airless chamber. Short of that miraculous intervention, I did not want to enter the chapel. I didn't want to see the fresco of the Presentation—not with Rosalie, not with Andre and his admirers, not while I was wearing Mitchell's watch.

Andre said, "This is an especially stately painting, with its six human figures aligned in the foreground. Their colorful robes, as you will soon see, bestow on each figure a singularity, a distinct habitable space, and yet the generous folds of those robes overlap, overcoming the space between them, uniting them in spirit. You will see that Giotto painted Jesus as an extraordinarily charming and slightly confounded child, a kid we instantly recognize as a kid. He and Simeon are raised slightly above the others, a status that is here ceremonial and yet also befitting the divine nature of that sweet child."

He took a pious pause—he even bowed his head slightly—which seemed designed to give everyone a chance to contemplate the wonders of the Incarnation and the humility of this shining star of academe. I didn't doubt his sincerity, but I did wonder if he saw himself reflected in the painted image of Scrovegni, hoisting up the chapel in exchange for a big reward.

"Now, look again at the fullness of time in this image, how Giotto balances the past and future in this moment," Andre said. "At the far right, Anna, who prophesied the arrival of the Messiah at the temple, is present, holding the scroll of her prophecy. Above her, the Angel of Death is present to confirm that Simeon's death is imminent, fulfilling the promise of the Holy Spirit to the just and devout Simeon—that he would not die before he met the Messiah. Each figure, in one sense, represents the fulfillment of prophesy, and thus their hands are extended toward each other and toward the child at the center of the frame, the center of all promise, the incarnation of the prophetic word. The Virgin reaches for her son, and at her side, her husband Joseph holds two doves, two earthly creatures that also live in the sky, a kind of mirror of the angel and the Christ child, creatures of this world and not. The woman at the far left of the panel provides symmetry in number, and balance in gender—three human figures on each side of the picture plane, three male and three female."

A woman said, "Who is she?"

Andre said, "We don't know."

A man said, "She looks like a servant."

But she didn't.

Andre said, "She is dressed in a very remarkable robe for a servant."

Andre was right. Shelby was clearly a companion to the mother of the Virgin Mary, and her peasant dress marked her as a servant. This pink-robed woman was no one's attendant.

The same man said, "I meant a handmaiden, attending to Mary and her child."

Andre said, "You will see that both St. Anne and the Virgin often appear with handmaidens in the frescoes, but this is clearly not either of those women."

I was already so deeply identified with that woman with no identity that I nearly stood up and announced that I knew her name.

A woman said, "She is not the first woman in history to be treated as if she is insignificant."

"She is not insignificant. She is unidentified," Andre said. "Indeed, Ruskin pointed out how beautifully she is drawn, how elegantly her gown is draped and colored. She has an honored place here in the chapel."

A very elderly woman said, "I'm sure she was happy just to be there."

It wasn't clear whether that woman was being cynical or sincere, siding with the feminists or with Andre, but most of the women and men in the room nodded their assent. Andre had the wit to let that inscrutable verdict stand, and then the doors behind him slid open and a guard said something rather complicated in Italian before he returned to the hallway behind the doors, where he was hurrying a small group out of the chapel.

Andre said, "There has been a mechanical failure, and the humidity in the chapel has reached a critical level, so I must ask you to reach under your chairs, collect your handouts, and follow me outside."

A woman said, "Is there a fire?"

A man said, "Nothing works in this country."

I didn't move until the room was almost empty. I didn't see the hand of God, but this emergency evacuation was an answer to my prayer. I would see the Presentation fresco in my own way, on my own time.

When I finally made it to the edge of the crowd gathered by the benches, Rosalie had disappeared. Andre emerged from the chapel with two men in suits, whispering furiously, and his arrival cleared the benches, so I sat down and scratched. Over the rumbling and grumbling of the paying customers, Andre said that the guard had informed him that air-quality issues were typically resolved in a few hours, and he assured us that the CPOCH staff had already agreed to give our group additional time in the chapel on Friday.

I had seen enough. I was itchy everywhere, but I decided to wait till I got back to my room and lined up the best of the minibar on the bedside table before I scratched out my eyes.

TWO HOURS LATER, I RAISED MY HAND AND WAVED UNTIL one of the young white-shirted men weaving through the tables in the Piazza del Something with a tray in his hand nodded. Like Giotto, I was getting good at the language of gestures. I pointed to my empty glass, and about fifteen minutes later, the waiter swooped by with my third Aperol spritz and a fresh bowl of kale crackers. I was sitting at the outer edge of his territory, where I could see the yellow awning on the other side of the crowded piazza. Despite the steady parade of thirsty Paduans shopping for an open cocktail table on their way home from work, I occasionally spotted Matteo's gleaming head under that awning as he nodded at potential customers, whom he greeted as old friends, most of whom he had surely never seen before—business as usual.

After a few cool slips, I was near enough to being drunk that it was no longer an effort not to think, so I read the new email from Rachel.

Dearest World Traveler—

I wanted you to be the first to know: I accepted an offer today. Am feeling dizzy (champagne in the boardroom, and again with David's parents). Maybe I was drunk when I agreed to spend at least one day a week here (and weekends) till I begin, and which I am sure to regret, but the kids will stay at the lake for the summer (happily), and David (sweetly) agreed to collect a bunch of stuff they can't live without (videogames) and drive it all up in that truck. He is either going to give the food truck a try at the lake this summer (his idea) or (my suggestion) park it in the South Bronx so it is stolen and we can collect on the insurance.

Daddy's gift. What can I say? (The money will come in handy. The boys have decided they want to live at the top of the Empire State Building.) I miss him beyond words. How did he do it on an academic salary? A scholar and a gentleman, that man. I know you must be missing him like mad over there, but I hope you are allowing yourself to have the fun he so wanted you to have. He'd have a ball reviewing the details of my offer, not to mention the reaction from my old boss in Cambridge. I'm rambling. This weekend is looking nutty, so call when you can or I will call you next week (in Rome, I think?) when I know where I am.

The little mess you made by leaking my job news to David—let's just forget it. I have. I forgive you.

Sending love from me and the boys your way.

This all went down rather easily with a couple of sips of the spritz. My second email was from Shelby. As I opened it, the henna-haired woman I'd seen with Ed outside the chapel tapped her knuckles on my table. She was even shorter and rounder than she'd looked at a distance, or else my perspective was less charitable after my last session at the chapel. She was still dressed like a sailor, but instead of Ed on her arm, she was wearing the handle of what looked like a little umbrella on wheels.

She said, "Marimekko."

I didn't say anything.

She said, "Vintage, yes?"

I said, "It's a relic." I knew she must be Caroline, Ed's sister, but she seemed so unlikely a wife for T. that I briefly wondered if maybe she was a nun on vacation. Either way, with that dye job, a veil would have come in handy.

"I saw you earlier today," she said, "or else there's a '70s revival in this town. I gave away dozens of dresses like yours, and curtains. Are you in the middle of a telephone call? I'm so relieved you're American. When we saw you earlier, I was going to tell you how much I liked your dress, but my brother said you might be Italian. I speak Spanish well enough. Or I used to. I am positively determined to learn some Italian while I'm here. I wish I'd learned more languages when I was young. It's meant to be easier for children for some reason, but I never found Spanish so easy in school. Latin—forget it. My brother knows enough Latin for both of us. He's a priest. Anyway, you finish your call." She didn't move.

"It's an email," I said. Now that I was certain she was T.'s ex-wife, I didn't know if I should run away or offer to buy her a drink.

"Go ahead and read it," she said. "I'd check my email, but I packed away my phone. Mine has a stylus, which is annoying. I should get one like yours. Read, read. I honestly don't mind."

I really thought she might wander away, so I opened Shelby's email. The subject was "Our Hero, Outside the Uffizi." There was no text, just a picture.

GIOTTO

I had never seen a likeness of Giotto before, and I didn't like what I saw.

Caroline said, "Is it bad news?"

I tried to relax my face into a casual smile. "Just a photograph of a statue in Florence." I held the screen her way.

"I'm going to Florence this evening," she said. "My name is Caroline, by the way."

I said, "To Florence with your brother?" I didn't give her my name. I knew I was inching into dangerous territory, digging around in T.'s past behind his back, but another sip of my drink sweetened the prospect of getting even with someone. "Have you ever been to Florence? Wouldn't you like to sit down and join me for a drink?" I swiped Rachel's bag from the chair beside me.

"I can't stay. I have a train to catch," she said. She lifted up the cane of her umbrella with both hands and shook it several times. Finally, it opened into a little stool—a tripod topped off by a white plastic disk. "Voilà! A chair for the lady," she said, though she didn't sit down. "Ingenious golf fans invented this thing because there are no bleachers near the greens." She slurred a few words, as if she had a slight lisp or a toothache. "It's a godsend in museums if you can convince the guards you have a disability." She turned the stool in a circle and nodded her approval. "Truth? I've never loved, loved, loved paintings, which seems to be about the best explanation for my daughter suddenly announcing she wanted to be a painter. I was a nurse a hundred years ago, and her father is a doctor. Could be she just wanted to prove that she had nothing in common with either of us."

I said, "Children are mysterious," which was as bland a rejoinder as I could come up with on the spot.

"I don't think so," Caroline said fiercely. "Children, divorce, death—there are no mysteries involved with any of them, just secrets people keep from you, things they could have told you and didn't."

This sounded like earned wisdom, something I could usefully apply to Mitchell's attachment to Rosalie if I understood the distinction better and how to make it stick. But I knew I had already gone too far with Caroline, and something about that crazy stool made me want to protect her, protect her from me, stop her before she went too far, before she said something she would only want to have said to a total stranger. "Since you wouldn't let me buy you a drink, please at least take my seat and enjoy your last hour in Padua. I have to be somewhere else."

Caroline said, "Is your name really Mitchell? If you don't mind my asking."

I looked down at my name tag. My cover was blown, even if Caroline didn't know it yet. "I ended up with my husband's badge," I said. "Long story."

"All marriages are," Caroline said. She was about to say something else when a phone rang—an old-fashioned ringing-bell tone— somewhere nearby. "That's my daughter's phone," she said, slapping her thighs. Finally, she pulled a white iPhone out of the pocket of her pants. She read something on the screen. "An Italian boy who calls every day," she said. "He listens to Lily's voicemail message and hangs up. Some of her old friends from back home leave sweet little good-byes, but most of the Italian ones just don't seem to know where she is or why she isn't returning their calls. That's the way Lily wanted it. Keep it secret. Keep them guessing." She pocketed the phone, and then she collapsed her portable stool and leaned on the cane end with both hands, surveying the crowd around us. Maybe it was the phone call, or maybe a pill she'd taken earlier had just kicked in, but she looked entirely at ease, becalmed, and, judging by the glances she was getting from passersby, a little loopy. "We'll both miss our trains," she said wistfully. She was fading, and she seemed pleased to be sinking beneath the surface of herself.

I said, "Good luck in Florence, Caroline."

She said, "Yes, you too," and started rolling in the general direction of the train station. I stood up to see how she was faring against the incoming tide of table-seekers. She was not looking steadier as she went, and I felt I owed it to Ed or T. to make sure she got to the train station. But as I pulled some cash out of Rachel's bag to pay for my drinks, I saw Ed rush out from under the yellow awning and angle his way through the crowd to his sister's side. He put his arm around her shoulder, and they veered off to the left, up an alley and out of sight. Maybe Caroline and Ed were supposed to meet up at Matteo's pizzeria, or maybe she had left him there when she spotted my dress again. Either way, Ed had to have seen me, and he hadn't wanted me to see him.

One more mystery, or one more secret, depending on your perspective.

I forwarded Shelby's picture of Giotto to Rachel and Sam without any comment. By the time I was back in my hotel room, I had a reply from Rachel.

> *As my boys would say—OMG.*
> *As Nana B. would say—that statue of Giotto*
> *looks more like Daddy than Daddy did.*

III

✳

I must have fallen asleep soon after I read Rachel's email. I didn't remember waking in the middle of the night, but when I rolled over in my bed at eight o'clock on Friday morning, I saw my dress puddled on the carpet, and my bra was on the bedside table, so I had to have sat up for long enough to pull them off. I hadn't pulled the curtains closed. Whoever had been out there on the balcony had seen more of me than even I considered essential viewing most mornings, and he had also shoved the desk chair back toward my end of the balcony and balanced a tall glass of latte macchiato on the seat, with a saucer on top to keep it warm. And he had left a note on Arena Hotel stationery beneath the glass: Metro @ 10.

This raised a number of questions, beginning with why T. was still in Padua, and why I was still there, and it also brought to a boil the simmering issue of his exchanges with Mitchell and why that history had been kept secret from me. But as I drank the cool coffee he'd delivered earlier, I mostly wondered exactly how much of me T. had seen from the balcony. When I went back out there in a bathrobe, I was encouraged by the distorting glare of the morning sun glinting off the glass doors until I realized I was able to read the green numerals on the clock radio beside the bed, which probably meant T. had enjoyed a clear view of all of my digits and dials.

In my prior life, this sort of exposure might have been reason enough not to show my face at the Metro, but I realized that the decent pastries at the hotel buffet would be long gone by the time I got dressed, and I was hungry. I finished my coffee and took all of my many questions for T. into the shower, where they were almost immediately washed away in a stream of blood that ran down the back of my legs and turned the water around my feet pink as it swirled down the drain. I got out and examined my back in the mirror. It was a little bumpier than normal from all of my scratching, but there were no gashes or scars. I did lather up with facial scrub back there, just to be sure, and after I dried off, I dug through my arsenal of unguents and applied a film of antibacterial salve and some moisturizer.

My three linen shirtdresses were hanging in my closet. This little surprise was bittersweet. I could spare T. the sight of me in stretchy jeans, but the return of my dry cleaning also meant I could pack up and leave at any moment. I had been cleared for takeoff.

My shoulders and back were still slick with moisturizer, so rather than risking damage to one of the shirtdresses, I convinced myself I could squeeze one more day out of the Marimekko, which I spread out on the bed and ironed with my hands. This worked reasonably well on the front, but when I turned it over I saw that the block print on the back was bisected by three thin streaks of my blood. It looked exactly like T.'s bloodied pinstripe shirt, which either meant we were both dying and didn't know it, or we were both saints who'd been selected for stigmata. Or T. had picked up some dread disease while he was out catting around at night and kindly passed it on to me.

I stuffed the dress into Rachel's bag and pulled on the navy blue shirtdress, which seemed least likely to show any leaks. The whole time,

I just kept telling myself, *He's a doctor, he's a doctor,* which somehow made sense of my bringing the bloody dress along for his inspection. As I left the room, my phone dinged. While I waited for the elevator, I read another email from Anandi.

Forgive me even as I begin, dearest friend, to intrude a second time on the peace and (so I hope on your behalf) joy of Italy. The truck did disappear, and as I said to Samir, is it not enough that she has managed to move vehicles around the East Coast of America while she is away? But Samir insists he saw a man in your house last night, and when Samir went across the street a second time and rang the front bell, a light upstairs did flick off. I don't want to call the police if you have a guest or a workman in there, but I did see a bald man enter and leave carrying something in a box just before midnight. I did not report this to Samir, who will be, gracious gods, going to the office today, so I will not have to act until this evening, at the earliest. I have been awake most of the night, not exactly on patrol but kept alert by the raging, roaring snarls of Samir's snoring. I have not seen the bald man again. There is a remedy for the snoring man upstairs—tomorrow, I will make rosewater. But the bald man across the street is why I have bothered to bother you. Perhaps you will waste a moment to assure me that no remedy is required?

I was exhausted by the time I got to the lobby. The only bald man I knew was Samir, and though I doubted he was robbing my house, I knew he was insulted I'd not left him a key, and I didn't doubt he was planning to spend his free time making me pay for that lapse in judgment. Rachel and Sam had keys, but Sam hadn't responded to my last two emails, and Rachel would not be sympathetic to my plight. She had urged me to have an alarm system installed after Mitchell died, and when it became clear I was not going to obey, she resorted to deception and purchased two signs warning burglars that they were entering an electronically protected property, and instead of sticking them in the lawn, I'd stuck them in the garage.

Someone should have arrested Samir, whose obnoxious snoring was audible well beyond his property lines every spring. Years ago, I'd tried to sell Anandi on my theory of sleep apnea, and I'd even downloaded a picture of a fantastically elaborate gas mask that was meant to cure the disease. Anandi said she thought his problem was allergies. I didn't really think it was either—I considered the snoring classic male territorial behavior.

Another woman might have left Samir. I liked the idea of stuffing his head into a big muzzle every night. Anandi made rosewater every year when her backyard came into bloom, put it in a dehumidifier, and the snoring stopped.

When I made it to the Metro, the bar was empty, and T. was standing near a table at the dark end, staring through the glass wall at Paduans passing into the arcaded path to the piazza. He was as crisp and blue as ever, and as I approached him, a young waiter delivered two espressos, two latte macchiatos, two bottles of fizzy water, and a heaping plate of *cornetti*.

T. orchestrated all of our encounters in advance. It was a charming habit. It made me feel he had been bearing me in mind. But this morning, the setup had a cartoon quality—not Beetle Bailey, more in the manner of Giotto, as if T. had already sketched the scene he imagined we would play out when he wrote that note and left it on the balcony. What actually happened at that little table would surprise us both—that was the art of him—but our scenes never exceeded the frames he had established, the vast stretches of life that passed between our meetings went unaccounted for in our conversation, and by his design our deep and complicated pasts never intruded into our time together, which stood apart from everything and everyone else, the memorable adventures of T. and E., a series of incidents involving two strangers, which resembled a story of intimates if you strung them together in sequence and filled in the blanks with a fictive architecture that appeared strong enough to support a genuine relationship.

After we sat, I sampled a *cornetto* filled with something that involved mascarpone and lemon, and then added two plain brioches to my little plate.

T. said, "I have a proposal."

I said, "I hope you have a pot of jam under that pile of pastries."

He dug around and found two little ramekins—strawberry jam and orange marmalade.

I slathered some of each on my plate for dipping. "Some bald man is carrying boxes full of something out of my house in Cambridge," I said.

"A curious juxtaposition," T. said. He scooped some foam out of his macchiato with a spoon. "The boxes mark him as benign, but the baldness seems sinister."

I said, "I really don't know if I should call the police or send the guy a thank-you note. There's so much in that house, so much I don't want."

T. said, "People sell houses."

I said, "Those people end up buying another house."

"Not all of us," he said. He scooped up some more foam.

I drank most of my espresso. Suddenly, we were both not talking about Lily, who hanged herself in her father's home. I wanted to tell him how sorry I was his daughter was dead. I wanted to tell T. he should join Ed and Caroline in Florence. I wanted to tell him I was going home to Cambridge. I also wanted him to know I knew about his secret conversations with Mitchell, with whom he had apparently never run out of things to say. Instead, for no reason at all, I said, "I met Caroline yesterday."

T. said, "Was she with Ed?"

This was not a gratifying response, which surely proved I had been aiming to unsettle him. I tried again. "He was with her the first time I saw her. I waved to them, and Ed acted as if he didn't recognize me."

"Maybe he didn't," T said. "Everybody thinks you're in Cambridge."

"Not everybody. People in Cambridge think I'm in Florence," I said defensively, as if my efforts to maintain two entirely separate lies ought to register in my favor. "Ed didn't want to see me."

"There's a lot Ed doesn't want to see," T. said. "He doesn't want to see what's become of his sister in the last twenty years. He doesn't want to see that no matter how often he conspires to bring us together, Caroline and I will never regret our terrific three years of marriage or our divorce."

I said, "You and Caroline were only married for three years?"

"Seven," T. said.

I nodded and finished my espresso—and two tiny *cornetti* filled with syrupy hazelnuts. "I still don't see why he wouldn't want to see me. But I think you do. After that lecture he gave—"

"That crazy lecture." T. lit up and took a big swig of his macchiato. "He wanted to impress you, I think."

I said, "Ed only has eyes for you." I hadn't ever formulated the thought so succinctly, but it seemed absolutely true. Ed was in love with T. This made Ed seem hapless and hopeless, which made him familiar, which almost made me like Ed again.

"After that lecture, instead of being mad at himself for making a mockery of his own amazing scholarship, he got blasting mad at me for compromising his immortal soul." T. paused to poke around in the pastry pile, and while he dithered I found it increasingly difficult to restrain myself from making a selection for him and shoving it into his mouth so he could get back to Ed, whom he'd left dangling between heaven and hell. Finally, T. chose a plain brioche, dipped it into my stash of marmalade, and ate it in one bite. And then, nothing.

"Meanwhile," I said. Still nothing. I took a swig of fizzy water. I said, "Does the story of Ed's immortal soul only come in weekly installments?"

T. said, "When I told Ed I was bringing you along to his lecture, he asked me a question about you, and I inadvertently revealed something I had meant never to tell anyone. And I exacted from him a promise never to let on that he knew. And he decided I had got him tangled up in a terrible lie, and that may explain why he didn't want to see you yesterday, or why he couldn't let himself see you."

I said, "Mitchell."

T. and I turned away from each other for a few seconds, as if the name were a comet shooting through the arcade.

I said, "Simon Allerby called me a couple of days ago, trying to track you down, and he mentioned that Mitchell had prevailed upon you to be kind to me. Which you have been."

T. didn't say anything.

"You made good on your gentleman's agreement," I said. "Well done." I was surprised by the force of my anger. I said, "Ed was right, of course. You should have told me."

T. said, "Really, E., he wasn't right."

I said, "I'm just trying to decide whether I want to know what Mitchell said about me, what he warned you about, how he described me so you could pick me out of a crowd." Whatever had erupted on my back in yesterday's heat was now roiling away in my gut, a toxic stew I wanted to expel. "I've been through most of Mitchell's correspondence, even his Harvard email, and your name never came up. Four months you were on the phone with him?" I couldn't control the volume of my voice, so I just let it go all the way up. "Did he take your calls in the bathroom?"

T. said, "Let's take a walk."

"You already took me for a walk," I said. "Your work is done here."

"Neither of us seems to know when to quit," T. said. "I had two telephone conversations with Mitchell, both initiated by him, and he wrote me three emails, one of which I responded to. The others I ignored. I'm sure I can dig them up for you." He downed his espresso and didn't say anything else, as if we'd have to wait until we were in front of his computer to continue the conversation.

I said, "We're here now." Admittedly, a very T.-ish thing to say.

"That's been hard to prove most days," he said. He repositioned our water bottles several times and finally left them standing next to each other very near the edge of the table. Significant? I'd already assigned those precariously perched bottles any number of identities— T. and I, T. and Ed., T. and Caroline, Mitchell and I, Ed and Caroline. T. said, "I had seen the workup on Mitchell's cancer in November, but I don't remember why my name came up again with Simon and Mitchell in December."

"This tour of Italy we're not taking," I said.

T. nodded. "That's it. And that's what Mitchell told Simon he wanted to talk to me about, though he really wanted to talk to me about Simon. Mitchell called me in December and again in late January, I think, or maybe it was early February. Both times, he slipped into paranoid fantasies about Simon and one of the male nurses in the office performing experiments on him, and I remember a recurring insinuation that Simon had forged the diplomas on his wall—none of it quite explicit, and none of it extraordinary. You give a man enough cancer cells and enough of the drugs Mitchell was absorbing, and his brain function gets a little unsteady and unpre-dictable. I did tell Simon he might want to dial down some of the dosages, and I think he did."

This made sense of what I had seen and heard at home. I also remembered waiting for the elevator after our first visit to Simon's office together, and Mitchell wondering aloud what kind of person would hang diplomas from a state school on the wall as a boast. Of course, this marked him as a pompous ass, not a paranoid madman. But I could see how such pomposity might have fueled a bout of real insanity, as it had in me. Mitchell's diplomas and citations were plastered on the walls of his home office, and mine were tucked into a box with Rachel and Sam's grade-school report cards. I didn't blame Mitchell for this. I could have hung my diplomas. But not hanging them separated me from normal graduates of not-famous colleges, a distinction both Mitchell and I understood as a sort of honorary summa cum laude. I said, "The emails?"

T. said, "The emails." He pulled a pastry from the plate and regarded it as if it might yield some wisdom. "They were fantasies. If he lived, where he wanted to have dinner in Padua, what kind of wine he'd want to be sure they stocked. One long passage I remember was devoted to his finally being able to complete the book he was writing about Dante."

I said, "And Rosalie?"

T. said, "Rosalie?" It sounded like a genuine question.

"Half-gay, redhead."

T. said nothing.

I said, "Beatrice?" I really thought Mitchell might have referred to Rosalie as his Beatrice. After all, he'd almost got the perfect ending to our romantic comedy. Before he got sick, he was planning to dump me, his ancient, blind guide through hell and purgatory, and waltz into Paradise with his beloved.

"Mitchell never mentioned a woman," T. said. For a few seconds he didn't say anything. "I didn't even know he had a wife." He wasn't looking at me. He was staring at the two little water bottles, which he pulled in a few inches from the edge.

I was still angry, but the righteousness was draining away, like paint fading from the scenes I had imagined, the story I'd invented in which Mitchell clumsily conspired with T. to orchestrate my time in Italy and make me feel at home when I was not. Instead, when Mitchell imagined Italy, I was not there. "He did have a wife," I said, but when I tried to come up with an image of myself in that house, a scene of Mitchell and me together that would anchor me in that marriage, I kept circling through a series of blank white walls, occasionally interrupted by the sight of that vast black TV that hid the hole Sam had made when he tried to make his father happy.

Maybe I hadn't been there—maybe that's why Mitchell couldn't see me, not since Paris, not since I'd first worn that black-and-white Marimekko dress that was crumpled up in Rachel's red bag, stained with my blood, the shroud I had put on when I first felt the life draining out of me, when I didn't object to Mitchell's betrayal of the life we had imagined for ourselves, when I let Mitchell trade our shared devotion to research for a bag of coins from Harvard's coffers. Maybe I had been dead long before I knew it.

T. said, "It was a month or more after Mitchell died that Simon called about something else and mentioned that he'd just had a great note from Mitchell's wife. Simon admired you."

I said, "Simon never actually spoke to me. He gave me orders. He considered me a serviceable nurse. Maybe Mitchell did, too." *She is not insignificant*, Andre had said. *She's unidentified.*

T. said, "It wasn't pity that drew me to you when I spotted you sitting at the back of that conference room, all alone. I wasn't trying to do you a favor. I had been drinking myself down all afternoon—"

"Gin and tonic and lemonade," I said. "The Perfect Marriage."

"You remember," he said.

I remembered every word the man had ever said.

"You were sitting there, but you weren't there, and that was the space I wanted to occupy," T. said. "I was poaching on your territory. I can't do what you do, E. I can't stop pretending I'm here. And it's exhausting."

"It's also exhausting pretending you're not here," I said. "I'm just warning you. It's very hard to remember everywhere I'm not every day."

"You're here now," he said. "With me, you're always here."

Instead of passing out with joy or leaning across the table and kissing him, like a normal person, I said, "Still, you should have told me—about Mitchell."

"I should have told the police that Lily was naked when I found her hanging from a beam above my dining room table." T. nodded. "I should have told them she had just taken a bath, which is why her hair was wet, not from sweat caused by the strain and stress on her upper body as they speculated." His gaze was fixed on mine. "When I found her, she had a towel wrapped around her bent head, and there was another damp white towel on the mahogany table. Probably, she had wrapped that second towel under her arms but the fold that was holding it above her breasts had come undone when the rope jerked tight around her neck. I should have told them. Right?" He wouldn't look away. "Lily took a bath, and then she hanged herself. I had to take the towel off her head to get her into the scrubs. She was naked, and I wanted her body to be at rest, not dangling above me, and most of all I wanted her covered. For most of her life, I wasn't there. That day, I was there," he said. He nodded. "I was her father," he said. He pulled the two water bottles apart, stood them at either side of his little white plate. "I didn't understand what the scrubs would signify when the story got out. She'd often worn my scrubs as pajamas. Significant? Lily was young and beautiful and talented and rather popular, and we were having a wonderful week together, and she took a bath and killed herself."

I said, "What's in Florence?"

T. said, "Nothing. Not Lily. Not the time I didn't spend with her. Not my house in Houston a few minutes before she got out of the bathtub. Just a house in the hills Lily shared with three young art students who are all still alive. Nothing. A big installation of blown-glass microorganisms she invented that no one seems to know how to disassemble without destroying. Surely, Ed or Caroline can make something poignant of that. I've made the whole city of Florence into something poignant, significant, the somewhere else I have to be, the one place I cannot go." His handsome, taut features had gone a little soft—the dark under his eyes sagging a bit, the skin of his cheek thickening at the sharp line of his jaw.

"Lily," I said, and I couldn't think of another word to say.

T. said, "Lily." He poured the dregs of his espresso into his macchiato and drank it down. "Now when you say her name, she's naked, right?"

I said, "She is."

T. didn't say anything.

I knew he thought this vindicated his covering for Mitchell, as well, but he was wrong. Every Virtue had another life as a Vice. Humility in one instance was Vanity in another. Ed could have told him that Chastity and Lust are twins.

A young waiter in a white shirt came to our table and raised his hands in surrender, uncertain whether we were done. T. nodded. The waiter pulled a tray from a stack near the windows and cleared everything away. T. and I watched him, as if something might happen that would mean something to us, about us. I tried to turn the two of us into statues of ourselves, an opposing pair, a Virtue and a Vice, but with the blurry reflection of the empty steel tabletop between us, we most resembled those two fictive chapels, plausible looking but uninhabitable, lifelike but forever separated by the chancel arch, the altar below us, the space between us where our lives had been lived.

The waiter returned and handed T. a cash-register receipt. I dove toward my red bag, as if buying him a coffee would even things out, but T. said, "I've taken care of it."

"Thank you," I said.

"You're welcome," he said.

It seemed like we would soon be standing, shaking hands, and going our separate ways, so I said, "I need your professional opinion." I pulled the Marimekko dress out of Rachel's bag.

T. said, "From here, I'd say the prognosis is not good."

"It's the stains on the back that I'm wondering about," I said. "And my back is sort of a mess."

T. said, "Hand it over." He expertly inverted it, as if he was used to dealing with women's garments, and he examined the stains on the inside of the back. He pulled the fabric very taut between his two hands and held it toward me. "Can you see the silver flecks in the blood lines? And what looks like lead or solder at the edge of each streak?"

The stains were shimmering.

"Cadmium, I think," he said, inverting the dress again and neatly folding it as he continued. "Definitely some formaldehyde. A good lab would probably find some benzene. You are likely allergic to all three elements. Thus the bleeding."

I said, "How do you know?"

T. said, "They're poisonous."

I said, "How did they get there?"

"Same way they got on my back," he said. "You were lonely."

"I don't understand," I said.

He handed me my dress, folded up as neatly as a flag. "Don't wear it again. Don't wash it. Get rid of it."

"It's a relic," I said.

"It's toxic," he said. "As are the rosary beads, medallions, and shiny, framed pictures of the Madonna della Misericordia that Matteo hands out to his mournful friends. Had I told you when you noticed the blood on my shirt, I could have spared your back. Forgive me. I was too embarrassed to tell you the truth. From the moment I put that rosary around my neck, I felt like a holy fool, and when I realized I'd done harm to myself, I took it as a sign."

I said, "A sign from God?"

"A sign from my body reminding me that I am allergic to religion," T said. "And a sign from my heart about how lonely I am."

In the space of a few minutes, we had acknowledged that we were both lonely, we were both fools, and we were both limber enough to reach around and scratch the skin off our own backs. By our peculiar standards, this was beginning to resemble a first date. I said, "Someone should tell Matteo he's killing off his friends with kindness."

"He claims I was the first to have a bad reaction. Which is unlikely, as he's been in the business of rosary beads for years. He employs a rotating cast of North Africans in his chapel. At night, they dip cheap souvenirs into vats of a silver shellacky goo, and then they distribute the stuff the next day, selling them to small shops and tourists on the streets of Venice and Padua."

"But their hands," I said.

"They wear gloves," T. said. "There are more immediate concerns."

"Their brains," I said. "And their lungs."

"Your loneliness," he said.

Instead of bursting into tears, I said, "We should contact the police." I was turning into Samir.

"Matteo employs two local cops as security guards for his chapel," T. said. "It's entirely legal. He's proud of the whole operation. No one else is offering those people steady work. Matteo considers it an act of charity."

I said, "He's a regular Scrovegni." It could've been worse. I would've been worried about more than my back had I slept with

Matteo. This thought made me itchy all over, so I said, "Is there any residual effect?"

"The chemicals will have leached out by now," T. said. "The loneliness may be chronic. When are you leaving for Cambridge?"

"This evening," I said, and I realized it was still true. "And you will go to Florence."

"I'm headed somewhere else," he said.

This was a twist in the familiar story.

I said, "Anywhere in particular?"

"I'm leaving soon," he said. "I have until September to decide where I'm supposed to be." From somewhere beneath his seat he pulled out a thin, square box that was covered in faded gold leaf and embossed with black script, something you might get with a pair of nylons if you shopped for them in the closet of a Medici. "I was going to propose a car trip," T. said.

The box itself was more elegant than anything I owned. Inside was an astonishingly pink silk scarf, a vintage Elsa Schiaparelli in its original box, something Gina Lollobrigida might have worn while being driven in a convertible to a film studio in Rome. I wanted to tell him it was the perfect gift, which it was. I wanted to tell him no one had ever given me something so delicate or pink, which was true. But I also wanted to tell him that even in a sleek little Alfa Romeo with the top down he could not drive fast enough, far enough, to cover the distance between me and the woman I imagined in the pink scarf in the seat beside him.

Before I said anything, T. said, "You can wear it on the plane."

I said, "I'll stick my head out the window."

"I'll keep my eyes on the sky," T. said. "Or you could stay here tonight. The chapel opens to the public again tomorrow."

"I have to deal with the bald man who's stealing stuff from my house," I said.

"Okay," he said. "But your work is not done here."

I didn't say anything.

"Someday, E.," he said, "someday soon, you're going to have to deal with me."

This was starting to sound like a genuine proposal.

T. said, "I have to be in Boston sometime before the end of the summer. I was thinking of coming next week."

I didn't say anything, but I felt my eyebrows shoot up right across my forehead to my hairline.

He said, "I have to give a deposition. Simon Allerby is being sued."

I said, "You'd be welcome to stay with me," but every time I imagined him in one of those rooms, he seemed too tall by several feet, his head whacking against light fixtures, his elbows poking through walls. And I could already hear Rachel banging on the front door, demanding to know who was sitting in her father's favorite chair. Toss in Samir with his nose pressed to one of my windows, and I was prepared to book myself a hotel room on the moon. I said, "Who is suing Simon?"

T. said, "Some pharmaceutical company."

Surely, it was Rachel's employer. That way, even if I didn't bring him home, she'd get to interrogate him.

"Simon is being targeted for publishing the results of a clinical study that was a bust. They won't win, but they will make him pay," T. said. His face was giving off nothing.

I could feel my face reddening and sweating. I didn't relish the idea of his seeing me as I really was, as I saw myself every day in Cambridge. I wasn't eager to watch T. try to rectify his impressions of me here in Padua with the reality of the hermit in the housecoat who preferred the sunken-in cushions on her sofa to a bucket seat in a sports car.

He said, "I was hoping I could buy you dinner one night."

"You don't owe me anything," I said. I wanted to spare us both the embarrassment of the grim conclusion of that dinner, a shared dessert neither of us wanted to eat, and after-dinner drinks we didn't need, and the other rituals that would follow on the realization that the promise of the evening had dried up before the appetizers had been ordered, that without the luster of Italy she seemed more opinionated than sophisticated, that she was a little older and a little heavier and a little more acerbic than he remembered, and that the door he had opened to her heart had since been sealed up and bricked over. I could live with myself in Cambridge, but I couldn't live with T. having to live with the truth of who I was. That's what I wanted to keep covered up. "I don't know, T.," I said. I wanted him to politely withdraw the invitation. "I don't even know what I want."

"Duck," T. said. "When in doubt, order the duck."

And we left it at that. He said he was going to have one more espresso. I said I was going to pack my bags. I knew it was likely I would never see him again. In characteristic fashion, we had made a date, but the date remained indeterminate. We didn't even shake on it. *Noli mi tangere.*

WHILE I PACKED, I REPEATEDLY FELT THE PRESENCE OF someone outside, but every time I looked at the balcony, T. was not there. An Air France agent who spoke with a British accent offered to sell me a business-class ticket for a flight that would put me in Boston just after sunset, for almost as much money as Mitchell had paid for the blue-and-white CPOCH badge I'd stuck in the suitcase with the Dante book and my poisonous old dress. When I begrudgingly gave the Air France agent my credit-card number, she asked if I might want to take a later flight and use my frequent-flyer miles—another of Mitchell's secret stashes. I thanked her, and she offered me an upgrade to first class for a few thousand more miles. *Mais, oui.* I was playing with house money.

I couldn't find the scrap of paper on which Margaret had written her room number, but I was able to locate her last name on the conference agenda, so I headed down to the lobby to dispose of the suitcase and try to arrange for a ride to the Venice airport.

"*Signora Berman!* You check out at last!"

I tried to match his enthusiasm. "Ricardo!" We had already tangled once with Mitchell's bag, and it hadn't ended well. "I have looked for you at night, to thank you for the glue—*colla.*" This wasn't true, but I knew we were going to need a surfeit of goodwill to get through this transaction.

"He is a day man now," Ricardo said. "And he brings the *portatile* from inside to here for you."

I said, "A promotion?"

He said, "No, *signora.* Is true. I insist on *portatile* at desk. Is Ricardo we have to thank you." The leather-bound ledger at the front desk had been replaced by a portable computer, which seemed to be the basis for his boast. He was already pecking at the keyboard. "Six days you been with us," he said proudly.

Not even a week. I had to get rid of the bag and get a ride to the airport before he checked me out. As urgently as I could manage, I said, "*Prego, Ricardo.*"

"*Pronto, signora. C'è un problema?*"

"*Sì, sì, sì,*" I said. "I need a ride to the airport."

He started typing madly. "Taxi? Limo? Hotel shuttling services? Is cheap and comes—we see right here, she comes next time in almost one hour more."

I said, "Okay."

He typed something else and pulled out a ring of red paper tickets and tore one off, as if he were admitting me to a movie.

This seemed improbable. I said, "What time?"

"We call you when five minutes is arriving," he said.

I said, "It's a van?"

"Automobus," he said.

More than ever, I wasn't convinced it was real. I said, "How much does it cost?"

"Pay only the driver," he said.

I said, "It goes to the airport?"

He said, "In Padova, the airport stays in Venezia, okay?"

I said, "Okay." I could draw the next frame of this cartoon: I was seated in the backseat of a taxi to the airport, watching the meter flip over into triple digits.

Ricardo was typing again, and I knew I would soon be checked out and locked out without my luggage or passport. "Now, Ricardo, this is not my bag."

He leaned over the desk and eyed the suitcase. I could tell he recognized it. He didn't say anything.

"I have to leave it here," I said.

He said, "Is broken?"

I said, "No. You fixed it."

He said, "*Certamente.*" His tone had cooled.

"Thank you," I said. I was prepared to grovel. "*Grazie.*"

Someone in the lobby yelled, "Elizabeth?"

I turned. I saw a man in shorts, a woman in a blue suit, and a doorman in a green vest. I didn't recognize any of them. I did see T. I was sure it was T., just outside the glass door. He was turning away as I turned to him. I said to Ricardo, "The doctor—" I could not recall T.'s surname. "With the silver hair."

"Harrington," Ricardo said.

"That's it."

"Harrington, T.," Ricardo said. "*Fantastico. Generoso.*"

"Is he still here?"

"*Elegante, eh? Così generoso.*" I had never paid Ricardo for the glue, or tipped him for fixing the bag I hadn't wanted him to fix, and I think he was letting me know that a thank-you wasn't going to win me any big favors at the front desk. "He likes to check out already."

I said, "Oh."

"*Estramamente generoso.*"

The woman in the blue suit waved. "It's Lisa," she said as she approached. "From the conference. Is that the bag for Margaret? She's going to be so pleased."

"She told you about it," I said. I don't know why I felt betrayed, but I did, as if Margaret and I had shared a secret about the fate of the Dante book that we had both vowed to take to our graves.

Lisa grabbed the handle of the suitcase. "I'll take this to our room, Elizabeth," she said.

Ricardo didn't say anything. He was eyeing Lisa as if she were a troublemaker.

I said, "I'm feeling silly about this now." Suddenly, I didn't want to give Dante up, not this way. "I'll take the bag from here. It's my problem."

Ricardo didn't say anything, but he did nod his agreement.

"Elizabeth, it's not a problem." She kept saying my name, as if she were trying out a new rhetorical trick for sounding more personable. "Really, Elizabeth, I'm tossing it right out the window." She turned to Ricardo and said, "All full! Full house! I know, I know. No room at the inn except the room with a dumpster under the window." She whizzed away to the elevator.

When I caught up to her, Lisa said, "They back in a big truck and empty the thing—at four in the morning, Elizabeth. Right outside our window. Margaret and I begged for a quieter room, but no dice." The elevator door slid open, and we both stepped inside. "I'm moving fast because I really have to pee. But we're thrilled—really, Elizabeth, thrilled—to have something good come of this ridiculous room." Lisa was only going up one floor.

I pressed 7.

Lisa said, "Top drawer."

I said, "Thank Margaret for me."

The doors slid open. Lisa said, "No problem, Elizabeth," and ran down the hall, pulling my past behind her.

Ed was wrong. T. was right. I could have lived without the gory details, with Margaret's way of covering up the grim truth of what she planned to do with the Dante book. While I waited for a phone call from Ricardo, I got an email from Shelby. The subject was "Worlds Colliding."

Dear friend—

I think of you everywhere in Florence, so much so that just now I squealed in delight when I saw this portrait of Dante in the Bargello—as if it was you standing next to me and not the very unpleasant young German thug with a nose ring who just snarled when I said, "He looks exactly like my husband!" (He does.) The German moved away in a huff. My pleasure, frankly. He smelled like a car air-freshener, but probably he can't tell because it all goes right out that hole in his nose. Giotto painted this portrait just before Dante was exiled from Florence. (You knew probably.) You couldn't know it from the tiny faraway picture of him I showed you on the bus the day we met, but Dante is a ringer for my Allen.

Truth? I sort of feel like an exile myself this morning, and I miss everybody, but it cheers me up to find another connection through Giotto to you.

Shelby had forgotten to attach the portrait of Dante. I was happy to let him disappear like that, to be replaced by Shelby's devoted husband. I sent her a brief thank-you. I almost attached a picture of the courtyard of the Gardner Museum, but I couldn't remember if I'd already rerouted that to her. This was another reason I was going to Cambridge. If I didn't get home soon and take some photos, I'd have to cut off our correspondence. Instead, I downloaded a copy of the Gardner's Giotto panel, *The Presentation of the Infant Jesus in the Temple*, and sent it her way.

IV

�֍

My phone dinged with a text from T. at noon on Saturday. I'd been awake for hours, but I hadn't made it past the bathroom yet. Before I went to sleep late Friday night, I'd drawn the blinds to prevent any surprise intrusions from nosy neighbors, so I was still feeling confused about whether it was day or night wherever I was and wasn't. And the Valium I'd saved all week for my return flight, the last of Mitchell's icebox stash, might have contributed to my grogginess. I was wearing nothing but my pink scarf. It was gossamer thin but not transparent, even when I held it up to the lamp, and it was big enough to cover most of the territory between my shoulders and my thighs. I had experimented with it as a sarong, and a bra, and a head scarf, which really was how it looked best. But I was feeling sorry for myself, and indulging a little Juliet thing, which is why it ended up as a kind of shroud.

T.'s text was brief.

Giotto @ 11:00

For a few seconds, I couldn't type. Sweat was pouring down my arms and legs. I blew the scarf to safety on the far side of the bed and got a towel to dry myself off. I finally managed to tap out a sentence.

I am in Cambridge.

Within seconds, I had his response.

Me too. Charles Hotel.

This was hot yoga, and I was sweating right through the towel. I turned off my phone. I got a bathrobe, and then I turned on the phone. I couldn't steady my hand enough to aim a finger at the tiny keyboard, so I put the phone on the bedside table and tried to poke out another sentence, but T. was much quicker.

8 blocks from your house.
Gardner Museum @ 11?

I needed air, all the air in Italy, so I shoved back the curtains and wandered out to the balcony. I was madly calculating how much time it would take to get to Venice, and then fly to Paris, and then on to Boston, and when I subtracted six hours, it seemed almost plausible. The sky was blue, and there was a dry breeze blowing in from somewhere, and that may have contributed to my optimistic math. When I started from scratch, I realized it was six in the morning where I wasn't, not where I was, and even if I got lucky I would not be in Boston until very late in the evening, hours after the museum had closed. And then T. upped the ante.

Or you could make me breakfast.

I was still half-hoping I might discover him in one of the other rooms along the seventh floor of the Arena Hotel, but I had walked the length of the balcony and back and spotted only a maid in one room, and then an elderly woman watching television, who waited with her slider open when I made my return trip to ask if someone had locked me out of my room. After I convinced her I was not a damsel in distress, I balanced my phone on the concrete rail and typed.

I'm not dressed.

T was relentless.

Just put on a scarf.

I was so utterly confused that I honestly could not remember if I had stayed in Padua because I expected him to know that I was never true to my word, or if I had stayed put so that I wouldn't ever have to see him again, especially not in Cambridge. So instead of typing something sensible (*Forgive me.*), or true (*I am in Padua.*), or provocative (*What happened to your car trip?*), or self-serving (*I've been kidnapped.*), I played for time.

Give me an hour.

T. was okay with that.

OK

"Okay," I said. That helped. I said it again when I went back into my room. "Okay." I folded up the scarf and put it back in its beautiful box. "Okay." I turned on the shower and waited for the water to warm up. "Okay, okay, okay." It got me into the shower, but I could tell it wasn't going to make it okay for much longer.

I found it unnervingly easy to imagine T. in Cambridge. He was precisely the man most Harvard senior faculty imagined themselves to be. But as the steam rose up around me, it was not so easy to see myself there. I just couldn't see it, see myself back in Cambridge, in that house, in that life, because I had never been fully there.

This was a secret I had kept for more than thirty years, a cover-up I'd masterminded from the moment Mitchell and I returned from our delayed honeymoon in Paris. I did it. It wasn't easy, but I persuaded myself every morning that the woman in the mirror bore a reasonable resemblance to the woman I had meant to be.

The hoax was elaborate and exhausting, often ingenious, and sometimes it even seemed virtuous. And I understood now that it had probably been a failure. My secret was out, almost from the start. I was the only one who didn't know. Everyone, almost everyone—second-grade teachers, wives of deans, next-door neighbors, the entire sales force at the Ann Taylor shop in Harvard Square—could not see me, did not remember me, would've bumped into me had I not moved out of the way. Everyone knew what Mitchell surely knew.

Finally, I saw the truth. I was never there in Cambridge.

But for three uncanny days, before my past and my marriage caught up with me, before Simon Allerby called and called me back to my old ways, I was here. I had been visible. I had been seen—beheld. I had died and woken up in Padua. And then I had the bad luck to rise from the dead, wander into the world in some indeterminate moment between my past and future, someplace where I was and where I wasn't, uncertain whether I was half-seen or lost.

Seven hundred years ago, Giotto painted two versions of the Presentation in the Temple. I had stood for countless hours before the panel that was housed in Boston, the version of this prophetic painting

whose final resting place was only minutes from my home. But until I responded to Shelby—sweet, sweet Shelby—I had never seen what wasn't there. I had known since Andre's lecture that the Angel of Death above the head of the prophetess was not present in the Boston panel. This made sense. Death did not enter the picture until I got to Padua. But more was missing than a heavenly herald. I had always known the Gardner painting was a revision of the fresco in the chapel, but I had never fully understood what was not there in Boston.

Sometime late Friday night, after the Valium had kicked in, I'd dug up Andre's stick-figure cartoon and glued it to one of the many blank pages in my *Journal of Discovery*.

I had never known that there was more to this story, more to this

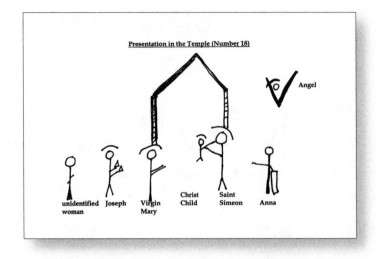

moment, a woman who was not there in Boston or Cambridge, a nameless woman elegantly robed in pink, a woman of uncertain role and status, a woman who was only present in Padua, not secret but mysterious—not insignificant, but not yet identified.

BY TWELVE-FORTY-FIVE, I WAS CLEAN, AND DRY, AND BUT-toning up my blue shirtdress, backing away from the mirror so I didn't have to see what a mess of wrinkles I was from behind. My plan was to run to the Metro for coffee and something involving bread to fortify myself for the chaos that was about to break out when I started reading to T. from my Book of Revelation, but my phone dinged with a text before I got out the door.

T. owed me at least another twenty minutes.

And then another text dinged in, and then another.

All three were from Sam.

Morning, Mom—

Thanks, thanks, thanks for the money. What a boon to get it now

when I need it. (I'm understanding from what you wrote that I can get
a lump-sum payout. Rachel mentioned a trustee, but maybe that's other
money coming to us at a later date?)
Why did you send that picture of that painter? (sorry to miss the point)

Oh—Sound the All Clear. I am the bald man.

I looked but didn't find anything stronger than aspirin in the house.
Rachel checked the freezer (?) but says you finally cleared it out.
Suggestions?

I dialed Rachel's number and got her voicemail, so I hung up and
I typed a text to Sam.

   1. Why are you bald?
   2. There is no more money till I die.
   3. Didn't that statue of Giotto remind you of anyone?

And then I dialed Rachel again, and got her voicemail again, so I
hung up and texted Sam again.

   4. Vicodin in an orange juice can in the freezer. Take one. Two if
      you're desperate and you don't tell R.

I dialed T. and got his voicemail, so I hung up, and then another
text from Sam arrived.

   1. Lost a bet. Told the girls I would shave my head if they won their
      first tournament game. (They lost the next day, or else it would be
      painted green and white—school colors.)
   2. Don't die.

3. Giotto=One of the Seven Dwarfs?

4. Vicodin=bonus.

And then my phone rang, and Sam said, "Do you think it would be weird if I borrowed a couple of Dad's old blazers? Rachel has been saying for months that I should take the suits, too, but I don't really wear suits anywhere."

I said, "What is going on there?"

He said, "I was here for Steve Kaiser's bachelor party last night, which is still going on. I told you I was coming back for that, didn't I?"

I said, "No."

Sam said, "I think I did. But I definitely forgot to cc Anandi and Samir."

I said, "Take the blazers. You should also look at the sweaters in the cedar chest. A lot of them are cashmere. Steve Kaiser is getting married?"

Sam said, "I know. That's what everybody thinks."

I said, "Why is Rachel in the house with you?"

"She's outside talking to someone," Sam said.

I felt the top of my head rise a few inches above the rest of my skull. I said, "Someone tall with silver hair?"

Sam said, "I have no idea. Hold on." And then he didn't say anything for several seconds, and I hoped he was peeking out a window to confirm my worst fears. I heard a lot of something going on. Sam said, "Is it okay if I just put the sweaters in this duffel bag in the closet? It's brown."

It was a handsome leather overnight bag I gave Mitchell when he got his first promotion and began to travel more often. "Take it," I said. I knew the sweaters had already been stuffed into it, probably with a few carpets. "Rachel?"

"She's talking on her phone with somebody," Sam said, as if he'd told me that already. "We drove down together yesterday. She was hoping she could get that trainer guy who lives two floors below her to buy her place this weekend. Don't ask. I don't know how that went. We were supposed to leave at six o'clock this morning, but I didn't even get back from Steve's till six-thirty, so she isn't officially speaking to me yet."

I had a text from T.

Sam said, "Did I send you the pictures of those two condos Susie found in Red Hook?"

I didn't say anything. T.'s text was brief.

Thirsty?

Sam said, "Mom?"

A green plastic bottle of fizzy water was balanced on the cement ledge of the balcony railing. I walked halfway to the open sliders. As I stood there, a cool breeze swept in from somewhere, and the bottle wobbled and finally tipped over and spilled onto the tiled balcony floor.

I said, "I have to go, Sam."

He said, "Who doesn't?"

"Before you leave, give Anandi your key to the house," I said.

"I'll give her Rachel's key," he said.

I didn't say anything.

Sam said, "Are you there?"

I heard a few sharp blasts from a car horn—maybe Rachel, maybe someone parked below my balcony. Sam hung up. I didn't move.

I heard T. say, "Very fizzy. If you were here, I'd offer you a sip of mine."

I said, "If you were here—" I couldn't speak after that. I was weeping, and I really couldn't see almost anything but the blurry lightness ahead of me. I walked to the open slider and leaned on the threshold. I think T. was sitting on the railing, or else someone had installed a statue overnight.

T. said, "Ricardo let me out here, but I think a maid may have locked up my exit. I'm going to have to leave through your room."

"Okay," I said. I still couldn't see him, but I recognized the bright blueness in front of me as T. I said, "I was thinking of going to the chapel."

"Oh, E.," he said. "We've both been to the chapel."

"Oh, T.," I said, trying to get some of the air blowing around out there into my lungs. "I don't know where else to go."

"Me neither," T. said. "That's why I rented us a car. There's a map in the glove compartment."

I didn't say anything. I was all packed. "Okay," I said.

He hopped down from his perch but left his bottle of water on the ledge. He took a few steps toward me, and I turned and walked into the room.

From behind me, T. said, "How's your back today?"

"Oh, it's fine," I said, and then I felt his hands on my shoulders, and I wasn't so sure my spine would hold me erect for much longer. But I didn't move. I sensed the smooth contours of his chest against me, and then his head was next to mine. I could feel the heat of him against my neck, which meant one of us was still breathing.

"Okay," he said.

"I couldn't agree more," I said.

"I would feel better if you let me examine your back," T. said. "We have a long ride ahead of us."

"Okay," I said, turning to him. I told myself I was in good hands. T. was a doctor in another life.

ACKNOWLEDGMENTS

✳

T hree images appear here courtesy of the Isabella Stewart Gardner
Museum, Boston:

1. The photograph of the central courtyard in the museum.
2. The downloaded detail of Giotto's *Presentation of the Infant Jesus in the Temple.*
3. The reproduction of Giotto's *Presentation of the Infant Jesus in the Temple.*

The map of the fresco program reproduced as "Sara's map" originally appeared in *Giotto* by Francesca Flores d'Arcais (Milano: 24 ORE
Cultura, 2011; English-language edition, New York: Abbeville Press,
1995). My gratitude and debts extend from the great Italian painter
Cimabue, who recognized and cultivated the unprecedented genius
of Giotto, to the devoted and welcoming staffs of the Isabella Stewart
Gardner Museum in Boston and the Scrovegni Chapel in Padua,
where my lifelong addiction to the work of Giotto ultimately took shape

as this novel. I am especially grateful to Kendra Slaughter, who connected me with Davide Banzato, who generously provided me with the most precious of currencies—time in the Arena Chapel.

My understanding of the history of the chapel building and the fresco cycle, and many of the ideas and opinions expressed by characters in the novel, was informed by the rich scholarship and endless speculation about Giotto that dates from Dante and extends through the indispensable work of Rachel Jacoff, who edited *The Cambridge Companion to Dante,* and James Stubblebine, editor of the oft-cited, much-admired collection *Giotto: The Arena Chapel Frescoes.*

The literature devoted to Giotto represents a vast and often contradictory treasury of facts, myths, analysis, and speculation. I'm grateful for every word of it. Two recent books are standouts: *The Usurer's Heart: Giotto, Enrico Scrovegni, and the Arena Chapel in Padua* by Anne Derbes and Mark Sandona; and *Giotto and the Arena Chapel: Art, Architecture and Experience* by Laura Jacobus. These are among the most original and illuminating books I've ever read on any topic. Both books were especially useful to me as I attempted to represent how our understanding of the history of the chapel has evolved over the centuries and to explore the questions and the controversies that still engage the chapel's most ardent and skilled interpreters.

GAIL HOCHMAN, MY AGENT, BREATHED LIFE INTO THE original manuscript—and its writer. My longtime editor, Jack Shoemaker, and all of his colleagues at Counterpoint made something beautiful of what I had done.

Mary Ann Matthews read and responded to every sentence I wrote, listened to every word I had to say when I wasn't writing, and opened her big heart and generous mind to me every time I asked for help. Michelle Blake read and improved every draft of the novel, and she repeatedly made me believe there was a book in there, even when I couldn't see it.

Many friends and fellow writers lent me much-needed support, and many went well beyond the call of duty. I am especially grateful to Alexandra Zapruder, who is as crazy about Giotto as I am, and much funnier than either of us; Jessica Francis Kane—again and again; Perrin Ireland, for lending me her pitch-perfect sensibility; James Lecesne, whose first response to the novel was to open doors into the wider world for it; and Elizabeth Reluga, Valentine Talland, Gisella Portelli, Maria Pia Cingolani, Verrall Dunlop, Valerie Martin, Elizabeth Benedict, Dennis McFarland, and Joan Wickersham.

Peter Bryant was, as always, my first and most trusted reader. He is first and most trusted in all ways.